KT-168-439

For Emile and Apple,
and all of their someday adventures in time.

THE LIBRARY
NEW COLLEGE
SWINDON
WITHDRAWN

Acknowledgments

I appreciate all of the support from other writers I've received for this project, including in no discernable order: Susan Jane Bigelow, s.e. smith, Kyle Jones, Jesse Kuiken, Riley MacLeod, and Malinda Lo. Special thanks go to Danika Dinsmore for her insights during editing and her ability to host a pep talk. Perennial thanks go to Lea Mesner for her coaching and enthusiasm. Other thanks go out to Top Pot Doughnuts in Seattle and the Colville Street Patisserie in Walla Walla for sustaining me with pastry while I wrote copious drafts of the story. And of course I have to thank Susanne Beechey who is a terrific life partner and a quietly effective motivator.

CHAPTER ONE

I FIRST JUMPED back in time on September 22, 1980, just a few weeks into high school, only I didn't realize it straight away. Time travel isn't supposed to be possible. Besides, I like car engines and the trees that line the streets in my neighborhood—stuff I can touch, not crazy shit like physics or magic. So I just ignored my experience until it became more important for me to face reality than pretend it wasn't happening. At least that's how it seemed as I was being chased through a dusty farm town, wearing shoes so thin I bruised the balls of my feet. Hallucinations shouldn't hurt.

Nope. It was a regular day at first. I woke up from my incredibly annoying alarm clock, which of course alerted King, our Golden Retriever, that he should burst through my bedroom door and lick me all over the face until I smelled like rancid dog. He followed me down the green hall like usual, standing behind me even when I whizzed into the toilet, lest, I don't know, he miss out on any of my fun. He and I didn't even notice anymore that the sink was wrapped in rolled up towels, held in place with duct tape. It had been that way since my parents had started letting me use the bathroom by myself.

I had epilepsy, see, which meant that on a surprise basis I lost consciousness as the neurons in my brain decided to start firing like a bunch of hyperactive kindergarteners hearing the recess bell. Problem is when they're misfiring that way all my regular stuff like walking, brushing my teeth, or pretty much anything else would stop, I'd lose control, fall over, and start twitching. But like the padding over the

2014002538

hard surfaces around the house, I'd gotten used to having seizures, even if I wasn't happy about them.

Sometimes—maybe half the time—the "episodes" gave me a tiny bit of warning, mostly by screwing with my sense of balance. The ground around me would drop out from under me, like a ship listing hard to one side. *Watch me do this impression of the* Titanic, *folks!* Or my own private earthquake. I mastered the art of quickly sitting down and putting my head between my knees, before I would fall over into humiliating twitchiness. Before the darkness could collapse over me.

In the kitchen that special day, my mother sat staring out the back window, surrounded by the orange flower wallpaper she'd hung a few years before. She drummed her fingers on the round table built by my father and me. There was a glob of varnish on one side that I liked to feel when I ate my breakfast, because it was smooth and irregular, and the wood underneath was more yellow. As usual, Dad had left the paper folded open to the comics section and put it next to my cereal bowl. I didn't have the heart to tell him I didn't read them anymore. I'd moved on to the *X-Men* and the *Fantastic Four.* Anyone with super powers, really. I wasn't choosy.

"What do you have after school today?" asked Mom, still looking out toward the poplar trees behind our house. They'd turned bright yellow, but hadn't started littering the lawn yet. It would be my job to rake the leaves when they fall. *Joy*.

"Nothing. I mean, hanging out with Sanjay, but nothing else. Why?"

Jay lived across the street from me. He was one of a very few people I knew who never teased me about my seizures, but we'd known each other since preschool. He was kind of an outcast, too, just because he was Indian. We had some stupid kids in our school district.

"There's a new study at the hospital for children with epilepsy. I enrolled you in it."

"A what?" I didn't feel like any extra studying, so I hoped this wasn't what she meant.

She turned to me. Her usual sad eyes looked bright today.

"They're experimenting with a new process to see if they can cure some cases of epilepsy."

"A process" didn't clear it up for me. I envisioned the taffy-pulling machine in Willy Wonka's chocolate factory.

"Is it a new drug?" I was on my sixth different pill. Most of them didn't stop my episodes, but two of them were particularly awful. Pill Number One gave me delusions that I was a doctor, even though I was still a toddler at the time. Mom had found me behind the living room sofa, cutting at myself with a razor blade, announcing I was doing "surgery." Pill Number Three made my extremities feel mushy and heavy all the time. I tripped a lot back then, which made for a lot of yuk yuks at my expense. The other pills just didn't work all that well, but I definitely was not a fan of Pills Number One or Three.

"No, it's like they have a new way of looking at your brain waves, and changing them. Dr. Barett told me about it."

Dr. Barett, my neurologist, was fresh out of some big name medical program, top of his class, said the nurses. He was nice and extremely fit, but he seemed to like nerve cells more than people. I wasn't surprised that this juicy new experiment to fix brain waves was his suggestion. But "changing" brainwaves sounded . . . intense. I nodded though, since Jay and I could hang out any time we wanted, and forgot about the appointment until I came home from school, when Mom hustled me out the door, jingling her car keys in irritation, like they were a cow prod instead of a device used to ignite our Ford's engine.

The first part of the study session was familiar to me, because every month since I could remember I'd sat in a similar oversized earth toned vinyl chair and let some nurse apply blobs of cold putty all over my head. The nurses smelled like soap and antiseptic and I tried not to inhale their breath as they hovered over my face. They took a long time to attach the long, thin wires all over my head. Unlike the nurses I had for my monthly checkup, these two women didn't talk to me while they worked. I wasn't sure if I liked the quiet or not. Finally I was ready for all of the electricity in my brain to be scratched out by a machine that looked like one of those boxes that measured ground tremors. Then for half an hour I sat as still as a scared rat while they watched the patterns of my broken neurons.

The second part of the study was different, longer, and involved the head of the study, Doctor Dorfman. He was a man with thick sideburns and gorilla hands, sending electrical signals to me to see if he could change how my brain responded. I could ruin the test if I moved so much as a pinky toe. I tried to come up with all of the ways that staying perfectly still could benefit me, but after two minutes had only listed Buckingham Palace Guard and mime pretending to be dead.

I sat frozen for something like ten minutes, which was a sure-fire way to drive me up a tree. Nothing like telling a guy to stay still to make him need to move as much as possible. My left elbow started itching, and my right foot was in full pins-and-needles mode. The glob of putty above my left eye oozed down my forehead as slow as a slug, or at least it felt that way. I tried to see the clock on the wall ahead of me, but with my glasses safely tucked away on the white counter behind me, I couldn't make out the position of the hands. It was just as well; knowing the time would probably have made me obsess about how much longer I'd be stuck in the chair.

A metal click and then dull hum came over the PA, but I stayed still.

"How are you doing, hon?" asked Cindy, the lab technician. She had bright red hair not to be found in nature, and said everything through a smile. I liked her immediately.

My father had always said, "Smile and they never know what you're thinking." So I worried I shouldn't trust her, for all of her grinning like a Cheshire cat. But since she'd asked me something, I answered her.

I hadn't even spoken yet when the seismograph thing set up next to me went wild, scratching out thick, dark lines on the paper. Alerting the world: It's alive!

"I'm okay. Itchy, and I think my right foot's asleep."

"Go ahead and scratch if it's not your head, and shake your foot a little."

I dug at my elbow through my shirt, which didn't cure the itch, but it would have to do. I couldn't dig under my sleeve without upsetting the wires that trailed from all over my head. I pounded my foot on the floor, trying to startle it enough to wake up. *Scratching and flopping my sneaker around, I am so cool.*

Without thinking, I reached up to stop the glop on my head from getting in my eyes. I knew better than to touch anything other than the tip of my nose, but once I'd started moving itches popped up everywhere, screaming for attention, and I forgot myself.

"Oh, hang on there, bucko," said Dr. Dorfman, who'd come into the room from behind me. He put my hand down on the armrest. His touch was heavy and cold; his hand a hairy giant on top of mine.

"Don't mess with the wires."

I took a breath and relaxed, having heard this a million times before. He walked over to the machine, running his hand over his sideburns. A long strand of connected paper had piled up in the basket next to the small monitor, and he bent down low to snag the printout in the middle until he had a ribbon of it to examine. Cindy came out from the next room.

"There's the abnormality," I heard him say to her, pointing at the paper in a few places. "Let's run one more test since he's still hooked up, only this time I want to make a change to the stimulus." They walked away, talking, and I was free to sneak in a scratch at whatever needed attention. At the moment, nothing bothered me. My body never cooperated. It didn't demand much when I was allowed to deal with it.

The doctor was back at my side, talking loudly to me as if I had hearing problems, not a seizure disorder. He was a lot older than my regular doctor, though in Dr. Dorfman's defense, my regular doctor was like a Calvin Klein model. Dr. Dorfman had gray streaks clumping together at his temples. Cindy said his work was the Rosetta Stone of neurology research, whatever that meant. I liked him enough, though nothing about stones seemed cutting edge to me. Weren't rock tools invented by cavemen?

"Okay, Jack, we're going to do just one more test. It'll only take a few minutes."

I nodded, sighed, and waited. *Always with the "few minutes."* A buzz zipped along my spine, which caused me to jerk a bit, and the machine roared.

I lost all sense of the room, the wires, the cold putty. In a flash of painful light I was on a hillside, in mid-step, running up a dirt trail, holding something in my hand. I wanted to know the shape of it, but couldn't figure it out. I had the impression that I held it a lot. Something felt wrong with how I was running, too, as if the effort it normally took to lift my feet had been recalibrated.

"Do you notice anything?" asked the doctor through the microphone in the other room. I blinked, saw the pale green walls around me and the fuzzy metal clock on the far wall. I was back. But of course I hadn't left.

"I saw something," I said. With each passing second, I felt less sure about where I'd been. Like a dream fading away.

"Can you describe it?" he asked, panting a little at the end of his question. He creeped me out.

I told him, feeling foolish, about the hill and the dirt path. A weird image came to me just then, that I had been wearing strange shoes. Leather moccasins, maybe. But I lived in these red Converse high tops. Why would I think of moccasins? Where did I even learn about moccasins?

He wrote down what I said, turning off his microphone partway through. I could see him through the observation glass, talking with Cindy. *This would be a good time to know how to read lips,* I thought. He stepped back into the room after a couple of minutes and told me I'd done a good job, clapping a hand on my shoulder. His palm took up all of the real estate I had there, but I sat there rigid. I wasn't sure why I felt the need to be tough.

Cindy unhooked me from the machine; I was grateful to end transmitting all my brain waves to everyone in the room, even if people couldn't exactly read my mind from the printout. She wheeled over a tray, and dabbed a hand cloth into a steel bowl of warm water. Wiping most of the putty off of my scalp and temples in silence, I noticed she wasn't smiling anymore. I looked at a picture of Olympic swimmers on the wall in front of me. What the hell was this poster about, and why was it here, of all places? Were we supposed to aspire to athletic greatness even if we could have a seizure in the water? Finally I was done and Cindy nodded to me that I could leave, so I wandered back to the waiting room.

The doctor was talking to my mother, who was hunched over an issue of *People*. She looked up at him and waited for him to update her.

"Jack was great today," he said, "and I'd like to see him next week if you can bring him in. I think we can isolate the source of his seizures."

"Oh, really?" she asked, looking me up and down. "He's such a good kid. It's just terrible that he has to deal with these episodes." She paused. "I'd hoped he'd outgrow them by high school." *Meet my son, the sweet failure.*

"Mom," I said, in an attempt to get her to stop.

"It's okay, Jack," the doctor said, now grinning, except he looked kind of in pain. It was clear he didn't make facial expressions all that often. "I'm really glad we got you in this study."

I wasn't sure how to respond, so I shrugged. But I was worried.

* * *

I'd almost forgotten about the weird sensation from the first day in the study. I stuck to my routine of Alert Against the Episodes. The rest of that week I took my little blue pills with even more care about timing, and watched where I was walking, as if I was extra prone to a seizure. Maybe my wonky neurons knew their days were numbered and would try to act up more than usual. I stared at my bike after coming home from school the rest of the week after the study session, refusing to pedal even to the edge of the subdivision. The dirt hills and slopes a couple of miles out of town where there was new construction in progress would just have to exist without me racing over them. I could feel little ninjas in my brain, getting ready to attack me the moment I lowered my guard.

Even though I stayed on watch against an ambush, I still had my routine to get through. Saturday morning as usual I stripped the padding on my bathroom sink and threw the towels in the laundry. One week was all it ever took for them to get moldy and the tape to disintegrate, and then little sticky gray strings would hang off of the towels, clinging to my hands and clothes. Not exactly the fashion statement I wanted to make. And that tape glue was wicked hard to get off my skin unless I wanted to bathe in lighter fluid, which was a bad idea for obvious reasons. So I tried to keep things tidy. After I'd repaired my bathroom I wandered around the house looking for tasks to do. It made it easier to ask for movie money if I could point to things I'd already accomplished.

That afternoon Jay found me in the driveway oiling the chain on my bike.

"Whatcha up to?" he asked, craning his head around. He was as much a motorhead as I was into beetles.

"Just keeping things lubed," I said, rotating the pedals. I clicked the tin can, watching drops of oil fall onto the chain.

"Sounds hot," he said, licking his tongue over his lips, and we laughed.

"Want to go for a ride?" he asked.

"Nah, I have homework still. But you could come over for dinner. Mom's got a chicken in the oven."

Jay was a secret omnivore, as his whole family was vegetarian. He was always happy to devour meat products.

"I could handle that," he said, sniffing the air.

"You can smell it from that far away?"

"Nope," he said. "Just your pits and the oil can. But I thought it was worth a shot."

* * *

The Monday after the seizure study, I inhaled my cereal and washed it down with a small wavy glass of orange juice, ignoring the newspaper. Grabbing my lunch sack off of the kitchen table, I scrambled out to the street, knowing I was late for the bus. The driver, Miss Glover, never waited for anyone. We were lucky she even slowed down enough for students to climb aboard. She'd clearly chosen an occupation that would put her in close contact with people she detested, just so she could challenge us twice a day.

Hearing the door bang shut behind me, my mother told me to have a good day. Through the screen door she was grayed out, slightly ghostly. I turned and saw the bus lurching down the hill. It would be a race to the corner. Would she break the speed limit in the subdivision? Her gunning engine answered me: *Oh yes. It's on.*

Our school bus was a Thomas Conventional model, built on an International Harvester chassis. Bright yellow, with a short, wide snout, it had a rear-loaded diesel engine with a lot of horsepower but not very good torque, and so it struggled on any serious incline. I pounded up the broken sidewalk, hoping I wouldn't trip or slip on any wet leaves. I figured everyone on the bus was watching me, but I didn't spend time worrying about what I looked like. I flew through the last ten yards, beating Miss Glover to the corner. I did a little dance as she opened the door.

"All right, Inman," she said, "stop celebrating and get on."

I walked around the front of the bus as the red lights clicked on and off. I'm sure I looked terrific panting up the steps, trying to catch my breath. I got ready for my classmates to start heckling me.

In the second to last row, I took the only empty seat and set my bag between my feet. This was my usual spot, because although we grumbled about too many rules at school, we were predictable as hell. Jay flashed me a "hey" from the last row. Woulda been great to sit next to him but The Nosepicker always flicked his nonsense there, so we avoided that spot at all costs.

"Spaz," said Kiernan Maloney. He was a stoner, in my grade, which he accomplished by getting held back one year. It must have been a shock to him that toking up behind the football field bleachers wasn't a fast path to the honor roll.

Kiernan had fire-red, thick wavy hair, and freckles covered every inch of his head. Maybe in another school he would be the target of bullies because of all those freckles, but in my school, he did most of the bullying himself. I closed my eyes and pretended not to hear him.

Sanjay poked me in the shoulder from the seat behind me. "Glover really had to slam on the breaks, man. Way to run."

"Thanks," I said, turning around to face him. My heart was finally starting to settle down in my chest.

"Did you do the algebra homework last night?" I asked.

"Yeah, why?" Sanjay fumbled in his backpack and pulled out his tattered algebra textbook. Catholic schools like ours held onto things like math books way longer than the public schools did—in my textbook were the signatures of previous owners going back thirteen years. The more basic math books were funny because the word problems gave their age away, with crap like, "Timmy needs 37 bolts for his wagon. If Tommy has 2/3 of the bolts Timmy needs, how many bolts does Tommy have?"

At some point our teachers relaxed about how carefully we handled our books, which we protected only with a brown paper grocery bag, taped to the hardback covers. Paper bags fell apart over the course of the school year, though, eventually disintegrating and revealing how beat up the book really was underneath. Jay's algebra text was missing part of the back cover; mine bared the inside of its spine every time I opened it, and it smelled like wet dog.

"I can't figure out number twenty-four," I said. Only the odd-numbered problems had answers in the back.

Kiernan leaned across the aisle, his white teeth showing against the tan polka dots on his skin. "Are you two queers cheating? You wouldn't be cheating, would you?" His undone tie dangled; Kiernan always waited for a nun or teacher to force him to finish dressing for class.

"Do you hear something?" asked Sanjay, keeping his head turned away from Kiernan. I stifled a giggle. Kiernan huffed at us and sat back, and Jay rolled his eyes at me.

We hopped off the bus, walking to the oversized front doors of the school.

"I thought high school was going to be so great, but it's just the same crap," Sanjay said.

"Why should today be any different," I said.

Two-thirty took forever to roll around because I couldn't stop thinking about returning to the brain study after school. I counted down the hours. None of the doctors before Dorfman had held out any kind of hope for me recovering. My mother had never gotten over her seizures, after all, but at least her medication kept her seizure-free, if not kind of tired all the time.

By the time I sat back down in the squeaky green vinyl chair, I'd mostly dismissed my weird hallucination, which is what I figured my experience was. Since it was a trick of my own mind, I thought it wouldn't happen again. Brains were all just a gross mass of chemicals and electricity, and at least outside in the world, lightning didn't strike the same spot twice.

Chapter Two

MOM HELD ONTO my arm so I couldn't leave the waiting room.

"You're such a strong boy," she said. I translated this into "You're as frail as a frozen petuna." She often told me the opposite of what she was really thinking. She'd managed her own epilepsy her whole life, and was always on the lookout for new medications to get my seizures under control. When I was younger she often broke down crying about how she'd "made me wrong," but other than that she didn't really talk about her own childhood or her brain stuff. We didn't have those conversations anymore, the ones with her blue eyes holding onto mine, searching for the defect inside me. I never knew how to respond to her desperation. I wondered if she'd ever talk with me about how she feared I'd get lost to my bad brain waves, but so far she hadn't brought it up.

"Mom, I'm almost fifteen. I'll be fine."

I reached over and squeezed her wrist, telling her I'd be back soon, and handing her an issue of *Time Magazine.* Something with a politician on the cover.

I waved as I walked out of the waiting room with the nurse because my mother still seemed nervous for me. Soon enough the machines would show the doctor that my heart was pounding, cause nothing beats having your body betray you to all the other people in a given room. Maybe by the time I was hooked back up to the chair, I would have calmed down.

"Okay, Jack, we're going to do the first part of the test now. Stay as still as possible. You know the routine." Cindy flashed me a quick grin. She was a Cheshire cat who'd convinced herself that she was just a nurse. I wondered who else was in this experiment. How many of us knew the routine? Were they all teenagers like me? Did we all have the same type of epilepsy? I had no idea. Other than my mom, I didn't know anybody with a seizure disorder.

As soon as Cindy started pressing putty onto my head, body parts that needed scratching sprang up like thirsty weeds. I resisted, trying to imagine I was at the beach with warm ocean water splashing over my feet. I could be a mean raft surfer. I didn't realize I'd started smiling. I relaxed my muscles and listened to the needles on the machine scribbling out my faulty brain waves. If the doctor minded me falling asleep in the test, a nurse would wake me up. But sometimes they wanted to catch me napping; I wasn't sure why.

Some time later the recording stopped and the Dr. Dorfman piped up over the intercom. He had a new moustache today that made him sound different.

"It's time for the next part of the test. You okay in there?"

I popped him a thumbs up. He had also gotten a hair perm since our last session and now looked like a cross between Wolverine and a standard poodle—two otherwise reasonably attractive beings that should have never combined into one.

"Good. Okay, here we go, Jack," said Dorfpoodle.

A light started flickering on off, on off, on off, in rapid succession. Blinking lights were known to cause seizures, but no medical folks had ever used them on me.

Tingles along my arms. I tasted a ham and cheese sandwich in my mouth, as if I'd just swallowed it. *What the hell?* I racked my memory for when the last time had been that I'd eaten anything approximating ham and cheddar cheese, but that was crazy, since I'd been sitting here for hours and it's not like anybody tastes something in their mouths that they haven't consumed in six months. *Slow down little brain.*

I wanted to say something to the doctor—*stop the test*—or the technician—*something is wrong.* But I couldn't open my mouth or move. The world jolted to the left, like the whole planet had crashed into a massive, interstellar iceberg, and then the room around me was gone. Replaced, somehow.

I tried to adjust to the very bright sunlight. I was moving, fast, still feeling like I was at an angle to the ground. Running, that's what it was. I stopped and grabbed onto the thing next to me to steady myself and my stomach. Maybe it was that stupid *Monte Cristo* sandwich memory. *Monte Cristo* sandwiches are greasy and gross, anyway.

I sucked up huge swallows of air, and then I told myself I was stupid, because hallucinations don't need to breathe.

Adjust, adjust, I told myself. I stood up straighter and looked around. I thought I'd been clinging onto a tree, but examining it more closely, I saw it was a pole. I was outdoors, on a hillside, the same as the last time. Maybe the pole had been a branch before, but at some point it had been whittled down and sanded, the kind of woodworking project I could see myself having. There were depressions in the wood under my thumb. I looked and saw a name carved into the side: *Jac.*

Jack is my name. It occurred to me that I should try pulling the wood from the ground. It popped out easily, and then I knew, like I'd only recently forgotten, that I had held the pole in just this way many times before. Calluses had formed on the insides of my fingers and palm where I gripped the pole. Not a pole. A stick. It was a walking stick. *My* walking stick.

I'd been running over a well-worn trail of dirt with tall yellow-green grass on either side. I wore soft leather shoes and no socks. Moccasins again. This was one consistent hallucination. *Go me.*

Behind me was a clearing, and past that a tiny village at the bottom of the long hill. Small wooden buildings bleached from constant heavy daylight lined up in a square, with small gray stones serving as a thin walkway between the structures. Most of them faced each other, built around the dusty courtyard. It was either early morning or late in the day, with the sun and moon passing each other in the sky. Birds chirped excitedly to each other but I couldn't tell if they were waking up or squawking their goodnights. I mean, because I didn't know anything about birds. Comics and car engines, okay, and bicycle gears, I had a sense of those, but chirping things and actual wildlife were not my forte.

I got a little more oriented. The scene felt slanted because I was on a steep hill. *Don't anyone call me Einstein,* I thought.

I searched the space around me for other people. For the most part I had caught my breath. I'd never had a dream before where I had any sense of control over it, but here I was making decisions. So I trudged up the rest of the hill, feeling my quads resist the hard-packed soil of the narrow trail. Larger pebbles pushed against the tender soles of my shoes. If I was going to have a hella intense mind trip, I might as well check out the scenery.

"You're tardy," said a woman coming out from a rambling, large yellow farmhouse on the left. "You worry me when you're late."

In the small town there couldn't have been more than two dozen buildings, but that was crowded compared to this. Up here was only this house, a bright red barn with white accents behind it, and expansive fields, until the land for the next farmhouse began, miles off in the distance, the silo next to it appearing only as big as my thumb.

Water trickled somewhere, but I didn't see anything like a river or waterfall. I looked for cars but all I saw were empty dirt or gravel roads connected around the courtyard, and one wider dirt road heading south out of town. The road collapsed on each side, the result of narrow wheels cutting into the soft ground on a regular basis.

"Sorry," I said, turning back to face her. I figured I should walk over to her, if we were going to have a conversation.

"Sorry, who?" she asked. Well, wasn't she precious?

She put one hand on her hip and stared at me. She seemed young, or at least younger than my mother, but she also looked more worn out, with ruddy skin and a streak of gray hair running from the top of her head into a tight bun at the back. She had the same build as my mother—lanky, but also with the slightest hump at the end of her neck where it met her shoulders, as if she'd spent a lot of time bent over.

"I'm sorry, ma'am," I said.

"Sweet Jackie," she said, a small smile spreading on her lips. "Come on, I need your help with the heifer." She paused. "Did anyone follow you?"

Paranoid much? I shook my head and she led me around to the back of the house. A few strands of her hair had fallen out around the bun, so it looked a bit like the frayed apron strings that hung down at the back of her waist. We walked past a few busted wooden buckets lying in the dirt and what I figured were bushel containers, all of them empty and dropped carelessly on the ground.

Nothing was familiar. And that was stupid of me anyway, since I was just in my head and not anywhere real. But this dream-mind gig didn't seem to be based in any memory of mine.

I thought about the valley—no green street signs, no traffic signals, no fire hydrants, no curbs, no telephone booths. I had a nagging sense that I should know why those things weren't there, but now I was having trouble finishing my thoughts. It was just so bright out here—

I woke with a start. Doctor Dorfpoodle was in my face, holding my eyelids open and checking my pupils with a penlight. I was surrounded by his massive sideburns. I could smell his perm. Perm didn't smell so good.

"Jack, there you are," he said, sounding worried.

"Yes," I said, trying to push myself into the back of the chair to get some space.

"You had a seizure," he said, putting the penlight away. *Maybe I should call him Captain Obvious.* His hands free, he began to stroke his beard. "We need to put you under observation for a few hours. But the good news is, I think we've found the source of the abnormality."

"I don't think I like 'put you under.' But this is good news?"

"Well, you're clever. Yes, it's a positive development." He didn't seem as happy as he should be.

He didn't know how annoying he was. But because I still felt out of sync with gravity, I figured I shouldn't tell him.

"Put your head between your legs and take deep breaths," he said. The nurse unhooked the wires from my head one by one as I sat with my knees up to my chest, my heels digging into the thin foam seat. Of course I'd learned to do this when I was three, but I pretended his suggestion was brilliant neuroscience I'd never heard before. I played with the worn out corduroy fabric at my knees.

The doctor looked at me. "I have to talk to your Mom, but you'll see her soon. We're just going to admit you for a little while. It'll be okay." He walked out and I waited to hear the door shut. I thought about my world history homework that I hadn't started yet. Now Mom would have to go home and come back to get my text book. *Sorry, Mom.*

"So I seized?" I asked Cindy.

"Yeah, I'm sorry, fella," she said, washing my scalp with a warm sponge. I waited for a fake smile from her but it didn't come.

She made a few more passes over my hair, and then another quick rinse in a small plastic bucket. Usually the nurses didn't take much care to get the putty off of me, leaving me to scream in my own shower with a gallon bucket of shampoo and a loofa, but Cindy was working to get most of it out on her own. I wondered if she was actually nice. *Maybe I should bother talking to her after all.*

Also, I had questions. "I was out a long time, huh?"

"Oh no, dear, just a second. We were in here right away and you woke up on your own."

"A second?"

"Sure, hon, just fifteen seconds total. You're totally fine."

I felt like I'd been gone for at least five minutes. I wondered if I should tell anyone.

* * *

At home, in my room, I couldn't stop thinking about the hill and the woman in the apron. I could recall with clarity the detail of the flower pattern on the fabric, the smell of the earth, the sounds of chirping bugs, the crispness of the air and how it felt inside my lungs. I'd run up that hill, pounding away and stabbing at the ground with my walking stick. Why would a dream in a seizure be so thick with details? I tried to focus on the US flag that hung on my wall, the pattern of stars, one for each state. But I kind of looked through it instead of at it.

I'd had weird non-memories invade before, all tied to grand mal seizures I'd had: a tool shed on fire, feeling the heat radiating toward me from the burning supports of the structure; getting to Contestant's Row on *The Price Is Right* and not knowing how much to bid on a curling iron and a year's supply of hair dye. In another seizure-dream I'd rowed across a broad, foggy lake in a leaky aluminum boat. Somehow, this experience was different. For starters, I'd never had the same false memory twice.

I got nervous thinking about it. What if I could get lost in a hallucination? What if I never came back? If the whole point was to find a way to end my illness, why was I having more seizures now? Adults sucked—always pretending to have all of the answers and then acting like nothing was wrong when clearly shit was falling apart. I didn't want to be in the study anymore. But at the same time, I wanted to know more about the weird place that inhabited a spot in my mind. I told myself I'd go to the study again and not make a fuss, because even though there seemed to be so much bad going on there, I needed to know more. Where was this uh, mind-space? One thing I knew for sure: I wasn't getting the whole story from Dorfman the Bearded.

* * *

My mother watched me push the food around on my plate. "You need to eat your salad, honey," she said. I poked at lettuce with my fork, as if I could digest it through the metal utensil.

"Jack, come on. Do what your mother says," my father said. I didn't need to hear him tell me twice, not that he would have hurt me. Dad never raised a hand in anger, and good thing. If he'd been the violent type, he could have done a lot of damage. He had two of the largest, thickest hands I'd ever seen on a person. They must have weighed five pounds each. When we went fishing I had to set up all of the hooks with bait, because he just couldn't handle little bits of squid on the tiny hooks. I didn't know why I needed to hear my father tell me to eat lettuce; it seemed ridiculous and at the same time, I wouldn't have taken a bite without him nudging me.

"Your Mom says the study is going well. What do you think?" *Why isn't anyone concerned about my seizure,* I wondered.

"Other than having an episode today, it's cool, I guess," I said. I picked up the two blue pills next to my glass of milk and popped them in my mouth. I took two pills in the morning, two at three o'clock, two at dinner, and two before bed. As I grew I'd had to take more of them, to keep my brain waves manageable.

"Well, Dr. Dorfman told us that may happen from time to time, but it's a sign they're isolating where the seizures come from."

"I didn't know that." *Because why tell the dumb kid?*

Dad put down his fork and knife, studying me. "We all have something wrong with us, Jack," he said. "If we can sort this out, great, but if not, you're okay anyway."

"Thanks for the badge of approval, Dad," I said.

He looked at me, his eyebrows furrowed like two angry caterpillars. "Jack, I'm serious. Don't mock me."

I nodded.

"I just wonder why I'm doing this study, is all. I don't like blacking out."

"See," he said, picking up his fork and pointing it at Mom, who had gotten up from the table again to wipe down the kitchen counter, "he says it's 'cool,' but it's really not. Is it at least groovy?"

"Don't say groovy, Dad, please."

Before he could protest I stuffed an enormous piece of lettuce in my mouth, knowing that he wouldn't ask me to continue while I was still chewing.

"Well, if it takes embarrassment to get him to eat well, so be it," he said to my mother. "You know what came into the shop today, Jack?"

I shook my head to show him I would love to hear his answer, and was grateful he'd changed the subject. Iceberg lettuce was harder to eat fast than it looked.

"A 1949 Chevrolet Deluxe." This was a sweet low rider of a car, the sweeping back fading over an old-style chrome bumper, something like a 216-cubic inch, inline 6-cylinder over valve engine that sounded like a factory at high production when it fired up, but was so powerful it was the engine standard at Chevy for going on three decades. Where the engine and body work was solid on the '49 Deluxe, the wiring faded fast and so my father probably had to start there if it was in his shop for repair or restoration.

"Really? Who owns that?" Dad knew nearly everyone in town with an antique car because he was on the regional classic car circuit. I took another horrendous bite of salad, in a show of good faith.

"Arnold Metchum bought it at an estate sale a couple of weeks ago, and wants to get it into running shape. The whole electrical system needs to be stripped out and redone, for starters." Arnold had a big plot of land near the border with Kentucky where he kept his nicest showcase pieces. My favorite was a 1924 Studebaker Big 8 Wagon, even if it wasn't a hot rod or racing car. The Big 6 was more common because it didn't have quite enough horsepower to drag the heavier 8 frame, but I appreciated the enthusiasm for size.

"Groovy," I said.

My father turned to Mom, who was tidying up the stovetop already, squinting at the counter to make sure she'd wiped up thoroughly. "I think he's mocking me again." She chuckled and sat down, placing a pitcher of iced tea on the table.

"No really, that's cool. And I bet you're happy to work a Deluxe, right?"

"I really am. I'm so sick of Pintos and Chevelles. All these crappy cars just because of the fuel crisis." He stabbed at his meatloaf and made a cube of it with his fork. *Meat cubes, mm.* "Nobody in town can afford anything else, anyway. I guess it doesn't matter. But stop by the shop if you want to help work on it. Armand and Frank like it when you come by. They get to show you things and pretend you don't know more than they do."

I laughed. My father's employees had known me ever since I was a baby. I'd always be a baby to them. It was frustrating and nice all at once.

My mother sat down at the table. "Jack, you look tired. Maybe you should take a nap before you do your homework."

"I'm okay, Ma. Besides, I did most of my homework at the hospital while I waited for them to send us home." She inspected me, like she didn't believe me or something.

"I'm just not sure you'd tell me if something was wrong."

"He's okay, Melly," said Dad. "He's old enough to know when he needs to rest, right, Jack?"

I nodded, and asked to be excused. I piled my dishes in the sink, not eager to wash them.

Back in my room I pulled out my history textbook, reading with great boredom about the Western Expansion. I flipped through the pages; three lessons ahead always seemed more interesting than what we were on at any moment. Staring at me from the page was a black and white picture of a man on a horse in some random town. Those stones in the street. *Cobblestones.* That's what I'd seen in my vision. Cobblestones. The ones I'd seen were configured in a different pattern than this, less fancy. *Who knew there were different ways to stick stones in the ground? How amazing-boring.*

Was I hallucinating cobblestones because of my textbook? I didn't know what it meant, or if it meant anything.

* * *

My mother had noticed something wasn't right with me soon after I started walking as a baby. I would stand, my eyes fluttering for long seconds while she waved her hands in front of me or patted me on the back, assuming I was choking in silence. I also had a habit of staring into space for whole minutes. Just as she would panic, I'd come around, either doing whatever baby thing I'd been engaged in, or with a blank look on my face that dissolved into some new interest as if I'd never been lost.

Because she'd had this same behavior as a child herself, she knew what it was, and she took me to the pediatrician right away, insisting they help me.

The doctor gave her a bottle of pills and a strict regimen, but wouldn't sit down and talk to her about my diagnosis. That's when she discovered me behind the pink living room couch, slashing my fingers with a razorblade, and declaring that I was going to be a doctor someday. We saw another doctor, this one a son of her coworker at Woolworth's who had just finished his residency. He had carefully slicked back hair and a Timex watch, so she knew he had aspirations but wasn't too smug with himself. He looked at the prescription bottle and ran tests on my brain so he could tell her about the nature of my specific disorder. She already knew about the haphazard firing of synapses that stole time out of my days and put me at risk as I learned to navigate the world.

That began the routine of pills, crushed and covered in chocolate syrup so I would take them, and the other daily precautions. My teachers and friends' parents were brought in by my mother on the vigilance against vulnerable alone time, so all of my episodes happened in front of other people. This did wonders for my social standing at school. I became a favorite target of freckled Kiernan Maloney, friendly neighborhood bully. At least I'd gotten good at avoiding him, for the most part.

* * *

"Okay Jack, ready to go?" asked Dr. Dorfpoodle, who was sticking with his hair permanent for the long haul.

I nodded that I was set to begin, and he put a hand on my shoulder. As if I was ready to bolt and run. *Maybe I was.*

"You don't have to be nervous. We're here to make sure you're okay."

I wasn't okay the last time, I thought, *but I'm here anyway, aren't I?*

I nodded. I nodded a lot without meaning it.

I wasn't even surprised that shortly into the test, I was zapped out of the lab room.

Once again I had hold of the walking stick. I felt the top part of the pole with my fingers and traced over the carved *Jac* in the wood. It was bright, like the last time, but I knew I had to wait to adjust to the sun. The same terrain came into relief. Hilly path, village in the valley. I saw that farther up, past the small town, the steepness settled out and at the top was the yellow farm house from before. It seemed more run down than the last time I'd hallucinated—maybe I wasn't as consistent an imaginer as I'd thought.

I turned around, noticing the uneven earth under my feet, and caught my breath—at the bottom of the hill more fields stretched through the valley in a green and brown checkerboard. Small white farm houses, most near bright red barns, a few with white or gray grain silos, stood out against the broad terrain. I'd seen farms beyond my suburban neighborhood, but never with such unbroken ground. I shaded my eyes against the brightness and faced the slope of the trail again. Crickets and birds harmonized all around me. There were no mechanical sounds in earshot. Birds couldn't come anywhere near the noise level of a jet engine, of course. Which was, you know, fortunate for the other woodland creatures and all. On Friday nights at home I went to sleep with the steady sound of the local race track humming through my window. The quiet here left me too alone with my dumbass thoughts. I could try to walk my way out of here. I needed to pick a point and head there.

Up the hill seemed better. I returned to that sensation of walking in a new way. I should be alert for a seizure. When gravity seemed shaky to me, it meant I was on a course to lose consciousness. I breathed hard, hoping to flood my brain with oxygen, and potentially stave off an episode, which was probably silly, because if I was here in this odd place I was probably seizing in the hospital clinic room. Early morning air rushed into me, crystalline somehow, refreshing. In the cloudless sky the sun and moon hung low, on a collision course. *I've been here before. Last time.*

Unsteady as I climbed the steep hill, I bent over, plunging my walking stick into the weeds and putting my free hand on my knee to brace myself as I went. My fingers explored the sides of my kneecap, noting differences. They were smaller, less pronounced than I knew them to be. *This is a vision,* I told myself. *Just a hallucination. It's a seizure-dream. It's okay to be strange in a seizure-dream. All bets are off, right?*

I straightened up and something shifted on my head. Reaching up, I removed a woven hat, frayed a little at the back. Something had taken a bite out of it. A thin brown strip of leather cinched the brim together, giving it a strong shape. Was I wearing a hat the last time I'd had a vision? I didn't recall. Yanking my stick out of the ground, I started back up the hill. From behind me, horse hooves drowned out the bird calls. Up from the village a young girl trotted along on a brown horse, calling to the animal to slow down as she saw me clambering along.

"Jac, you're usually early," she said. This must have been directed at me, since there wasn't anyone else around. "I don't believe I've ever arrived before you."

"There's a first time for everything," I said, huffing.

"That's a strange response." She looked down at me from her perch in the saddle. "You look unwell. Do you wish to ride with me?"

I'd never ridden a horse before and had no idea how to get up there with her.

"I can just walk."

"Clearly, you are capable of walking," she said, and she laughed, flinging her long blond hair around behind her with a whip of her head. She had on a tattered but mended dress, mostly white with blue piping, and brown ankle boots. *Well she's a strange bird,* I thought.

"Here, I'll drop the stirrup." With that, the girl took her feet out of the leather strap where they had been braced, and held out her hand. She pulled her dress away so I could see what I was doing. I didn't know where to begin.

"Good Lord, Jac, just stick your toe in the stirrup, grab the saddle, and pull yourself up."

I did what she said and was surprised to find myself sitting on the butt of the horse before I even knew what had happened. The girl laughed and tossed her hair again.

"You even sit on a horse like a boy, Jacqueline. What an odd girl you are."

Chapter Three

GIRL?

It took a second for what she'd said to sink in, but fortunately I didn't say anything while I processed this information. Not like I knew how to respond or anything.

As soon as she said "girl," I understood all at once that I wasn't in my own body. Yes, I was wearing scratchy trousers, an indigo button-down shirt, and a woven hat, but I wasn't a boy. I had a braid of hair slapping my neck as we galloped along, and the bouncing of the horse made me extremely aware of which parts of my body were different here.

I tried to snap myself out of it, first by shaking my head around, which just reinforced the evidence that I had hair past my shoulders. I told myself I shouldn't worry about it; any moment now Cheshire Cindy or Dr. Dorfpoodle would wake me up.

At the top of the hill we came to a small red schoolhouse, with long windows on either side of a central set of steps leading into the building, but it wasn't the school that caught my eye. Two white boys with shaved heads, wearing faded overalls and beat-up shoes pulled at the old rope attached to the flagpole, raising the flag for the day. Something about the flag was different. The stars were aligned wrong, not like the flag in my room. Before I stumbled to the ground in my attempt to dismount, I counted up the stars, multiplying the even rows of them. Forty-six. *Why would I imagine a flag with forty-six stars?*

The bell rang out from the small steeple at the top of the school, and my friend yanked at my shirt sleeve.

"What are you waiting for? Honestly, Jacqueline, you're in a daze today."

I walked inside, dragging my feet, and now that I'd at last adjusted to outdoor light I was unprepared for how much darker it was in here. I walked into a desk. Two young girls giggled.

"Good morning, Miss Jayme," said the student who'd given me a ride to school.

"Jacqueline, Lucille, take your seats," said the teacher at the front. She was a tall woman, with her red hair neatly pulled back and a stern expression that obviously loved its location on her face. Twenty-five students of varying ages sat at their desks, children as young as kindergarteners and a lanky boy sporting teenage acne the oldest. Everyone had already sat down, and most had turned around to look at us. They were clean at their hands and the better part of their faces, but I could see that soil and dust clung to their hairlines, wrists, and ankles. There were more clothing patches in the room than at Clown College.

"Nancy, Marcus, Sirus, and Myrtle, open your readers and turn to chapter six," commanded Miss Jayme, reading from some kind of list on her desk at the front of the room. "Three grade, come here and collect your history examination, and I hope you all remembered to bring your pencils."

Up stood six or seven kids who walked straight to her desk without making a sound, and I started to worry that I could hallucinate such a frightening version of school in my own mind. Outside horses whinnied and crows called to each other, but none of the students seemed to notice. Miss Jayme handed out more instructions until each of us had an assignment. Lucille and I and two others were all doing mathematics. Apparently math is easier if it's three grade levels below one's current level.

I kept sitting at my desk, and then I wondered why. If I was in my own extended dream, why not just . . . go? Instead I got distracted staring at the ink well in the corner, wondering how many children had dripped on the edges around it as they practiced their penmanship.

I kept waiting to pop back out of this fantasy into the history of education. But I'd been sitting for at least an hour and somehow, I was still here. This was one sucky illusion if I was working on long division.

My hands started trembling. *That's a sign of something. I can't just sit here like an idiot.*

I bolted out the door.

The teacher called out after me, rushing to the front of the school. I untied Lucille's horse from his post and jumped up on him again, this time struggling to get my hips over his back because he was already galloping. He was more than happy to race off, back down the hill. I hunkered down with my arms around his thick neck, and heard Lucille's voice, no longer so cheery: "Mrs. Jayme, she's stealing my horse! Jacqueline, stop!"

I looked over my shoulder and watched the already small schoolhouse shrink before the curve of the hill blocked it from view. We passed a wooded area on our right, and I listened to the horse's hoof beats as we traveled outside the edge of the village. At the bottom of the long hill the animal slowed and then stopped to nibble on some weeds growing next to the road. Cars definitely had an advantage over this shit. I heard rushing water, so I pulled the horse's neck toward it and we trotted over, through weeds and brambles that got thicker as we went. I had to grip the saddle tight with my thighs to keep from falling off. And once again I was reminded that I didn't have my boy junk. My stomach considered revolting. I had passed the tree line and under the lush branches, finally felt a little more at home. Maybe these were the same woods where Sanjay, Jeannine and I relaxed after school, and I was re-crafting them here in my mind. We didn't have a river, but we had the same humid air and cushiony, moss-covered earth. I threw myself back over the saddle and crashed to the ground. Bad, bad hallucination. The horse, for his part, seemed content to nibble at the green stuff that grew next to the tree roots.

When would I be back home? Why was I in this place? Couldn't I have created a nicer environment if I had to be seizing?

Seizing. I wondered if I was having a terrible or worst-ever episode, and if this whole series of events was evidence that I was sicker than usual, or dying. Maybe I'd wake up in the doctor's office, or maybe inside an ambulance. Well, that didn't make sense, since the study took place at the hospital. *Dumbass.* I stood up, brushing off old leaves and clumps of dirt, and wiping my hands on the front of my wool pants. My hip, which stuck out farther from me than I was used to, ached from where I'd landed on it. I had wandered away toward a sharp curve in the river. It wasn't as large as say, the Mississippi, but at this spot it was a good twenty yards across. Cool water met my skin as I put my hand in the river, and I could see the polished stones that sat at the bottom. Next to the flow was a puddle, some kind of spot where water occasionally overflowed here and got stagnant, and grew mosquitos.

I leaned over the puddle and looked at myself. Angular features, small nose, dark brown eyes and hair. A similar but less full jaw line than mine. I wasn't very old yet, maybe eight or nine or ten, but I could discern how different this girl's body was from my real one. My hands curled into fists tightly enough that I yelped from the pain of my fingernails in my palms. Geez, even my hands were different—slender, with tiny knuckles. Vision or not, I didn't care. Without thinking I picked up a rock and hurled it into the river.

"Careful," said a voice from behind me, "you'll hurt the fish."

I swung around, another stone in my hand, searching for whoever had spoken.

"Up here," said a boy sitting high in a tall tree.

"Leave me alone," I said. "I don't care about the fish."

"What an angry girl you are."

"Go away." For a place as desolate as this, I sure ran into a lot of people.

"Pray tell, why are you so upset?" he asked, shifting his weight. The branch fluttered.

"You wouldn't understand."

"Why not?"

"Shouldn't you be in school?"

"Shouldn't you?" he asked. Even behind the large leaves I could tell he was smiling. God, I hated smiling.

"If you don't leave, I'll throw these rocks at you!"

"I don't think you can throw that far." He kept one hand on the tree trunk. He wore torn brown knickers cinched at his knees, a gray button down, collarless shirt with the sleeves rolled up, and thin laced shoes that each sported a small hole where the balls of his feet had worn through the hide. His messy, dark bangs clapped against his forehead and suggested he was not fond of a barber's chair.

I considered showing the little brat that I didn't throw like the girl he thought I was, when all of a sudden he came crashing out of the tree. It was a twisting, snapping fall that elapsed in several portions as his body hit strong branches and by the time he smashed onto the forest carpet I had made up the ground from the river bank to his tree.

He was breathing, wincing with each inhale. His legs flexed at terrible angles. Tears cut lines over his dirty skin.

"I've never fallen before," he said in a hoarse whisper. "You're bad luck, you."

"You have to get out of here. We have to get you to a hospital."

"A what?"

"A doctor. Your legs are broken. You could have internal bleeding."

"I don't see how you could know such a thing."

"It's obvious!"

"I'm done for, then. Just leave me be." He lifted one thin arm a little and waved me away. *What a strange child. Who talks like this?*

"Why do you say that?" I looked around for branches I could lay on the ground so I could drag him up to the horse. I tried to remember the first aid health class I'd taken last spring of eighth grade. I knew how to make a cravat and deliver CPR, but he wasn't bleeding badly anywhere and his heart obviously was still beating. His legs were a tangled mess, though.

"If it's past noon, our doctor is in the tavern." His words came out as tiny grunts.

"He's drinking?"

He frowned at me. "My father owns the tavern. Doctor Traver shows up every day at noon and stays there until we close."

I laid out a loose-knit set of leafy branches, and had them more or less woven together as quickly as I could manage. "Okay, I'm going to move you now, uh, what is your name?"

"Why are you still playing games with me?" he asked. "I'm Lucas."

"Lucas, I'm Jacqueline," I said, even though the name seemed foreign to me. "And it's going to hurt when I move you."

"Jacqueline, you are a strange girl and you enjoy stating the obvious."

I crouched behind him and slipped my hands under his armpits, pulling him to the mat as he screamed. I worried about not lashing Lucas to the branches, but he seemed to be staying put as I hauled him up to where the horse waited. Every few feet I apologized for hurting him. Instead of answering me he just grit his teeth and moaned like a stuck cat.

Now out of the woods, I could see just how far we had to ride to get into town, and I was having trouble wrapping my head around how to move him. If I rode the horse we could go faster but I wouldn't be able to keep him from sliding off. If I stayed next to him I didn't know how to steer the horse. In any case I didn't know how to secure Lucas to the animal, until I saw the small coil of rope at the back of the saddle.

"I hurt so much," said Lucas, who had turned pale. He was shaking a little, which I imagined added to his awful pain.

"I know, I'm so sorry. Try not to move." I fumbled with the rope and yanked on it to tighten whatever kind of knot I'd fashioned. I had never been interested in the Boy Scouts. Sanjay, the Eagle Scout, would have known what to do.

Freaking Sanjay. When is this nightmare over?

From the top of the hill an older man driving an uncovered wagon bore down on us, his two large horses at full tilt. He wore the same dour expression as the schoolteacher, but masked by a full, yellow beard. I could tell he was tall even though he was crouched over the horses at the front of the wagon. Dust billowed up from behind him; the ground vibrated. He assessed that we were in trouble, and he softened a little, letting his shoulders relax at the top of his barrel-shaped chest.

"Well, so there's the Griffith's horse," he said, jumping down and taking the reins. "Kentucky hasn't killed anyone for horse stealing in a while, but the penalty's still on the books, young lady."

The word "lady" sliced into me.

"Uh, okay. Can you help me before you arrest me? My friend fell."

He bent down and brushed Lucas's bangs out of his eyes. "Took a tumble, eh, son?" I thought I saw a moment of shock in his eyes as he noted the boy's broken legs.

"Let's get you to the doc. I expect your dad will be there as well."

Lucas looked even smaller as he scooped him up, held in the driver's arms like a stringless marionette. The boy screamed again as his legs jostled. It made my own legs hurt to see it.

"We'll talk about the horse later," he said to me, motioning for me to sit at the front of the wagon. He hitched Lucille's horse to the others, and we raced into town, the same square I'd seen during my last brain study session. My mind was nothing if not consistent.

The horses slowed once we pulled up to the tavern, and the driver leapt off his perch from behind them.

"Tie 'em up," he told me in a gruff tone, going to lift Lucas out of the wagon bed. I did as instructed. Lucas was past screaming at this point, mumbling mostly to himself and saying he was disappointed his father should know of his gracelessness.

I double-checked the reins and pushed one heavy door open, letting the light stream into the musty space. Lucas lay out on the bar counter, crying. In the darkness, his father, the bartender, rushed to him, dismayed at the sight of his crumpled son. They resembled each other, with their blue eyes, underformed chins, and small frames.

The wagon driver noticed me in the doorway. "Girl, get over here and make the doctor some coffee." *Girl.* I wished they'd stop calling me that. I walked behind the bar and asked where the coffee was.

"It's out in the back office," said Lucas's father, pointing toward a door in the corner. "You'll find the pot back there, too." He took a small tumbler away from the man I assumed was the doctor.

I looked around the room, not sure where I would find what I needed. A desk, heavy with papers, a metal typewriter, and a large glass that looked like an hourglass over a bowl of mostly clear, off-white liquid. An oil lamp, that's what it was. Towering bookshelves crammed with novels, a dog-eared encyclopedia, and a MacMillan book. Curled up under a table was a brown and white cat that looked at me with one eye, the other intent on sleeping. Why was I in here making coffee while that boy was stretched out in pain on a bar, maybe dying?

At least it was something to do, not that I had any idea how to make coffee appear in a cup. In the corner of the room, a few feet past a pile of papers, I found the wood stove, with a dented, black iron kettle sitting on top. I fumbled to find some matches to light a few logs, then dropped the box when I heard the screams. I ran into the bar. One of Lucas's legs was now straight, for the most part.

"What are you doing in here, girl? Get out of here and don't come back until you have coffee with you!" The wagon driver turned back and held down Lucas, who had a belt in his mouth, while the doctor set his leg. I hurried back into the office and looked for a coffee container. Why was I still here? Who would come up with such awful things in their mind like broken boys, and alcoholics, and shit, what was wrong with me that I'd imagined myself as a girl?

Hearing Lucas yell again brought me out of my thoughts and I stumbled over to the wood stove, lighting the chopped logs on fire. The kettle was about half-full, so I left it on the top of the burner to get hot, and found where Lucas's father kept his provisions. A yellow bag on a low shelf read *Arbuckle's Ariosa Coffee,* so I put two spoonfuls of that in the tin mug from the desk, and as soon as I saw steam rising from the kettle, I filled the cup to the brim and came back out to the bar.

Lucas's dark hair lay matted against his sweaty forehead. He turned to me and watched while I handed the hot cup to the doctor, who looked sober enough already if not a bit unsteady from dealing with the gruesome details of this patient. The leather strap was gone from Lucas's mouth and now lying at the end of the bar with deep bite marks. His legs looked reasonably aligned, and perhaps he had a little color back in his face. His eyes had a wild expression.

"Jacqueline, hold my hand." He sounded haggard, shredded. *I must really hate myself to have a hallucination like this,* I thought.

I did as he asked. His fingers were tiny and frigid and it felt like cupping a frightened mouse.

"I think I'm dying," said Lucas. I turned to the doctor.

"You're useless! Why aren't you helping him?"

Dr. Traver looked worn out, as if he had spent the whole morning walking here from the bottom of the valley. He was thin and reeked of cheap liquor; his fingers ended in clumsy clubs, and they would not quit shaking. He narrowed his eyes at me in a frown, and said through his stubble that I should just leave him alone and button my lip.

"You're not going to die," I said to Lucas. "You just—"

Bright lights, blinding me again, while I tried to adjust to the invasion in my eyeballs.

"Okay, Jack, there you are, buddy." Dr. Dorfman, leaning into my face so closely I could see the pattern of his nose hair.

"Hi," I said. It was all I could manage.

"You just had a little seizure, is all," said Cindy. "We're done for today. Try and relax, honey."

Words came out of my mouth; I heard them as if from a great distance.

"What did he just say?" asked the doctor.

"I think he asked for someone named Lucas. Who is Lucas?"

Then darkness fell over me, and I was gone from the lab, the saloon, all of it.

Chapter Four

THE ADOLESCENT ROOM of the neurology ward was full when I was brought in, so I'd been admitted to the pre-teen room, which had six beds facing each other. Disney characters were painted on the walls, their smiles frozen forever against the puke yellow paint color. I could only imagine what travesty of animation was plastered in the teen room. The Disney cartoons looked creepy at night with the main lights turned off and the flickering fluorescent bulbs over each bed giving everything in the room an undead blue tinge. I lay on my flat mattress and counted my worries—I was missing quarter exams at school, my brain was somewhere between mush and Lala Land, and I wasn't sure what body I was in at any given minute. *Nice list!*

Mom had taken to sleeping in a stained orange chair that had broken sometime in the last seventeen years and no longer fully reclined. She heard me sit up in my bed, and stirred.

"Oh, Jack, you're up. I'm so glad," she whispered. The worry lines in her forehead seemed to have deepened.

"I'm fine, Mom."

"You are not fine. You haven't been fine since that day in the lab."

"Mom—"

"Don't 'Mom' me," she said, and a nurse at the station just outside the door looked up at us.

"Something is wrong and nobody's talking about it, and I don't like it." Her nails were bitten past the beds of her fingers, and the skin there was uneven and raw. In better light I could have told if it was red or not.

"I've only been here a couple of days," I said. I didn't have the energy to help her settle down.

"Oh, see? You have no idea, Jack. My poor boy."

One of the nurses walked in, smiling all fake at me. "Look at you, doing so much better."

"So what he's awake," said my mother. "He thinks he's been here for two days. You tell him he's been in that bed for a month. You broke my son!"

* * *

Slowly, the people in my life relayed the story to me: I'd had a fifteen-minute seizure during the study session and Dr. Dorfman worried that I was at risk for brain damage, as I spent some of that time not breathing well enough. Hypoxia, he called it. The staff brought me to the emergency department of the hospital where they flooded my system with whatever drugs they thought would settle my synapse activity. I spent the next month in and out of consciousness, mumbling about coffee grounds, a boy named Lucas, horses, and one-room school houses. People pondered what I meant by all of it. My friends Sanjay and Jeannine came by most days after school, telling semi-conscious me about all of the stupid things on the bus and in class that I'd missed. And my father and mother took turns staying at my side in case I woke up, even though before my bad seizure, my Dad spent most of my life at his auto shop. I had caused everyone to focus on me.

A simple EEG gave the doctors hope that I was better from whatever funny business had ensued in my head. Dr. Dorfman came in to talk to me. He stood at the side of my bed as still as a statue.

"Looks like you're ready to go home. I hear you got out of your midterm exams."

"I guess so," I said. This was news to me.

"So we're not going to keep you in the study any more, Jackson. I'm sorry about that."

What am I supposed to think about this?

"So that's it? I'm going to have seizures forever? Like Mom?" My throat hurt.

Dorfpoodle stared at his shoes in the least helpful way possible, thinking I don't know what.

"Well, most people who have epilepsy in childhood outgrow it in adolescence. You may still see a shift in your alpha waves—become non-epileptic."

He stared at me some more, and I thought about telling him that he was creeping me out.

"You still seem worried," he said finally.

Why, because your doctor-speak isn't reassuring?

"The seizures I had in your study…were different. Like long hallucinations."

Dorfpoodle pulled up a plastic visitor's chair that had a big Mickey Mouse on the seat. I wondered why anybody would want to smother a beloved, famous mouse just by sitting down, but maybe chair designers knew something I didn't.

"It's common for the brain to insert flashes of images or memories in the midst of a seizure. It happens to a lot of people."

I pushed myself up straighter in the bed.

"These weren't flashes, this was a full-length movie." *Don't tell him any more, he'll think you're crazy.*

Instead he cleared his throat. A lot. Like, for ten seconds. I was about to hit the nurse call button, or I thought about it, at least.

"Some patients report having more involved images during a seizure, it's true. You are a bright young man, I'm sure your brain wants to do all it can to reconcile the hyperactivity with whatever material it has."

He really needed to work on his bedside manner. I gave up arguing with him. He was the neurologist and I was just the child, right?

Half an hour later, some woman dressed head to toe in purple came into the room and handed my mother a paper saying I could go home. I said goodbye to the kids in the room with me who felt they knew me. I had no clue who they were, having slept through most of my stay there. One girl, only five, had a heart condition and couldn't leave her bed. Her almond-shaped, dark eyes reminded me of Lucas's—pleading, vulnerable. She smiled and waved. "Now I won't have to listen to you snore anymore."

Walking into my house I felt like an intruder. The stuff was familiar but weird, as if they weren't mine to touch or use. My mother noticed I was taking in the surroundings.

"You want a pop?"

"Sure, thanks." I turned on the television and flopped down on the couch, which was orders of magnitude more comfortable than the bed at the hospital. Someone had stacked my textbooks and notebook on the coffee table; on the top was Jeannine's neat script with a list of homework and study assignments. I picked up the phone on the glass end table and dialed her house. Jeannine was the daughter of a Cuban immigrant who had fled to the US when Fidel Castro took power. Which was like, all her dad could talk about, so Jay and me tried to stay as far away from him as possible. It's hard pretending to be completely shocked when you've heard the story for the twelve-thousandth time.

"So I can't take a few days off from school without you peer pressuring me to do homework?"

"Hey you! Are you home? You want visitors?" I could see her face in my mind, perfect white teeth, long neck hidden by her straight chestnut hair until she swept it away to twirl it, and cheekbones that framed her many intense expressions. I suddenly felt every minute of the month I'd spent conked out, and wanted to see her.

"Sure, I'm accepting visitors."

"Oh, your Highness, of course."

I laughed.

"Besides, I'll enjoy getting you to redo all the homework from the past month for me."

"Of course you would. I'll tell Jay to join me."

"You know, I think I'm more in one-on-one mode today, if that's okay."

"Oh, sure, okay." A brief pause. "Give me half an hour."

"See you soon," I said, and hung up.

I didn't want Jay around when I talked to Jeannine, because I had to tell someone about my experience. And I couldn't share with Jay that my brain had made me female in my vision. Though come to think of it I wasn't sure I could reveal that to Jeannine, either.

* * *

Weeds invaded the old concrete slab where our suburban tract ended; the area just past a boundary fence was a hangout we'd discovered in grade school. We walked to the rusted iron fence and pushed ourselves in between the gap where a few supports were missing. Daylight flickered through the trees here. Compared to the forests in my hallucination, these trees were mangy, sad leftovers from whatever woods were originally here before the houses. In the distance a jackhammer tore the shit out of concrete and occasional trucks rumbled by on the freeway half a mile away. I'd kind of missed the noise of home.

"You look too thin," said Jeannine. She was in nurse mode.

"Hello to you too."

"I'm sorry," she said, playing with her long hair. Like most of the other girls in school, she wore it parted in the middle and pulled around her face like curtains. I gave her a look that I hoped was reassuring.

"No, it's okay. I think I've forgotten how to take teasing."

She smiled then and I thought about not telling her about my unreal time in the valley. I mean, talking about it would make me look unhinged, right?

But Jeannine asked me what I wanted to talk about just a moment too soon, before I could come up with a cover story and there I was, unable to think of a good lie. I should have prepared before she showed up at my front door. *What a schmuck.*

"So what if I had a really insano story to tell you?"

"So what if you did?" she asked, sitting carefully on an old stump.

I told her about the first two neurology test sessions, about the snapshots of images and snippets of conversation that haunted me before my third appointment in the study. She nodded, leaning in and listening even though I worried I sounded like I'd lost all sense of reality.

"Well, but you've seen weird things after your seizures before, right? Weren't you witness to some fake forest fire?"

"It was a blue shed," I said, correcting her. "But this was different, especially the last time. Way more intense."

I wasn't selling it very well. I was a rambling maniac. I tried to give her better details. That yellow coffee container, the sound of Lucas's legs snapping, how the horse smelled.

Explaining that I'd spent several hours in the same place, done things I'd never experienced in real life—down to the feeling of the smooth river stones in my hands—I noticed that Jeannine was puzzling through my story in the same way I was.

I stopped talking and looked at her.

"So now you think I'm crazy."

"Si, creo que usted está loco," she said, and laughed, waving her arms around in the air as if she would fall off her perch.

"No, no, I don't think you're crazy, Jack. But there's probably some other explanation. There has to be."

"Okay. Like what other explanation?" I was ready to hear a believable answer from her. Because while I'd told myself this whole time that my experiences were strange seizure-induced visions, I was realizing just in this conversation that I didn't believe my own explanation. *Holy shit, holy shit. What if… what if the town and all of it were… real?*

"Well, you certainly know what horses look like, even if you don't know how to ride one."

Good point, Jeannine! I thought back to that morning. Had I ever seen a valley like that, or a town square? The inside of a tavern? Maybe in a western movie? I wasn't a fan of westerns. Maybe I'd seen something like that in ads for *Little House on the Prairie*? I supposed brains were capable of creating new scenery based on things they'd experienced before. But then goose bumps sprang up on my forearms.

"I was in an office in the back of the tavern, looking for coffee, and I found a package, wrapped in yellow paper. I think it was called Arbuckle's. How would I know that?"

She sat quietly, computing some idea. "Okay, here's what you do. Today is Friday. Come to the library with me tomorrow and we'll see if we can find it there. And in the meantime, draw what you remembered. Then we'll check it out."

"It's a date," I said, without thinking. Jeannine blushed. *Dumbass alert. Idiot child of auto mechanic and worrywart says something ridiculous, news at eleven.*

I agreed, nodding like a bobblehead, but I knew already that I'd never heard of this coffee brand before.

Even if Jeannine was sure there was some other explanation for my experiences, I was worried. What if, just if, I wasn't hallucinating? What if all of this wasn't my spazzy brain cells, but something else?

What if I'd really jumped back in time?

* * *

The public library was in the middle of town, at the center of the extremely boring historic district. The one-story building looked like an oversized brown shoebox, magically plunked down next to a small lake. Well, "lake" was a bit of an overstatement. It was little more than an overgrown pond, tiny enough to be ignored for most of the year until it froze over in winter, and then screaming for anything to do, people with ice skates would descend on it, scraping along every inch, most of them waving their arms wildly for balance. An "outside" library reading room looked out on the lake, which really meant we could get a lot closer to the stinky water if we wanted, which we didn't. We left our bikes in the rack outside the tall glass front doors, and Jeannine heaved one open and looked relieved for the inside heating. She marched up to the card catalog, and of course she was a library regular so she already pretty much knew where everything was. She pulled out a skinny drawer by its tiny brass knob and began flicking through the subject headings, two handed, each flip of an index finger giving her half a second to decide if the card had what she wanted.

"Here we go," she said, scribbling the location number on a scrap of paper. She tucked a pencil stub behind her ear. *Lucky pencil.*

"Shockingly enough, it's in the history section."

"Be still my beating heart," I said.

"Do you have your drawing with you?"

I nodded and patted my shirt pocket, and we scoured the bookshelves until we came up with the title Jeannine had found—*A History of Coffee in the Americas*. It was navy blue and the size of a checkerboard and smelled like old men reading. She opened it and we combed through looking for the section on coffee brands.

"If only the pictures were in color it would be easier to spot," I said, running my pointer finger along the page. No sooner had I finished my sentence than I gasped, unsnapping my pocket and yanking out my crumpled paper. I placed my sketch on the page, next to the photo.

The heavy black writing against the light background, words scrawled across the package in an arc: they were the same. I mean for real, my drawing was hideous, but it was clearly an attempt to represent the label.

"Wow," said Jeannine.

Oh no

If she were convinced, then maybe my experience was real. Like really real. Her eyes darted back and forth between the images.

"It is quite a coincidence," was all she whispered.

We walked our bikes back home for the last quarter mile; it had rained while we'd been in the library, and the leaves on the roadway made biking uphill too slippery for us. Ice puffed out from in front of our faces as we made the steep climb to our development. At the end we stood in the street between our two houses. Her hair didn't look much different from the rain, but I looked like a misty rat.

"Look, you must have seen that box somewhere else, and then remembered it in your seizure," said Jeannine.

"I guess so." I hid my disappointment. Jeannine was the smartest person I knew. If she wasn't entertaining the notion that I'd traveled through time, I figured I shouldn't, either. Maybe my epilepsy was playing with my memory. Or maybe I had crossed the line into delusional raving lunatic. How would someone know if they were out of touch with reality, anyway? Wasn't that like, in the definition?

"I just. . . it seemed so real. Not like a dream." *Way to sell it, Jack.*

"I know you want to believe that something actually happened to you during the study, but honestly? There's no other explanation, Jack. You were in the hospital, you seized, the doctors admitted you, and you woke up. You didn't go anywhere else."

That was a good point. Doctor Who had a T.A.R.D.I.S. for his time travel. I didn't even have my own phone line.

She continued.

"You must have forgotten that you'd learned about that coffee name. I've been reading up and our subconscious minds are way more powerful than we realize."

I nodded.

"I know, I know, there's no other way to explain it. You're right, I saw that label at some time in my life and forgot about it."

She gave me a long look. I tried not to cringe by her sizing up of me. "You're agreeing with me too easily."

"What? What does that mean?"

"You really think you traveled back there, is what I mean." I made a mental note to start hanging out with stupider people.

I shook my head, but she stopped me. She took hold of my handlebars.

"The mind is a mysterious thing. You know that better than anyone. It plays tricks on us. We see things—we see all kinds of things all the time and they don't even register, but our brains pick up on them and store them away."

"You sound like Mr. Garrison in biology."

"I've had a whole month of classes that you got to skip, silly."

"Right."

"Didn't you say you tasted a sandwich once, that you hadn't eaten?"

Ham and cheese, on grilled rye bread with the rind of the ham still attached, yes, I thought. I remembered it like I'd just eaten it again. It was like a super-memory. "Sure."

"Well, brains are powerful things. It takes a whole room to hold a supercomputer, but our computers are all in our skulls." She tapped on her temple to illustrate her point, which frankly, I understood before she demonstrated it.

"But it felt really real." *Way to go, Shakespeare. What a way with words.*

"I'm just glad you're back, Jack. I missed you."

"You did?"

"Yes," she said, and she started walking again. "Jay missed you, too."

"Oh." I missed him too, and I hadn't spent any time with him since coming home from the hospital. "Well, I'm here now."

"Good." We were outside her house across the street, four doors down from mine. "Now that you're back, you can forget all about that whole ordeal." She gave me a quick hug, and told me she'd see me on the bus on Monday.

Forget, I should just forget. If I could have forgotten the town and Lucas, I would have. I doubted, however, that it was possible to pretend it didn't happen.

I was in this alone. Whatever the hell "this" was.

Chapter Five

I TRIED TO GET GOOD at pretending everything was normal, but most mornings I woke up with the sounds of tree branches snapping and Lucas staring up at the sky in a crumpled heap. Jay and Jeannine and I had taken to hanging out even more often in the wrecked concrete factory, before it started getting too cold outside. We nursed hot mugs of coffee, discussing which rock groups we liked and how awful our algebra teacher was. Sister Cordelia should have retired years earlier; now she just snapped at us. And she couldn't even remember how to write the quadratic equation.

I zoned in and out of the discussion, wondering if I'd be let back into the epilepsy study, because maybe I could get to the bottom of what was going on with me. I stopped daydreaming long enough to notice they were talking about *The Fog*.

"I don't want to see it," said Jeannine, waving her arms in front of her as if in some sort of defense from bad movies.

"Come on, it's going to be awesome," said Sanjay. I smiled at both of them, glad enough to talk about horror movies. Something was still off though—it wasn't entirely unlike the sensation when my neurology was thinking about betraying me again. *I hope I don't start seizing out here.*

"I bet it won't be as scary as *Night of the Living Dead*," I said.

Jay rolled his eyes.

"Oh come on," he said, "it'll be way better. The killer's not going to stagger around like a stupid zombie."

"Stagger or not, those zombies can take out a whole town."

"All you need is a flamethrower and blam, movie over."

"Come on Jay, are you saying the creature in *The Fog* would survive a flamethrower?"

"I'm saying most things know how to get out of range of a flamethrower, geez."

"Okay boys, I have to get home for dinner," said Jeannine. "Take care of your hand, Jack."

"Yeah, or you'll turn into the living undead," Jay said, hanging his head and raising up his shoulders to approximate the bad posture I'd have as a zombie.

We squeezed through the break in the fence and Jay jumped on his bike, waving as he pedaled off around the corner.

"I think it's good that you're getting back in the swing of things," said Jeannine. "But you still seem a little off-kilter."

"Yeah, maybe I am. I shouldn't be, I know."

She stopped walking and put her hand on my forearm. She was warm.

"What?" I asked.

"Jack, you spent nearly a month in the hospital. You're worrying that you actually went back in time, which is impossible. You're behind in your classes and wondering if you're crazy? I don't know, that sounds like a lot of shit to worry about. Give yourself a break."

It sounded so reasonable when she said it. But I couldn't just relax and take things in stride. Something was wrong, something had changed inside of me, and I needed to figure out what it was. I didn't really care if it was a stupid electrical impulse or if I'd really for real jumped through time and space. I had to figure out what had happened because right now, everything around me felt fake and stupid.

I looked her in the eyes, her pretty almond-shaped eyes, and I lied to her.

"You're right. I need to settle down. Everything's really okay."

"Exactly. You've got friends, you should lean on them. It's okay."

"I just have to ask you one thing," I said.

"What's that?"

"Please don't start singing."

She gave a fake gasp and pushed me away. "Like I'd waste my breath on you!"

"Not your breath, your art!"

She was already well ahead of me. "Either! Both!"

I walked up the steps to my house, my stomach nagging me for dinner the moment I smelled my mother's cooking. It smelled like barbequed rib night.

I pushed through the front door, kicking off my shoes in the foyer and bracing myself for King to rush at me. In seconds I had a wet-nosed retriever all over me. I knelt down and hugged him.

"You're a good dog, King. A very good dog." *And you don't look at me like I've lost my mind.* At least I felt some connection to him, even if I was struggling with the rest of my existence.

Soon enough though, I'd leave them behind again.

* * *

I set the thin plates around the table and plunked the utensils, tucking white paper napkins under the forks. Mom sighed.

"What?" I stared at the table, wondering what I was missing.

"It's nothing."

"No, it's not nothing. What's wrong?"

"It's just that my mother's dinner table always looked so much nicer. Maybe we should buy new china. Get some linen napkins. I don't know."

"Well I think it's great," said Dad, walking into the kitchen. He used a loud voice, which he usually brought out when Mom was in one of her blue spells. She gave him a little smile.

"Well, you are easy to please," she said, and turned to the counter, picking up a bowl of potato salad. And then she pivoted again to face me.

"Jacky, you're feeling better?" Once again she was inspecting me head to toe.

"Sure, Mom."

"What aren't you telling me? Be honest."

Okay, don't blink. If you blink or look up or sigh or anything she will claim you're lying. She has some secret mother skill, the knowing skill. Smile. Sell it.

"I wish I were still in the study and they could get rid of my epilepsy. But I'm happy to be out of the hospital and back home." *As long as she doesn't ask me to say more, I'm okay.*

"All right. You know, being a teenager is hard. I remember."

Oh god, please don't talk about this, Mom.

"Great. Gosh, I'm so hungry. Who's ready for dinner?"

I put down the platter of chicken and Dad grabbed the cornbread. I tried not to drool all over the table. The food tasted so good we ate mostly without talking and Mom asked for the first time in a long time if we should play cards. If Dad was surprised he didn't show it. I didn't want to be the wet blanket in the group, so we went through round after round of gin rummy and then it was time for me to take my bedtime dose of medicine. I headed up the stairs knowing that the pills would knock me out in twenty minutes, but three steps up the dizziness swamped me. I grabbed at the wall on one side and the railing on the other, the brown shag carpet still under my feet. And before I could reach the landing and sit down, I was gone.

Crickets chirped around me. I sucked in what smelled like thick summertime air. In the night I couldn't see through the dense trees to the sky, but there was enough light coming through the leaves for me to see a little in front of me. It must be near the full moon. I took stock of my situation. Who knew crickets could be so damn loud?

I was wearing thin leather lace-up boots that stopped just below my knees. And I had on riding pants, or some sort of trouser that had a padded inseam, and a dark button-down scratchy shirt. I patted myself. I sighed, taking it in that I was not in my body anymore. *Not again. There's being a mixed-up teenager, and then there's this shit.* I stood up. I was taller, whoever I was, than the last time because the ground was further away from me and my legs took longer to bring around with each step. I patted my head, felt a braid in the back.

I was wearing a bra. A very uncomfortable, way too small for my frame bra at that. I dug under my shirt and tried to find the closure with my hands. Having never undone one of these I was totally confused about how to get it off of me, so I opted for the always classy ripping it to pieces technique. It was flimsy enough and collapsed under my shirt. I didn't really have a chest that needed it anyway, or at least, I knew I didn't need it to sustain life. Wasn't I supposed to be excited to be this close to breasts? Isn't this what the guys were all talking about in the locker room at gym class? As if any of them knew what the hell they were describing. I pulled my shirt open and looked down.

Yup. I had boobs. There they were. Just hanging out, wondering where their friend named bra had gone. Maybe I'd been wearing it just to protect them from this wool shirt. Because wow, the shirt was super itchy.

It was too much. I wanted to get a handle on what was happening to me, not have it happen when I least expected it. I hadn't even been in Dorfpoodle's hospital chair. What the hell? How long would I be here this time? Was I lying on the stairs at home, hoping my parents would notice me? *Poor Mom.* Neither of us was ready for this junk.

I leaned against a tree, trying to snap myself out of it. *Jeannine says it's impossible that what I'm experiencing is real. I'm just in a seizure or a coma. I'm not really here, smelling warm bugs and old horse shit. I don't really have breasts. I'm not here, I'm not here, I just want life to be normal again, even if normal means I have epilepsy. A cure isn't worth this.*

I leaned against a tree, crying. Maybe the brain study jiggled something loose in my head? How would my parents handle it if I was even sicker than before?

The howling of wolves snapped me out of it. *Do wolves hunt people? No, right? Can I get some agreement here?* I wondered, knowing that I was just talking to myself. I knew they hunted in packs, but not how many that would be, exactly. Probably they were after some woodchuck or whatever kind of small furry things lived in the forest. Baby deer. Then the howling came again, from a different place in the darkness, closer to me. I squatted down, not daring to move a muscle. All that sitting still for EEGs had finally paid off. So huzzah for that. My eyes adjusted to the low light but even so I could only make out the trees around me and the uneven ground. Recently rained on from the feel of things. The walking stick, was it near me? I felt around and found it propped up against the tree, next to me. At least I could thwack a wolf if I needed to, for whatever that was worth. I would most definitely be great at pissing off a wolf pack by bopping them with my stupid stick, so I hoped I could get out of the woods before we found each other.

I listened for the river, and heard it come from behind me. I picked a direction uphill and hoped I'd made the right choice. My blood pulsed past my ears loudly enough that I worried I couldn't hear everything around me. I just wanted to be back playing gin rummy with my parents at the kitchen table. Maybe this was my punishment for not appreciating my life enough.

I walked slowly, small rocks pressing uncomfortably against the soles of my boots. My feet ached, my knees made clicking sounds as I hiked up the slope. I tried to watch out for brittle twigs because I wanted to stay quiet. Bats chirped in the trees above me, searching for insects to catch, and I hunched up my shoulders in defense, should they not notice me and fly into my head by mistake. *Maybe I shouldn't complain about the suburbs so much.* I was thirsty. How I was going to press on or reorient myself, I wasn't sure. If this was a hallucination, I just needed to wait it out, however long that took. But if this shit was for real and I was actually clambering up a hill, then I didn't want any close encounters with bats.

The sky seemed brighter somehow, mostly because the trees were thinning out. There was a clearing ahead, maybe even the last of these woods. The trunks of the trees were smaller, too, as if they'd begun growing more recently than in the thick of the forest. Fallen branches and the dense carpet of leaves gave way to tall grass and thistle that stuck to my sleeves and legs, but it had trouble piercing any of my clothing. That explained my ridiculous outfit. At least Jacqueline was an intelligent person, if not a fashion queen.

I heard another sound, like a snort, and ready for an attack, spun to my right. Tied to a small birch tree was a horse. She looked at me and lowered her head a little. I walked up to her and stroked between her eyes, and she pushed into me. Then she nuzzled the pocket of my shirt, and whatever was inside mashed against my skin. I fished out a sugar cube and set it in my palm, which she ate in half a second. I untied her reins from a tree branch, and planted my left foot in the stirrup and hoisted myself up. Pulling hard, I turned her around from the edge of the woods and nudged her, hoping she'd know where to take us.

We half-trotted along the edge of a field where a low stone wall ran miles ahead as far as I could see, and then the horse slowed to a walk. At some point I fell asleep on the back of the horse and wound up lying on her shoulders and mane. When I opened my eyes, we were underneath the doorway of a stable. The soft snores of other animals greeted us. I jump-slid off the horse and peeked outside, but nothing reminded me of the last time I'd been here. Of course that was nonsense anyway, because this wasn't a place. This was just the interior of my jumbled brain. I was Jack Inman with a dog named King and a boring case of epilepsy. I wasn't some girl named Jacqueline. *None of this is real.* Jeannine knew it wasn't possible, so I needed to just deal with what was a delusion from a seizure.

Delusion, delusion, I told myself.

And yet, I still tried to find something familiar. I tied the horse into one of the stable stalls, and crept over toward the farm house, a three-story white building with a porch that ran along the front. Was this my house? It wasn't like the house I'd seen at the top of the hill.

As I walked I stumbled over a tree root and flew headlong into a pile of garbage and dirt. From somewhere, a dog barked, alerting the occupants to my dangerous stalking of their tree roots on the side of the house. *If it's not the freaking wolves, it's an attack dog.* I tried to collect myself and get out of the bin, but this was taking much longer than I'd have liked. Bits of eggshell and potato peels clung to me, along with a good measure of soil.

I tore around the back of the house, intending to get back to the stables and race away, but I stopped short, seeing the double-barreled shotgun pointed at me.

"Hold it right there!" Then a quiet gasp. "Jac, Jacqueline? Is that really you?"

"It sure is," I said. I didn't recognize the man for a minute, and then realized it was Lucas's father. I'd never learned his name. He looked more wrinkled, with wide gray streaks running through his hair. *That is a classy imagination,* I thought, *that can age someone in a later episode.*

He lowered the gun.

"Imagine that. Well, what brings you back to town? You ah, you don't smell so good." A half-grin crept onto his face. It was the same grin that I'd seen Lucas make from up in the tree the day he fell. Before he fell, of course.

"I had an appointment with your compost bin. Have you always lived here?" It was a stupid question to ask, but it left my lips before I could retract it.

"No, we're just boarding for the moment. The tavern has shut down."

"What? Why?"

He walked closer to me, speaking in a whisper.

"Jacqueline, where have you been? Nobody can drink alcohol anymore. I'm doing what I can to make a living, but I couldn't afford to keep the building." They must have lived in the tavern, too? I hoped it wasn't in the tiny room with the cat and the stove.

"Oh, of course," I said, trying to remember from my U.S. history class when exactly Prohibition happened, like when Congress banned making and drinking alcohol. For some reason it was all wrapped up with my memory of the Teapot Dome Scandal, even though I was pretty sure they were entirely unrelated. U.S. history was first period, taught by Miss Peckerman, who also taught gym. I thought she preferred gym because she could just shout and blow her whistle, and in history those pretty much weren't allowed. I was lucky I retained what country we were studying from all of her hatred of reading and using an inside voice.

"I'm sorry," I said. "It sounds really hard for you."

A bit of stale bread fell out of my hair and we laughed. *Look Ma, I'm a freak even in my hallucinations!*

"Why don't you come inside and we'll get you cleaned up?"

I'd caused his son to fall out of a tree, so why was he being nice to me at all? Then it occurred to me that he hadn't said anything about Lucas. What if the boy hadn't survived?

* * *

Lucas's father boiled water on the stove, walking back and forth several times across the squeaky floorboards in the hall to bring it into the bathroom, where he poured it into the deep claw foot tub and mixed it with the much colder water from the tap. The pipes clanged and rattled every time he touched the faucet.

"Here are some clothes," he said, handing me a pile of dry cloth. "They're men's clothes but well, you wear those anyway." He smiled at me sheepishly.

"Thank you."

"Take your time," he said, shutting the door behind him quietly. I swung the metal latch into a hook on the door, locking it more or less.

Even though I wasn't a fan of the rotting garbage smell I'd taken on since landing in the compost pile, I didn't want to see myself up close again. I could be dreaming or not, but whatever this was, there was only so much I could handle.

I took off my shirt and a worm fell to the floor. *Freaking terrific.* Making sure I was looking elsewhere, I lowered myself into the tub, relieved at the hot water. I watched the steam swirl upward all around me. There was no padding around the porcelain in here. Maybe this was all one big fantasy about not having seizures. After all, I'd spent how many "hours" in the woods and on a horse and I hadn't taken even one little Klonopin pill.

A brick of soap looked hand cut and had way more perfume in it than seemed chemically possible, but that was an advantage when dealing with eradicating the smell of decomposing food and earthworm entrails. I couldn't help but breathe in the floral scent. *Guess I should take the plunge into perfume overkill and wash my hair*. I was not ready for the experience. First of all I had a shitload of hair, even if it only barely reached my shoulders. Second the long locks were like rubber bands, tangling easily, and I fought through sharp pain as I snagged my fingers in the mass of knots, yanking too hard on the roots.

Jacqueline had a grown woman's body at this point; it was certainly different than I'd ever seen in a dirty magazine. All of these bones were beneath a layer of softness I wasn't used to. I wanted to avoid contact with myself so I flapped in the water, building up as many bubbles as I could produce. Once I was halfway covered, I slid deeper into the tub and let my skin burn a little. I worried I was invading someone else's body, even as I wanted to be back in mine.

I looked at my feet, each of which had a bright red line on the outside, along the edge, from where the boots pressed too hard against them. No wonder they ached so much.

I stood up in the tub and gingerly got out, one leg at a time, cuddling the towel against me. *Oh my god I have to dry under my breasts? Get out of here.*

I dressed quickly, noticing how ill-fitting men's underwear were on me, but I was covered in clothes soon enough. I found a brush in the medicine cabinet and ran it through my hair, the way I'd seen my mother do, exclaiming again when it got caught up in tangles. I wiped the mirror with my hand and took a good long look at myself. Jacqueline was attractive, but probably called plain by the people who knew her. Her chocolate brown eyes were big and round on her face, and there was a small curved scar under her bottom lip. I wondered if she fretted about it when I wasn't like, inhabiting her. If that's what I was doing.

Here you go acting like you're in a real place again.

I let the steam fog up the mirror so my reflection became a blur, and then I padded back into the kitchen to find Mr. Von Doren.

"I knew you'd come back," I heard behind me, from the living room where I'd just been. I turned and saw a young man holding himself up on two braces, familiar, dark long bangs dangling in front of his crystalline eyes in a way that I presumed annoyed him. His once angular face looked more square now, and a light dusting of stubble stood out on his chin and above his upper lip.

"Lucas?"

"I suppose it has been some time, hasn't it?"

"Yes, it has. How are you?" I winced because I'd asked yet another dumb question. He was standing on crutches, of course he wasn't fine.

"I'm well, thank you. It's really good to see you again."

"How is that even possible? I made you fall out of a tree."

"What?" he asked, frowning. "I slipped, that's all. I should have known better than to put myself in danger."

"Well, I'm sorry your legs were ruined forever."

He stared at me.

"The crutches?" I pointed at his legs and then heard my mother's voice in my head telling me not to point, so I dropped my hand quickly and pretended I hadn't been such a dumb ass.

Lucas laughed and didn't seem in the least annoyed with me. "I recovered just fine after the accident, Jacqueline. These are from polio."

"Oh, I see. Well, I'm sorry about that, and if I hurt you after your fall."

"Some people get polio," said Lucas. "As for you, well. Jacqueline, you saved my life. I owe you everything."

Chapter Six

I SAVED HIS LIFE. *I mean, I saved his life?*

I'd thought I was at fault for distracting him, for making him fall. And here Lucas was telling me that he regarded me as a hero. My cheeks got hot, thinking of how I was stuck in this place. Well, maybe not stuck. I'd popped back out before, so maybe I would again. I started fanning my face with my hands, because all of this thinking was getting me flustered.

"There, there, where did you go off to?" asked Lucas, leaning toward me. He smiled a little bit like he knew a secret.

"I need a drink," I said, turning back toward the kitchen.

"We can't—"

"Of water," I said, knowing he was about to remind me that alcohol was illegal.

"Oh, sure. Of course." Lucas took a glass off of a shelf and crutched over to the large sink, the glass suspended between his fingers. He wasn't slowed down at all by his weak legs.

"Mr. Rushman got indoor plumbing last spring," he said, holding the full glass out for me. "And this is the second house in town to own a telephone. I'd think of it as magic if there weren't other people listening in on every conversation." He pointed to the large black box on the wall. I'd only seen pictures of the phones with the cylinder ear piece and the cone-shaped voice receiver. It looked heavy, like it could pull the wall down with it.

"Nifty," I said. I didn't share that phones were no big deal in my time.

Outside the sunrise had made it over the top of the valley, making the rooms in here a lot brighter. I didn't hear any farm activity in the field, though. "Where is this Mr. Rushman?"

Lucas sighed. "We should sit down."

I followed him into the living room, which seemed at odds with itself. Low ceilings made it feel cramped, but large picture windows let in the prettiness of the fields and the woods at their edge. Furniture that bordered on fancy stood atop a scratched wooden floor. The wallpaper sported vines and flowers, but was bare of pictures. Looking out the front windows, I saw that we were in the lower valley. From here I could see that the town I remembered had doubled or tripled in size since I'd escaped school on Lucille's horse. The old walking trail had become a paved road. Two black cars trudged into town with as much energy as their small engines could handle, rattling the whole way. I hadn't seen any automobiles the last time, but Lucas had grown up, so I guessed that plenty of other things had changed in the interim. Lucas, grown up. He'd always seemed serious to me, but now there was something else about him, and I couldn't put my finger on what it was. I figured I'd just try to get a date out of him.

"Lucas," I asked, running my finger along the side of the heavy blue glass, "what year is it?"

"My goodness Jacqueline, have you been out of civilization this whole time? But of course you have." He patted me on my knee, as if I were the child. "It's 1926."

I racked my brain for any knowledge of that year. Flappers and secret drinking parlors—speakeasies, that was what they were called. I nodded my head without realizing it.

"So okay, it's been a long time. What are you not telling me?"

Lucas sighed and stared at his hands nestled in his lap, his wooden crutches leaning against the sofa next to him.

"Mr. Rushman is missing. Along with a few other town leaders. He let us stay here when father shut the tavern, but he disappeared from the field one day two months ago, and we haven't seen him since."

"But why? He's just a farmer."

"He had a vote on the city council. And he resisted going along with changes to our town's civil and criminal code."

"Civil and criminal code?" I had no idea what he was talking about.

Lucas listed the new laws, counting on his fingers.

"No dancing, no businesses allowed to be open on Sundays, no gambling, no smoking, oh there are a bunch of others but those were the notable ones."

"Sounds like someone wants to make the most boring, uptight town ever, sure, but why should he disappear because of that?"

"Well, it's more complicated than that." He looked me up and down, like he was checking if I was real. *None of this is real, my friend.* "You have been gone a while, I reckon."

I wondered about that. Where did everyone think I'd gone?

"David Rushman, Earl Wise, who owned the general store, and Maurice Johnson, the attorney in town, were all members of the city council."

"And they're all missing?"

He nodded.

"Because why, they like dancing?"

Lucas frowned. "You may not want to take this seriously, but some of us don't have that luxury."

"I'm sorry. You're right, I've been gone a while." I mean, apparently. "Please tell me what's been happening."

He inhaled, looking at me out of the corner of his eyes, sizing up if I was worth his words or something.

"They were the majority of the city council, and there was this group of people who were really rather insistent about making changes to the local laws, who wanted to require everyone to sign an oath of religion and agree not to drink or smoke and such, and well, Mr. Rushman, Wise, and Johnson wouldn't go on with that.

"And now of course alcohol is illegal everywhere, but this group, led by Dr. Traver, has gotten lots of other things stopped in town."

"Wait, Dr. Traver?" I asked. "The town drunk?"

"He's made an amazing transformation," said Lucas. "Now he's 'The Prophet.'"

"Get out of here," I said, and Lucas looked at the front door.

"It's just an expression."

"You are such an odd girl."

"That's why you like me," I said. Good grief I was awkward no matter what time or body I was in. At least I was consistent.

"So, 'Prophet' Traver somehow became more popular? Because I don't remember anybody thinking he had the answer to anything."

"Well, Dr. Traver did have a way of capitalizing on people's fear. He would stand in the town square on a soap box with the holy book held up to the sky, and preach about how we were all going to hell."

"An actual soap box?"

Lucas leaned in again, looking me straight in the eye. "Yes, Jacqueline. An actual soap box. I think you don't actually want to know what's gone on in your absence."

My heart quickened up in my chest; I noticed he was touching my knee again.

"No no, I want to hear it. It's just, people say soap box and mean it as a … oh, never mind. So somehow people cared about this ranting guy in the street?"

"There weren't many followers at first, but over the years he's built quite a church for him in Marion. Once he got the Sheriff on his side, many other community leaders joined him, some out of fear, some because he makes them feel important."

Marion—the little town in my hallucination had a name. I tucked it away in my memory.

"Then Mr. Johnson, who mostly handled wills and helped people with land sales, didn't show up at his office one day."

"Okay," I said.

"His secretary, Miss Marker, a dour woman, traveled to his house at the top of the hill, certain that he'd keeled over from a heart attack or a stroke. She found flies collecting on dried-out scrambled eggs and some toast, and a mostly evaporated cup of tea sitting on his kitchen table. A streak of blood led out the back door and disappeared in the dirt. Shaken, she went to your mother's house."

My mother? I tried not to make any expression as he continued, but little switches started flipping on in my brain. The top of the hill overlooking the town. And older woman who lived there. I'd seen my mother in that flowery house dress. Or rather, Jacqueline's mother.

"Your mother was in the backyard, but Miss Marker asked if she had seen Mr. Johnson, she responded that the world worked best when people minded their own business. And the week after he disappeared, an unsigned note showed up at the tavern, shoved under the front door after closing. All I know about that is that after Father read the note, he closed the saloon. And a year after that Congress put an end to alcohol in the whole country."

"What did it say?" I asked.

Lucas looked at the buttons on my shirt instead of my eyes. Or maybe he was staring at my chest. I stifled a gasp. *Look at my eyes, mister!*

"He wouldn't tell me. Mr. Wise and Mr. Rushman vanished last Tuesday," said Lucas.

"Whoa, so he's still grabbing people?"

"He's never going to be satisfied with his level of control. He wants impossible things, extreme obedience. We're trying to find David and Earl, but we suspect we won't ever track them down. Traver may have some hideout on Black Mountain. We're looking into it."

"Who's 'we?'" I asked.

"We call ourselves The Underground," said Lucas.

"Like the people who smuggled slaves out of the South?"

"Yes, just like them. As you know, Marion was part of the original Underground Railroad."

I didn't know. But I nodded.

Wait a minute. I didn't know that. We hadn't covered the Civil War in our US History course, not yet. I'd heard of the Underground, but had I ever learned about a town named Marion, or Black Mountain? I racked my brain, searching for some scrap of memory.

Nothing.

Oh my god, this is real, I thought. *I don't know how it's happening but it's really happening. I mean, maybe it's like dreaming you're speaking French in your dream even if you don't know French in real life, and really you're just saying le le la le blasé chauffeur, but you wake thinking you were speaking full French.* What I really needed was to wake up in my own reality and then check this shit like Marion and Black Mountain and Underground Railroad groups. But right now I was sitting on a couch talking to someone who was either completely made up or completely real. It was nuts.

"So he got what he wanted," I said.

"Trouble is, once a man has power, he always wants more," said Mr. Van Doren, walking into the living room. His boots and jeans were soaked up to his knees.

"Hello, Father."

"Hello you two," said Mr. Van Doren, who headed to the front door and pulled off his boots, leaving them and a small puddle on the entry floor. "I see it's story time. Catching Jac up with our latest developments?"

Lucas nodded.

"Although she keeps interrupting me with nonsense."

"Well," said Lucas's father, scratching his chin, "I can assure you it's not nonsense. I have just returned from checking the creek behind Mr. Wise's property, to see what may be there."

"What did you think would be there?" I asked.

"My dear, I was looking for Earl Wise. But I fear he may be far away, if he isn't to be found here in town."

"You mean like on Black Mountain?"

He nodded, and he looked sad. This was heavy. If I was traveling through time, I'd landed in a really crappy spot. What did it mean? What was I supposed to do?

"I think we should explore Black Mountain, father," said Lucas. "If only our automobile were in working operation."

"You have a car? Where?"

"It's in a safe place," said Lucas.

I tried to be casual, but I was excited. "What…what about it doesn't work?"

"I would need to know anything about mechanics to answer you, Jac."

"Just take me there and I'll fix it."

The two men looked at each other. Whoever Jacqueline was, the notion that she could repair a car wasn't impossible for them. Jacqueline was apparently a badass.

And I had found a purpose.

"We can take you to the automobile, but we don't have any tools," said Mr. Van Doren.

"We can probably find what she needs," said Lucas. I was missing something.

"See, Jock Edwards, the mechanic in town, is in league with Dr. Traver."

"Oh. Of course he is. So let's steal them."

"You can see why I enjoy her so," said Lucas. *Enjoy me? What am I, a bottle of Coke?*

"I can indeed. Jacqueline, that is a whole other matter. I'm sure we can figure something out."

"I could just walk in there and grab at least some of what I need. I know what to look for."

"We can't let anyone see you, Jac," said Lucas, touching my leg again. He was warm.

"What? Why can't they see me? If I haven't been here for years, Dr. Traver can't have anything against me."

Lucas took my hand. "Well now, of course he could. But more importantly, Jacqueline, everyone thinks you're dead."

CHAPTER SEVEN

"WHAT?" I ASKED, "Why do people think I'm dead?"

Outside, a rumbling motor cut into my shock, and Lucas scrambled to stand up. "Come quickly." He crutched toward the hallway, back where I'd bathed. I bounded up after him.

"Where are we going? Who is that?"

Mr. Van Doren stood up and peered out the front window.

"Traver's men. Go." He waved at us.

"Jac," said Lucas, turning around to face me. The engines at the front of the house cut out; we heard car doors clanging shut. "No time like the present; let's go see about those tools." He opened a door in the hall and I saw a staircase leading down to the basement.

"But your father?"

"He will hold them off. Come along now!"

Loud knocking on the front door of the farm house made the windows on either side of the door shake in their frames. *Good grief have you builders ever heard of energy efficiency?*

"Hurry!" He pointed to the staircase.

I pounded down the stairs as Lucas shut the door and set a lock from our side of the door. *Whoever heard of a basement you could lock from the inside?*

First I only heard our breathing, but quickly enough the shouting began. I found a grimy small window at the top of the stone foundation. Pushing a few old fruit boxes to the wall I climbed up and held onto the sill, peering out in case I could see anything.

Mr. Van Doren had managed to get three men down from the porch to the front lawn, back to their cars. That they all had on gray suits and black fedora hats made them look like they were in some kind of uniform. All of them were still yelling, and then Mr. Van Doren walked down the porch stairs and pointed at the far end of the field. One man, the oldest of the three, got in his face and said something to him, but Mr. Van Doren kept his composure. And then they returned to their cars, speeding off as fast as they'd arrived.

A slam from the front door, and pounding on the floor sounded above us.

"That's the all clear," said Lucas, who unlocked the door.

Mr. Van Doren opened it, and he and Lucas had some whispered quick conversation. Then Lucas turned around. Picking up his braces he slid down the railings on his arms and landed hard on the floor. Instead of complaining he scrambled back to his feet before slipping again. This time he giggled in response.

"Come on," I said as I pulled him to his feet.

"You always make life more interesting, don't you?" he asked.

"Oh no, I'm boring. It's you two who are the barrel of laughs. What did those guys want?"

"They wanted to know if Father had been looking around Earl Wise's house, and they were asking questions about who came riding to this house last night."

"They saw me?" I'd slept for much of the ride, not bothering to take stock of who was around me.

"Probably not them, or they'd have intercepted you. My bet is it was old lady Heinrich, that busybody on the corner. Let's go."

"What did he say to them?"

"That the rider slept in the stable without our knowledge, and when we spotted her at sunrise she fled on horseback into the Wannaker Woods down yonder. I don't know what he said about his trip to Mr. Wise's house."

He waved me over to a coal pile in the corner of the basement. His fingers ran along the mortar line of heavy, large, soot-stained bricks, and I gasped as they slid into the wall. A quiet click, and a section of the wall pulled out toward us to make an opening just a couple of feet wide. We slipped inside and Lucas pulled a handle to shut the door. *What clever little Prohibition and abolitionist people.*

"There's a lantern by your feet," he said. I fumbled in the dark and felt around until I hit on lacy metal. A brief flash of light as Lucas struck a match on the wall, and then lit the wick. The dank passageway stretched out ahead of us, sloping downward and curling around until I couldn't see any further. It was barely wide enough to allow our shoulders through. He handed the light to me and I gripped it, leading us into the retreating darkness. I was even beginning to appreciate the soapy cologne from my bath as competition to root rot and mold.

"So, can we talk now?" I asked, knowing I sounded frantic. Behind me, Lucas kept up a quick pace. "Because I have something to tell you."

"Yes, this clearly is an appropriate moment to converse," he said. We'd arrived at the bend in the tunnel, and I could see that it had started to climb upward again toward the surface. "You can relay your tale to me soon. But we have a rendezvous with a certain piece of machinery. And then we need to meet up with someone."

"Who?"

"Your mother," he said, giving me an exasperated sigh.

I manually displaced the image of my mother in Ohio with this woman I'd "seen" in one freak dream. If I'd somehow literally jumped into another person, if all of this was real, then I needed to learn quickly what this whole world was about. If this place was real, could I get hurt here? Die? I quit rushing up the slope and put my free hand against the wall to steady myself. Lucas stopped short behind me, not expecting my sudden deceleration.

"What is it, Jacqueline?"

I had started crying.

* * *

Lucas's arms were around me, squeezing me in a way that felt at once comforting and a little strained, as if my burst of emotion had frightened him. In return, I put my arms around his, clinging onto both of us at once. It was weird but I didn't care so much right at that moment.

"Now, now, this too shall pass." He reached up and smoothed my hair, and I nuzzled into the crook of his neck, which smelled of lye and coffee. And then I pulled back, hard, remembering that none of this was right. The sensations of warmth and fear in my body ceased and I was left realizing I was really a boy myself, supposedly attracted to girls my age, or at least, Jeannine. I wasn't this person. I pushed at him and dropped the lantern, spilling the oil out on the dirt floor and extinguishing the light. We stood in darkness, neither of us able to see anything.

"We must be careful about what we pretend to be," I said. Sanjay was a big Vonnegut fan and had made me read *Mother Night*

"You continue to confound me," he said. Of course he'd never heard of Kurt Vonnegut. *Although if Lucas was a figment of my imagination maybe he could have.* Instead of saying anything else he just dug in his pocket for another match.

"I'm sorry," I said.

"If that is so, then please, for the love of God, just walk with me so we can get somewhere safe. People are waiting for us. Honestly Jacqueline you didn't used to be this weepy and existential."

I frowned into the pop of light and tried to flatten my expression before he caught me. He looked at me, frowning.

"What 'people' are those?"

"The people who are trying to get rid of Dr. Traver and his band of thugs," said Lucas, handing me the lantern. "Try to keep a grip on it this time."

We carried on, and the tunnel took another turn. Now we'd come upon a locked door. This time Lucas pulled out a small skeleton key and unlocked a large iron shackle. The key struggled with the tumblers inside the lock. He grunted as he wiggled it and turned the key at the same time, and then the lock sprang open. "Okay."

I reached out and touched his muscular upper arm. "Lucas, I don't want to get you in any trouble."

He smiled a little and wiped his bangs out of his eyes. "We are well past that point, Jac, but don't fret. None of this is your fault."

At least there's that, I thought.

We were through the door next and Lucas closed it firmly; I could see from this side that it didn't look like a door at all but rather part of a rough-hewn wall. We stood at the cross bar of a T intersection, water running through the lowest point of the tunnels. It stunk like old garbage cans. Lucas blew out the lantern because there were electric lights here running the length of the corridors.

"We're in the sewer?" I asked, having no idea where to go next.

"We are indeed," he said, and one brace slipped on a damp stone. "I hate it in here."

"It smells terrible," I said. Even the cologne soap was no match for the stench. "Why does the tunnel under the farm house lead to the sewers?"

"This was part of the Underground Railroad."

"Wait," I said, interrupting him. "*The* actual Underground Railroad?"

"Yes, of course that one. You really did not pay attention in Miss Jayme's class, did you?" In my defense I only was in her class for half a morning, but whatever, I didn't want to argue with him.

I suddenly felt foolish.

"Anyway," continued Lucas, "years later, when the township started planning for a plumbing system, they built the storm drain here. Mr. Rushman saw to it that he was on the city council so he could help survey for the sewer and leave the secret tunnel undiscovered."

"He was a clever man," I said.

"He certainly is," he said, correcting me. "Now then, we go this way. We need to be quiet now because our voices will travel from here up to the street."

I nodded and followed him through the Underground Freaking Railroad, which was way more interesting than anything we'd ever discussed in Miss Peckerman's class, but I had to pretend not to see the rats, whether they were alive or skeletal. Rats were gross. They seemed to have no problem eating their fallen friends. We hurried along until Lucas came to another part of the wall that I now could tell was another hidden door. Again there was a soft click, but this time the slab only moved a little.

"Give me a hand," said Lucas. I braced against the door and grimaced because I no longer knew what kind of strength I had. I walked back a few paces and then ran into the wall, expecting to throw my shoulder out of joint. Instead it flew away from me, and we were in another corridor, weak beams from the gas lights flickering down to us from the street above.

Lucas closed the wall behind us that had sprung free of whatever had been impeding it. "Well, you're as tough as I remembered."

"Don't you forget it," I said.

"I shan't."

"You shan't?" I laughed at him, the sound echoing around the chamber.

Lucas hushed me, and looked at the ladder. I wondered if he would be able to climb up. He must have figured out what I was thinking, because he leaned into me and kissed me on the back of my fingers before telling me that he was pretty strong himself. His lips were just as warm as his hands, and left a spot on my skin that lingered. But I didn't reach over to touch it. All of those times I'd sat perfectly still for the EEG machine had trained me well.

"Hold these," he said, handing me his braces. He set his feet onto a step of the ladder and yanked himself up. It was slow going. I worried that at any moment more pursuers would crash into the room, while we were in such a vulnerable position. I calculated that I could use Lucas's braces like baseball bats; they seemed sturdy enough to take a few hits without breaking, if I needed them for that. I hoped it wouldn't come to that.

I followed Lucas up the ladder, gripping both braces in one hand. He had reached the ceiling.

"I dare say, I think you're gazing at my bottom," he said from up above.

"Don't flatter yourself," I said. He laughed a little and pushed the metal cover up and over, and more sunlight burst into the hole. I covered my eyes to give them a chance to adjust.

Pulling ourselves out of the sewers we found ourselves on a quiet side street. It looked vaguely familiar. Maybe this was a section of the original town square that I'd seen before. I held him up while he steadied himself on his crutches. He pointed to a building at the end of this block, away from the main street. "We're almost there."

"We're almost where?" I asked. I was no longer clean from my bath. "Somewhere where I won't notice you smell like rotting trash?"

"I would almost say you're not appreciative of my efforts."

I put my hands on my hips and then was distracted by their shape. "I would almost say you just dragged me through a hill for the sport of it."

He made an expression I couldn't place, and before I had time to recognize it, he was off toward the wood structure. We ducked inside and I saw it had once been a bank. A long counter ran the length of the room, protected with dark brass bars that every so often were interrupted with sections mounted on hinges so the tellers could open them when needed. Everything was covered in dust, including the tables that customers had used to fill out deposit and withdrawal requests, and which had been pushed up against the teller windows to make room for something large and bulky in the center of the building. Whatever it was, Lucas was pulling off the canvas that covered it. A cloud of dirt flew up into the air, making us cough.

It was an Auburn Beauty, early 1920s, gun metal gray and burgundy, with extra room for the chauffeur and a snappy leather box mounted on the back. I was pretty sure the trunk wasn't standard. I ran my hand along the body, feeling the slight changes in density that hand-hammering created. Wild. I'd never seen a car from this era in such good shape. On the other hand, someone had removed the roof, probably so it could be used in racing. There wasn't a safety belt in sight. I looked at the steering wheel and dashboard. There was a lot of empty space, because other than headlights, the gear shift, and the emergency brake, there wasn't much to this car. The wood paneling was gorgeous. It was a strange mix of luxury and plain.

"Where did you get this?" I asked, running my hands over the dash. I hopped back out and lifted the hood to take a look at the engine.

"It was Mr. Rushman's. He bought it after his horses got too old to pull the wagon.

It dawned on me that Mr. Rushman was the man who rescued Lucas after he fell out of the tree. I'd met Mr. Rushman. *Holy crap.*

"It must have cost a ton."

"A ton of what?"

"Money, Lucas. I'm just asking, was he rich?"

"Of course he was—is—rich. The town is named after his mother's family."

"Oh. Right." I flashed him a smile like I'd been playing with him. I looked under the hood.

The engine was covered in greasy dust. Or dusty grease, it was hard to tell. The fan attached to it was almost larger than the engine itself. I figured the heat coming off of this thing was intense. Continental, six cylinders, probably not more than 100 horse power, but for a man used to a two-horse wagon, it must have felt like aiming a rocket down the street. I looked around at the distributer cap, the hoses, tugged on the belt to see if it held enough tension, checked the leads coming from the battery. Everything seemed to be in order, so why wasn't it working?

I found the hand crank behind the front bumper and pushed it into the grill, nearly breaking my thumb as the crank sprang back at me.

"Careful," said Lucas, like a reflex.

"Thanks so much."

He rolled his eyes at me and I jumped back behind the wheel. I went through my rusty knowledge of early mechanics. I didn't want to look nervous in front of Lucas. *Check that the brake is on. Check that it's out of gear. Okay. Check that the ignition is on. Press the starter button.* The engine cranked two, three, four times and died, even though I pumped the accelerator.

"I told you it was on the fritz," said Lucas.

"Did you know there are seventeen different kinds of fritz?"

"I beg your pardon? No, I did not."

I giggled. Maybe it needed gas. I tapped the fuel gauge. The needle had been pointing to a quarter of a tank, but now it dropped to the far left. Ha.

"I see, you're teasing me again."

"Just a little. But I can't figure out what's wrong if I don't play around with it."

He crutched over to the front window and peeked outside at the street.

"Well, try to make your deductions quietly, please."

It was a good point. I nodded, and stopped myself from holding up a finger to my lips.

"Do you have a gas can in here?"

"Um, yes. Somewhere." He walked over behind the old teller counter and brought out a small can. It was also covered in dirt and dust. If this were Dad's auto body shop he would have fired the staff. I felt his fingers touch mine as he passed the can to me.

"So this is oil, but thank you."

Lucas glowered at me.

"I mean, are there more cans back there? I can just go look." More silence. Terrific, now I was pissing off people in the real world and in my own mind.

I found four cans of gas, popular before gas stations popped up everywhere. I felt around on the shelving—what did bank tellers need shelves for, anyway–and came up with a can opener. Two cans of gas and the car seemed close to full, if not pretty stinky from the fuel.

"I think it'll work now," I said, full of bravado. This time I was ready for the crank recoil. The engine rumbled to life.

"Jacqueline, help me with the doors," said Lucas, heading to the rear of the bank as the building filled up with exhaust. I hopped out of the car and helped him unlatch two wide wooden doors that had been bolted into the floorboards. Leaves and other debris twirled into the bank. He headed over to the car's passenger side and waved at me.

"We have to hurry."

He wanted me to drive.

My driving knowledge wasn't as limited as most of my friends' because my father had put me behind the wheel many times before, starting with go carts when I was seven. But I really hadn't driven much beyond a flat track or a parking lot. And I hadn't tried to shift into gear yet, so if there was an issue beyond needing gas, we could be in trouble.

If Lucas worried that a young woman in the 1920s wouldn't know how to drive a car, he didn't say anything. I pushed down the clutch and ground the stick into first. The gears inside bucked at me and then I eased off the brake. We popped past the doors and then second and third gears were easier. He pointed to a rutted road and the car bounced along kicking up dust and revving until I'd find a new gear. The ride was hard; I made a mental note to put more air in the tires.

I guessed we had rudimentary shocks but every pothole threw the car and jolted us. It was like having hot popcorn drive a car. Lucas tapped me on the shoulder; in his hand he held a pair of goggles.

"Don't forget these," he said, yelling over the noise of the engine. I fumbled with the strap as I kept one hand on the steering wheel.

"Where are we going?" I hoped I would hear his answer over the noise.

"To your mother's."

Too bad I didn't quite know how to get there. I hoped all roads led to Rome. At least I knew she was up the hill from here.

According to Lucas, she needed me. The woman needed me and thought I was dead.

* * *

Lucas had me take a roundabout route to the farm house to make sure nobody followed us. I guessed people really did think I was dead, or someone would be watching the house for signs of my reappearance.

"What is she going to say when she sees me?" I asked. I didn't want to give her a heart attack.

"We'll find out in a few minutes," he said, scanning the road behind us. So much had been built up between the farm and the town that now most of the city streets were obscured by outlying buildings. What was once a straight shot from the valley to the hill top, was now a series of turns on farm roads. It wound up being a little bit of cover for why I didn't know how to get to my own house.

I pulled up to the farm house, and at first only a few brown hens were there to greet us, clucking at the ground and scattering to get away from the dust cloud the tires kicked up. The engine cut out roughly as if it didn't want to stop chugging. We lumbered out of the car and an older woman came out from behind the house with a basket of laundry in her sun-weathered arms. Her mouth fell open, but she refused to drop the garments, instead setting the basket on a tree stump. She brushed her house dress as she walked over to me. I thought I could see a resemblance in her jawline and eyes to my image in the mirror.

She gripped my elbows, holding me in a way that suggested she'd sized me up like this many times before.

"Jacqueline? My Jacqueline?"

"Hello, mother," I said, because the obvious was clearly the best. *Sigh.*

Her expression turned sour, and she looked around at the line of trees that had sprouted up on one side of the long driveway. "Get inside," she said, pushing me toward the house. "You too, Lucas." As we hurried up the porch steps, I saw her brush aside a tear.

"I knew you weren't gone," she said, and followed us in.

In the small foyer, she shut green curtains and wrapped her arms around me, rocking me. This was not something that happened in my family, but I tried not to squirm. She smelled like powder and clothes dried in the sun. There was no stemming the flow of tears now. After some time, I realized I was crying, too, figuring I'd add that to the layers of weirdness of this whole situation. Lucas walked to the back of the house and I heard the clatter of plates and cutlery. My mother pulled away from me, holding my shoulders this time and inspecting me.

"You're a grown woman now," she said, and then she laughed a little. "And you still insist on wearing men's clothes. Tsk."

"They're comfortable," I said, happy to tell her anything that wasn't a lie. *Which is weirder,* I wondered, *the grown part or the woman part?*

"You need to eat something, I'm sure. Your friend has already made it to the kitchen." With that, she put her arm on my shoulder and we joined Lucas.

The years had not been kind to her, carving deep lines next to her eyes that dove down her cheeks. Her knuckles were knobby and her back slouched. But she still seemed proud. Was it just her in this enormous house? Nobody ever mentioned my father in all of my time here. *Oh, those absent dads of the 1920s.*

Each room I could see was like a museum. Wallpaper was lined up perfectly, even though the print in the living room was of small diamonds. The floorboards weren't varnished, but someone had taken care to put up chair railings. In the living room crown molding ringed the walls. I couldn't spot any nail holes in the finish work. A line of windows with small panes ran along the wall to the end of the house. The trim was painted white, but none of the glass showed any stray paint marks. It was once a very proud house, but it was clearly too much for her to continue to maintain.

Lucas moved a brass lever and opened a square door in a dark wood cabinet on the wall of the kitchen. He grinned, seeing what it contained, and pulled out a small amount of ham. It hit me that this was an ice box, the thing before people had refrigerators. It was like living in a colonial reenactment. If this was all in my head I had super fantastic reading comprehension that I'd never seen in real life.

He made each of us a plate with ham and buttered sourdough bread, and as we sat at a long table in the kitchen, we talked about how life had changed for my mother after Dr. Traver and his associates took control of the town.

She held up her hands and counted on her fingers. "No music allowed, except from the hymn books in church. No hand-holding between unmarried couples. No dancing, celebrating of birthdays, or associating with those deemed outcasts by the prophet. Of course no drinking, but I was never one for the bottle."

"Associating?" I asked "How could anyone stop that?"

"Don't act like I raised you to be a dummy," she snapped at me. "People shun you like you never lived here your whole life and they don't know you. It's so bad now I can't even get anything at the grocer's on Main. Lucas and his father bring me food in the middle of the night now."

"You do?"

Lucas nodded, pretending he couldn't talk in the middle of his bite.

"But isn't your money as good as anyone else's? What do they care?"

She shook her head at me, pulled apart her piece of ham and started making a pile of little pink strips on her plate.

"They closed my account, girl. Gave me what little I had in a bag and told me to have a nice day. I made a good go of living off my land, for a while, anyway. I still have the three hens, though they don't lay much anymore. I kept mating the pigs until they were too inbred. When the cow stopped milking I led her to the corner of the pasture over there—" she pointed with one crooked finger, through the wall of the kitchen and toward the back field—"and shot her through the eye with my shotgun. Her meat lasted me for a long time, through the winter mostly, but it was a bitch to make a hole big enough to bury her. Lucas's father helped me with that, too. That man is going to heaven for damn sure."

Lucas smiled but said nothing.

"Wow. All of that is awful."

"Sure was. Not as awful as the July day that Western Union boy pedaled up here, sweat pouring down his face from under his cap. I knew it was bad news if anyone dared venture all the way up here. Like the day the US Army sent two soldier rejects up to tell me your father died in France in the trenches."

So that's what happened.

"This telegram boy thought he looked all official with his black boots up to his knees and his full-length trousers instead of his knickers, but I laughed at him. Maybe I'm a mean old lady, I don't know. He read the note from some sheriff four towns over saying they'd found your body in a creek, and I just couldn't believe it. My baby. I knew you had a stubborn streak but you've always been smart. Your father and I never'd thought we could have children, but you'd come along and then I lost him, but … I just wasn't ready to give you up."

I looked at her hands trembling on the table, her fingers interlaced with each other. She must have been devastated. I reached out and took her hand and squeezed it.

"She wasn't doing well," said Lucas finally. "Father found her one night when he was bringing over a box of groceries. He says he helped her inside and made her a meal and drew her a bath."

Like he'd done for me. *Thank goodness we have Mr. Van Doren for our family hygiene.*

"He stayed with me for a week," she said, and for the first time she looked ashamed of herself. "That kind man brought me back to health. I told him about the telegram, and he looked me straight in the eye and said he didn't think you were really dead."

"What? Why not?" I asked.

"Because nobody came up with the body, and he said he'd learned that the sheriff who wrote the telegram was agreeing to set up another church for Dr. Traver, one in his town."

"But why tell you I'm dead?"

"Who knows how this crazy man works. Maybe it was to break me, or maybe it was a threat that they could get to you if I kept acting up or if I didn't move away. If you're trying to put the fear of god into people, you can't have some dissenter hanging out, thumbing her nose at you and your followers."

Who knew was right. I nodded and tried to think about how someone had gone from lush to total control freak like Dr. Traver.

"You were a dissenter?"

"Don't act like you don't remember. Ain't nobody calling themselves the Messiah or a prophet really so. Yes, I told my friends he was a snake oil salesman, pure and simple. I wrote letters to the newspaper, reminding them of scripture, and I told him when he was on his ridiculous box that he belonged in an asylum and not a church. So yes, I dissented. Every chance I got."

I laughed out loud. If Jacqueline came from this woman, no wonder she had such a reputation for being stubborn.

"Once she was better I came up here every few weeks with more supplies," said Lucas.

"In the car we drove?"

"No, in a three-wheeled cycle I have. I pedal it with my arms." He gave me a big grin, figuring I'd ask how he could ride a bike. *Oh my god you're not kidding,* I thought.

"You industrious young man," I said, and I smiled back at him.

Mother shook her head and stood up from the table, shuffling to the sink to rinse her plate.

"Nobody ever saw you or stopped you with these deliveries?" I asked.

"Oh it stopped," he said. "Recently."

"I suppose we couldn't have gone on with this forever," mother said from the sink.

"Mr. Traver's followers grew, with all kinds of people coming into town for his Sunday sermons, which lasted all day. At some point he became aware that Old Lady Bishop was receiving help from neighbors in town, might even be running some kind of bathtub gin operation out of her home. He told people I must be stopped.

"One evening I thought I heard Mr. Van Doren or Lucas coming to stop by with monthly groceries, so's I went out to the front porch, and instead of a friendly greeting I watched men skeeter by the house throwing rocks through the front window. One of 'em had a note attached telling me I wasn't welcome anymore."

I looked toward the living room, and noticed for the first time that one of the windows had wood in it instead of glass.

"And I decided right then and there that I had to drive the so-called 'Prophet' out of town."

I'd been wondering all this time, if this wasn't a hallucination but a real place, why I was here and what I supposed to do about it. If I'd somehow fallen into the life of Jacqueline Bishop, daughter of an outcast in a town run by zealots and murderers?

Maybe her goal ought to be mine, too.

Chapter Eight

DARK BROWN EARTH STRETCHED OUT before me, and I'd never noticed before that high quality soil has a smell. Of course nothing in my subdivision came close to being farmable dirt, so I'd never had the exposure, but now rich soil was all up in my nostrils, getting friendly. The broad field was dotted with green plants that while kind of pretty, didn't look especially appetizing.

"I didn't know potatoes were this ugly," I said.

"The leaves are drab because they're poisonous," said the old woman named Darling. She was the daughter of a freed slave, and so tiny I thought I could put her in the pocket of my overalls. She wore her hair very short, and every so often she fiddled with a pair of wireframe glasses that kept sliding down her nose. But Mother admonished me to listen to everything Darling told me about gardening and not to give her any lip. I squatted down next to her while she gave me instructions for harvesting potatoes. Darling yanked a plant out of the raised row. Bits of the ground dropped onto our shoes.

"Potatoes are related to nightshade," she said, knocking clumps of dirt off of the roots. She took a quick glance to see if I was paying attention. "Nightshade is a poison. The only part of the potato plant that people can eat are the roots." She tossed a pair of dirty white gardening gloves sideways to me and I caught them. "Put these on when you go down the row to gather them. Understand?"

"Yes ma'am," I said. The gloves hung loose on my hands and smelled moldy. I lifted up the basket and moved down a few feet to start harvesting. Darling stood up, not gaining much height by doing so, and dusted off her blue dress.

"You got the right idea wearing those boy clothes," she said before walking back into the house. I kept my head down and pulled potatoes out of the ground, not wanting to fret about my progress or lack thereof. After my basket was loaded up, I dragged it to a long table behind the kitchen door and sat down to pluck the roots from the plants. A woman about my age, maybe younger, walked up to me from around the side of the house, her apron filled with raspberries. Small cuts on her arms stood out, just beginning to clot. The raspberries and her blood clashed with her bright red hair. There was way too much red going on here for my eyes. She took care to fill up a metal bowl with her load, not spilling a single berry.

"Hi, Jacqueline," she said, sitting next to me. She held up her apron to dry her sweaty forehead. *Raspberries and perspiration, yum.*

"Hello," I said, glancing at her sideways. Lucas, his father, and I had been here for a few days and I hadn't seen this person yet. But she knew who I was.

She laughed at me. I could see older scrapes and bruises on her arms, but I wasn't sure if they'd come from earlier escapades in the raspberry bushes or if she had some more general tendency toward maiming herself. "I'm Lucille, remember? It's been a while, I suppose."

Lucille. I'd stolen her horse the second time I jumped back. The day I met Lucas and rushed him to the then-drunk Dr. Traver.

"Sorry about your horse," I said, snapping another potato off the stem.

Lucille laughed again, taking some of the vegetables from me. Cackling was more like it. "We never took that horse anywhere interesting. He was probably thrilled he got to have an adventure."

"Well, that's nice of you to say. I'm glad nobody threw me in jail for taking him."

"Mr. Rushman got the sheriff to look the other way, remember? Back before the sheriff we have now."

"Yes." Finally, an actual memory I could share with someone here.

She looked at me, probably wondering how someone who seemed so intelligent at times was really this idiotic. *Get in line, lady.*

"I don't know, I guess he reckoned you were doing a good thing trying to get Lucas to the doctor. Besides, my Pa told the sheriff to take it easy on you." She shrugged her shoulders and screeched out another laugh.

"Thanks, Lucille's Pa."

"Lucas is right about you," she said as she tossed potatoes into the finished pile.

"What's that?"

"You are an odd and fascinating girl."

"You have no idea."

* * *

Gathered around the supper table were the members of the Underground—Mr. Van Doren and Lucas, Lucille Gifford, Arnold Dawkins, who was a friend of the missing lawyer, Mr. Johnson, and Darling Madison. And now me.

"You think we are such a daring group," said Lucas, seeing me taking in the table of people.

"What do you mean? They seem pretty regular to me."

He harrumphed. "We're regular until someone sees us white folk eating dinner with Darling."

"Well," I said, trying to cover my shock at him, "maybe we shouldn't be too proud of ourselves." This was not a good time to bring up Rosa Parks and the civil rights march on Washington. A lot more racist shit was going to happen that he didn't know about.

Mother sat down at the head of the table; I figured her place was assigned as such because this was her house, not because she was the leader of the group. I couldn't determine who was in charge actually, because it seemed like everyone brought some special experience with them. It was certainly a larger supper gathering than I ever had at home. *Home.* I missed simple dinners with my parents.

We passed around bowls, each with a bit of our haul in them—mashed potatoes, mid-season zucchini and tomatoes, stewed together, grilled pork sausage, and biscuits that were too dry to eat alone, but better with vegetables on top.

"Because sawdust is always more edible when it's wet," Lucas whispered to me.

I gave him a shocked look, as he'd just insulted Mother's cooking. I kicked him under the table.

"Ouch," he said to me, passing the potatoes to Mr. Dawkins, who had spent so much time indoors he looked like a white sheet.

I felt Lucas's left hand on my knee, squeezing me. He was trying to get back for my kick, but instead of hurting it felt good. I didn't want him to take it away, but he did after only a second or two. *What the hell is wrong with me? I shouldn't like this. Stop it, Jack.*

I sighed and put vegetables on top of my biscuit. My real mother would have been impressed. I really just wanted a box of mac & cheese or a pepperoni pizza. And Lucas's hand back on me. *Damn it.*

I turned away from him and his messy bangs and tuned into the conversation around the table. Compared to the meals at my parents' house, it was loud. Seven people created a lot more noise than three, especially when one of them was as quiet as my mother.

"How are you adjusting?" asked Mr. Dawkins. He held his elbows off the table as he ate.

"I'm fine," I said with as much cheer as I could gather. I caught a glance from Mother, who seemed to think she knew better than to believe me. "Thank you for asking."

"Well, I know we're all glad to have you here, Miss Bishop. We understand it may be quite the transition. Our sweet town has seen a lot of changes in the last couple of years."

Transition? I figured he meant it was better than me being dead. *How is someone supposed to respond to a comment like that? Nodding? A little head dip and a "Yup, it's great to still be alive and kicking"?* I wound up giving him a half-smile, half-shrug.

"I'm grateful to be back with Mother and ready to get Dr. Traver out of here."

"Well, we need to be careful about that," said Mr. Van Doren. Maybe I sounded too excited. It was hard to know what these people expected.

"He's more dangerous all the time," said Mr. Dawkins, nodding.

"Well if he'd had plans to kill me, I'd be gone by now," said Mother, getting up and collecting plates from the table. "But I'll sure as I'm standing here not go down without a fight." For an older woman in a threadbare housedress, she was intimidating.

"I still think we need to increase your protection, Octavia," said Mr. Van Doren. "Doctor Traver doesn't realize Jacqueline is back. He thinks she's off in the big city."

She set the dishes down next to the sink and marched back into the dining room where we sat, her chair creaking under her. "Pray tell, Jacob, why does it matter?"

"Because with your daughter back, he might presume you have more to fight for now. You were a little more … vocal before you thought she was deceased. There are still people in town who would listen to you, if they thought they had enough numbers to deal with Traver."

"You're an articulate man, Jacob. They would listen to you, too."

"I think we all know they would not. With all due respect, I moved to town and opened a tavern and never really was a part of the council. You are from Marion and your family helped put it on the map. If you were to get traction for your ideas to retake leadership, well, Traver must see you as a big threat."

This remark was met with silence. As soon as he said it, we all knew he was right. My presence was putting all of them in greater danger, at least if Dr. Traver found out I was back.

"I should leave so he doesn't find out," I said. I fiddled with my fork, a thin piece of aluminum, barely bent enough to hold food.

Mother walked over to me and drew it out from my fingers, then collected the rest of the silverware from our place settings.

"You will do no such thing."

I opened my mouth to protest, and she shushed me. "I won't hear of it," she said. "I've already spent too much time away from you." She waved the cutlery as she spoke, and then walked back into the kitchen, where she stood over the sink, choking back tears.

I couldn't do anything without hurting people.

Mr. Van Doren spoke up, and he didn't look unkind as he made eye contact with me. "When Dr. Traver decides to take us on, and he will at some point, it won't be because he knows you're alive, Jacqueline. Although I'm sure we're all touched by your offer."

"Aren't you tired from this?" I asked. The tablecloth sported several stains from where food had fallen onto it from the course of the night, but I guessed that it would be perfect and clean the next time she set it out. After subsisting on next to nothing for years, I guessed she was honored to have these people in her home. I ran my hands over the cloth.

"Oh honey love, of course we're tired," said Darling, across the table from me. "But we've made the decision to stand up to this man, so tired it is."

"Please tell me we have a plan," I said.

"Yes, Jacqueline, we have a plan," said Mr. Van Doren, and he sounded a little irritated. *Don't get snippy with me, mister,* I thought. *You're my hallucination and you will not speak back to me!*

"We're going to discuss it in a few minutes, after supper."

I nodded and brought more dishes into the kitchen. Mother was filling up the sink with hot water and soap. Darling came in behind me and set down the last of the chipped blue and white china from our meal. She patted me on the back.

"Come see me by the stables when you get a minute," she said in my ear.

Mother turned around and with wet hands gave me a hug. "I love you, Jacqueline."

"I love you too, mother," I said automatically, with her arms squeezing me. What would the nuns back at school in Ohio think of all of this lying I was doing? How many times would I have to recite the Hail Mary at this point?

You'd have to get them past the time travel first, schmuck.

"I know it's been difficult since your father's death," she said. I wished she'd let go of me. I was running out of air.

"Yes, maybe we should talk about that some time."

She pulled away, cupping my shoulders in her hands. "Well, there's no point in rehashing it, dear. It was a terrible war, and you were so young."

"I'm just going to get some air before the meeting, if that's okay with you."

She nodded and went back to scrubbing a dish with a tea towel.

Outside the night was filled with cricket chirps and bird calls I didn't know. Darling stood next to the horse I'd rode in on, and she had to reach up to pet his cheek.

"Are you happy to be back?" she asked me, still looking at the horse. They looked pretty content with each other.

"Of course."

"There is a lot of work for us to do. Judging from how you dig up potatoes, you're not afraid to get your hands dirty."

I tried to interpret what that meant. *Does she want me to make a mob hit on someone? What the hell?*

"I have a cousin who lives three towns to the west. I can't call him to ask him to come out here because Dr. Traver's friends would find out. But if you wouldn't mind, you could go see him and bring him back."

"I don't know where I'm going. I mean, uh, I'm not good at directions."

"I know you're out of your time," she said, and she turned around to face me at last.

"What? What are you talking about?" *Holy shit, she knows?*

"You really belong to another era, dear. You're ahead of your time."

"Oh. Sure, I guess so."

"You are a strange girl."

I sighed. "I know, because people tell me that all the time. I'm getting tired of hearing it."

"Well, now I have more to say, so how about you button that lip and let your elder speak?"

"Uh, sorry." I stabbed at the dirt with my boot.

"Strange doesn't mean bad, it only implies that you're different. You are both selfish and other-oriented; it's merely a strange mix, like a butterfly and a wasp."

Now we were talking about bugs. I wasn't sure why.

"Butterflies and wasps are both pollinators," she said, reading my confusion. "We need them both for the harvest, even though they go about their work in different ways."

"So…you're saying, what, exactly?"

"That you have more than one option open to you. You can charm people or you can push them away and sting them. Be selective in your tactics."

"Oh, okay. Why didn't you just say that?"

She shook her head and laughed at me.

"I set up your horse for you," said Darling, and she pointed to a large pack on the railing next to the animal. "You have supplies for both of you for a few days. Head west out the old farm road, follow the railroad tracks. You'll come to an old red barn two towns away where you can spend the night, but get out of there before dawn. Keep going to the next town and find my cousin, Jack. He lives in the first house on the right in the town of Joy. If you hit the Ohio River, you've gone too far." She winked.

"Tell him to get out here and bring that jalopy of his."

"He'll come just because some woman in trousers tells him to?"

"He'll come."

"Why are you so sure?"

"Because you're bringing American pie. Honestly, girl, where your brains at?"

I figured I was missing something, but just nodded.

"And don't tell anyone you're going, or they'll tell you not to. We don't need a fight on our hands, we need a crafty man like Jack. Especially don't relay any of this to that little sweetheart of yours."

"He's not my sweetheart."

"Oh please, he's got a shine on you and you on him. I think I know young love when I see it. Just get out of here before we wake up in the morning. Now let's get back inside. You first."

I walked back to the kitchen door, kicking dirt off of my boots before heading inside. Lucas was at the work table, drying dishes. Mother had left, so it was just the two of us.

"There you are," he said, giving me a flash of a smile.

"Here I am," I said. "Need a hand with those?"

"Yes, actually." He tossed me a tea towel. How many of these did Jacqueline's mother own?

I stood next to him and dried the gravy boat.

"Lucas, I need to talk to you."

"We have already established that we are both here together," he said, "and that you are capable of speech."

"Do you always need to be so sarcastic with me?"

He put down the china. "I suppose not. I apologize. Pray tell, what would you care to discuss?"

I side-stepped once toward him so that we were inches apart, the pile of dishes in front of us. "Do you like me, Lucas?"

"Are you asking if I fancy you?"

"Um, yes."

"You never fail to surprise me with your directness. But yes, I do fancy you. I thought it was obvious."

"Well, I worry that I'm making it all up in my head." *Boy, do I ever.*

He took my hands and held them to his chest, and I could feel his pulse, rapid fire.

"I was not expecting to ever see you again, after you left, and like others I wondered if the telegram about your death was true. And now that you're back, well…" He trailed off.

"There are so many things I need to tell you," I said.

"I know. You keep telling me you have to talk to me, and yet we never seem to have time. Let's take a walk after the meeting."

Precisely when I was supposed to trot off to some guy's house at the end of Kentucky. *Great timing, this guy.* I didn't know which way was up anymore, but I wanted some time with Lucas.

The meeting started with Mr. Dawkins calling us in to sit down in the living room. Darling closed the curtains. Mr. Dawkins leaned forward into the middle of the group, his leather suspenders pulling against his shoulders. He knew the Attorney General of Kentucky, who would probably be sympathetic to helping us stop Dr. Traver and his thugs.

"But we need to bring him evidence of Traver's criminal acts."

"Do we have evidence?" I asked, hoping it wasn't too stupid a question to pose to the group.

Silence. Why couldn't I just keep my big mouth shut?

"I saw something," said Lucille in a quiet voice. "A handwritten note from Dr. Traver to a congregant." Judging from the others' reactions, I was the only person in the room who didn't know this already. A spring in the couch started gouging my leg so I moved over a little to get out of its way.

"What were you doing in his church?" asked Lucas's dad.

"She's a spy," said Darling, coming into the room and sitting next to me. She dried her hands on the towel and folded it up as she spoke. Lucille continued, looking at the ceiling like she was trying to remember the note.

"The esteemed Dr. Traver requests that Mr. Rushman be brought to his spiritual retreat on Black Mountain."

Well, that sounded ominous enough.

"We reckon that's where the other missing men disappeared to," said Mr. Dawkins. "It's not so much a retreat as a small cabin. We don't know where on the mountain it's located, however."

"What is the plan?" asked Mr. Van Doren.

"Well let's work that out here. I think a few of us should try to find this cabin and discover whatever we can so that we can bring it to the Attorney General."

"Black Mountain is a large piece of rugged land, Arnold."

"Yes. We're hoping Lucille can learn a more precise location from Dr. Traver's church office here in town." *Maybe it's just me, but does this sound far-fetched to anyone else? Anyone?*

"It's too dangerous to just sneak around his cabin," said Mr. Van Doren, leaning back in his chair. He was the skeptic of the group, I guessed. "We need to find the location and then watch it for a while. If he holds people hostage there, there must be guards or someone keeping watch. We can't just walk up and find some smoking gun and take that to Frankfort as evidence."

I liked Mr. Van Doren. If he was all in my mind, he was a smart part of my mind.

We agreed to give Lucille three days to figure out where the spiritual prison was and then another few days to watch the cabin. But Mr. Dawkins and my mother were worried that the longer Mr. Rushman was at the cabin, the more likely he'd be killed there, so time was of the essence. And that meant that I had very little time to find Darling's cousin and get him back here. I hoped my horse was fast.

We had our assignments, though I was pretty much on light duty preparing food for the others. I wondered if Darling planned it that way, knowing I was about to leave. She looked like a little old lady, but she knew a lot. Or something.

We were silent for half a minute, each of us thinking. I was wondering if I would find the town of Joy. I figured some of the others were steeling themselves for a showdown.

"Let's go over the plan again," said Mr. Dawkins.

* * *

After the meeting the Underground members turned in for their rooms in the rambling farm house. It would be easier for them to leave once the dawn broke. Instead of heading to bed I went to the stable. My horse turned to look at me and without worrying about it I pet his muzzle. He gave me a satisfied huff.

"I thought I'd find you here." I turned around to see Lucas walking toward me.

"You thinking of running off?"

"No, why?"

"Because that pack is bursting at the seams, like for a trip."

"You are one astute gentleman. Please don't tell anyone."

He stepped closer to me and stood up straight and I was annoyed that he was so much taller than me. *I'm tired of being a short guy…oh, wait.*

"You have so many secrets, Jac. You should share some of them. I want to know what is going on with you."

He was close enough to me that I could sense his body heat, smell him. I felt dizzy, but not in an epilepsy way.

"I'm afraid, Lucas, if I tell you everything, that you won't like me anymore."

There. I said it. What would he do with it?

"Jacqueline, if you tell me the truth, I will probably like you even more."

"Okay. Here goes." I took a deep breath.

And kissed him. His lips were soft, although having never kissed anybody but my mother on the lips, I guess I didn't really know what to expect. He inhaled sharply because I'd surprised him, so his mouth opened, and then mine did, too, and I could taste him, sweet and earthy. I started to fall over, but he caught me and pulled me up against him. I wanted to fall into the kiss even more. A strange ache filled me, like I wanted to pass through his body. Finally we came up for air.

"You are even more beautiful when you are one inch away," he said, and he seemed shy all of a sudden. "But I notice you're not talking if you're kissing me."

"Good point. How about one more kiss and then we can talk?"

He obliged me. I wanted so much more from him. I pushed myself away.

"Lucas, I am from another time."

"You're, what? I'm afraid I don't understand."

"I'm really Jackson Inman, and I'm from Ohio, and I was in a hospital in 1980, and then I was here when you fell out of the tree. And I bounce back and forth between then and now but I don't know how or why or what it means or what I'm supposed to do about it."

"Jacqueline, stop. Why are you doing this to me?"

"I'm not doing anything—"

"Stop it! First you kiss me like a, like a woman of the night, and then you give me this nonsense story? You are too cruel."

"No, Lucas, it's true! I told you it was hard to believe. But it's true."

"You are impossible." He turned and started to walk away.

"Wait—"

I grabbed his arm, and he yanked himself out of my grip.

"Don't lay your hands on me. You embarrass yourself. I'm going to bed."

He walked away and I cried as I watched him. I pet the horse's head.

"I'll see you in a couple of hours," I told the horse. I wiped my eyes and trudged into the house, glad that everyone else had turned in already. *This has to be real or I am a total jerk even to myself.* I was so exhausted it was easy to fall asleep.

* * *

I don't know how long I'd been conked out for before the shouting woke me, but I heard Lucas's voice first, followed by loud thumping as he and Mr. Van Doren pounded open people's bedroom doors.

The house was on fire.

Running out to the upstairs hallway, I saw smoke billowing up the stairwell from the first floor, flames licking along the banister. Darling and Lucas had already wet some towels from a basin in the upstairs vanity, and were holding them over their mouths. I couldn't see where any of the others were. Darling handed me a wet hand towel and I held it over my face.

"Where is everyone else?" I shouted to Lucas. I hadn't realized fires were so loud. From downstairs wood popped and snapped, and the dull roar of the blaze grew louder, as if it had a way of turning up a stereo knob.

Where were the others? Maybe they'd gotten out already and it was just the three of us left up here.

Curling around the corner of the wall at the bottom of the stairs, the flames told me our time was short. The smell of burning fabric and wood hit me in a wave of heat. Timbers began snapping under us.

"I don't know where they are," he said. Darling took hold of us and pushed us into her bedroom. For the moment we could breathe, but we'd also backed into a corner.

Crashing sounds from below as part of the second floor collapsed into the first. I didn't need to see it to imagine what those rooms looked like now. I looked out the window to the back yard and fields behind us, and saw that the stables were also fully engulfed. *Those poor animals.* It could only be Dr. Traver, trying to stop us from turning him in to the authorities. Darling dug in the small closet, pushing aside a crate of winter clothing.

"Help me," she said, and I took two steps to reach her. On the floor was a crude metal fire escape ladder, bundled up in a roll.

"I peeked in the closet last month," she said. "I just remembered this was here."

Lucas had shut the bedroom door to keep the fire out, and he crossed the room to open the window. I hauled the ladder over, setting the grips on the sill and letting it unwind against the side of the house. Smoke poured out from the dining room window below us, but this was our only option.

"Darling, get out of here," said Lucas, in a low, commanding tone I'd never heard from him before. She nodded, and scrabbled down the metal rungs.

"You next," he said to me.

"No, you go. Don't argue with me."

He stood close to me, and put his hand on my collarbone. I felt the fire under his skin as he pushed me toward the window, and in my field of vision, I could see the smoke forcing its way under the door.

"You're the one on crutches," I said.

"You're the only one who ever notices," he said, and he kissed me on the cheek. *I cannot be wanting to kiss him right now, what the eff,* I told myself.

"I'll be right behind you," he promised.

I went down the ladder as quickly as I could, jumping to the ground when I had five feet left, because the ladder wasn't long enough. My relief at reaching dirt ended as soon as it had begun, because when I looked up, I saw her. Mother, about to be overtaken by the fire, staring out into the darkness from her bedroom window looking resolved. Resigned. Something. A fireball exploded from the kitchen, raining down glass and wood splinters onto us, which I tried to avoid by covering myself with my arms. And then Mother was gone.

Chapter Nine

I WOKE, FEELING A HEAVY BLANKET over me that reeked of flowers. Detergent. I fumbled on my nightstand for the matches I'd left there and instead my fingers found Object Too Large for Matches. As my eyes adjusted to the dark I saw glowing red numbers: 5:35. I was home, like home home, in my bed. I still smelled the burning farmhouse in my nostrils. My mind retraced my last steps—chased by Prophet Traver's henchmen, fleeing with the Underground to the farmhouse, plotting against him, running from the intense fire and Mother looking down at me like a ghost from her bedroom window. Mother. *My mother.* My mother was in the next room, with my Dad. I was Jack. Jack, I was me again. I put my hands on my chest, feeling skin that could only be described as dry, covering ugh, budding chest hair? I bolted out of bed.

I stood in front of the mirror that my father had glued to my closet door. Fumbling for the light switch I clicked it on and looked at myself. A stupid thought about the convenience of electric lights crossed my mind before I took in my image. I wore only a pair of pajama pants. I was older, more mature, with some pointy stubble at my chin. My biceps curved away from what had once been scrawny arms and my Adam's apple bulged out from my neck. The room smelled like too many substances at once—plastic, vinyl, deodorant—all of them were noxious to me, almost as toxic smelling as the smoke from the house fire. I wanted to breathe in the fresh air from Jacqueline and Lucas's time and flush all of the junk out of my system.

Without realizing it I sat down on the corner of the bed. Lucas. Jacqueline's mother, Mr. Van Doren. What had happened to them? None of it had been a hallucination. Those people were real. Was I real then, or now?

I scanned the room again. It was mostly the same as I'd left it, but there was a *The Who* poster in the corner that shouldn't have been there, and a small television on my desk I didn't have before I left. This time around I wasn't moaning in some hospital bed, stuck in a coma. I was me later in my life. What had I been doing? What year was it?

Oh my God, Lucas. Did he make it out of the house? Mother, looking like she was already a ghost. *No. No no no no.* What was I supposed to do now? *I need to go back and help them.* I sat down on the floor, staring at my room and trying to put all of it together. My knees were folded up against my chest, my very different-than-Jacqueline's chest.

I hate landing into bodies like this, I thought. *Even mine.* And there were weird things in my room. I found an essay on US history I'd written and learned there was a new President I'd never heard of before. A copy of *Rolling Stone.* An album from *Queen* I couldn't remember owning. Those people in Marion had been through a nightmare. *As have I. I was going to help them bring down Dr. Traver and now I'm here. And selfishly all I want to do is kiss Lucas again.*

I had wanted to come back here. I'd missed my family, and Sanjay, and Jeannine, my own time. I'd cried myself to sleep knowing even Jeannine didn't really believe I had gone to and come back from another time. Seeing myself in the mirror now should have made me relieved, but instead another emotion was tugging at me. I needed to undo the tragedy I'd seen. I had to make things right for Lucas, for them, for me.

I tiptoed downstairs, the once-familiar shag carpet tickling my feet, then walked into the kitchen. King saw me from his curled up position in the corner and lumbered up to me, wagging his tail and seeming like a slower version of himself.

"Hey buddy, how are you?" I asked him, petting him between his haunches where he liked it best. He sniffed me, inspecting me, and then moved in for the full slobber. I gave him a vigorous pet on his chest, his favorite spot.

I checked out the kitchen. New, white appliances greeted me. The black and silver wallpaper had been torn down, replaced with cheery bright yellow paint and white trim. Ivory linoleum with small, light pink diamonds lined the floor; the room looked like Easter had thrown up in here. In the middle of the room, I stared at the appliances, trying to recollect what each of them did.

"Hey, Jack," said my father, walking in from the garage. He wiped his greasy hands on a work towel. I did a quick comparison and saw that my hands were almost as large as his.

"Hi, Dad," I said, and clutched at my throat. My voice was a full octave lower than it had been.

"Sore throat? Don't give it to me!" He poured a mug of coffee from the black coffeemaker, which declared itself Mr. Coffee. Maybe all kitchen appliances had names for themselves.

"I'll try not to," I said, massaging my neck, trying to make like I had a crick. Perhaps if I whispered I wouldn't have to listen to myself as much.

"You're sure up early," he said, stirring something marked Half and Half into his cup. Half what and half what, I wasn't sure.

"School doesn't start for another ninety minutes."

"You know," I said, as casually as I could, "I kind of can't remember what day it is. Is it Thursday?"

He laughed and turned to face me. He'd grown a little at his waist, but he seemed as strong as ever, and he still wore the same cologne he'd used my whole life. English Leather. And holy shit, I was taller than him now. This was too weird.

"I wish it were, Jack. It's only Tuesday. Don't get ahead of yourself."

"I'll try not to, Dad." That awful voice again.

I could smell the house in flames, and hear Mr. Dawkins's screaming to get everyone out of the house. I didn't know if any of them other than Darling had made it. My stomach turned itself over inside me. *Lucas.*

"Well, get cleaned up, and stick your head out in the garage to say bye before you drive off to school," he said to me, his face turned back to the open hood of the car.

I said okay, but I didn't mean it. And then it dawned on me.

I drive now?

* * *

Clearly I had some kind of issue with grooming, or at least, that's what all of the bottles and jars of products lined up on the bathroom shelves told me. Waxes and shampoos and hair conditioner stood at attention, soldiers in the battle against hair on my face. I had set up shaving gel and aftershave next to the sink, and uh, two different razors. Why did I need two different razors? One for each side?

I leaned on the sink, only then noticing that there was no padding on the porcelain. The faucet had regular old handles. If I wanted to leave the hot water running now, I could. And still, I was actually me. *Maybe.*

I rooted around for the bottle of Klonopin, but couldn't find any little blue pills. I studied my face in the mirror, feeling stupid. Yes, I was the same, if not a lot more developed. I was solid, with a firmness I'd lacked in my earlier years.

I didn't like it.

In the shower, I let the hot water run over me until I turned red. *This isn't right. I need to be somewhere else. I have to get back and help them.* After showering the plush towel covered up my nakedness and I breathed a little easier. As I didn't have any experience with shaving, I didn't know what to do with the razor, so I skipped any attempt to rid my face of hair, hoping nobody would comment. I found my school uniform—in larger sizes—and headed downstairs. I was not ready for what had happened to my mother.

"Hi, Jack," she said in a sing-song from the kitchen. It was a fake brand of happy. She glanced my way, looking at me only for a second or two. I sat down next to her, trying to take it all in.

"Good morning, Mom."

"Sure," she said. Her coffee was losing steam, but she only stroked the handle of her cup, not drinking it. Most probably my father had poured it for her. I wondered sadly when he had taken over the task from me, or maybe it was today he'd done it.

Mom's skin looked gray and dry, especially around her fingernails, which she had bitten to the quick. Her robe was stained and smelled a little, mostly of spoiled milk and body odor. She looked lost somewhere inside herself. I reached out and held her hand. She didn't notice it immediately, but then she pulled away from me.

"Mom?"

Silence.

"Mom? I have a question."

"Sure, Jack." The melody had evaporated. She was all monotone now.

"Did something happen to you?"

"What?"

I asked her again. She drew in air. I felt a rock in my throat waiting for her to speak.

"Oh. You know. My pills don't work anymore. We're trying new medicine." Each word out of her seemed to take great effort, and she faded away again at the end of the sentence.

She was quiet, still fingering her mug. I kissed her temple fast and pulled away. Sinking my hands into my trouser pockets, I headed out to the garage to see my father. I hoped he could give me answers. He slid out from under a 1970 Camaro Z28, one of his favorite muscle cars. Bright red with two broad white racing stripes, the body was in good condition except for some rust over the wheels. Its position in the far-side parking spot of the garage meant it was his current pet project. Dad didn't like to work on his own cars at the shop, unless there was some special piece of equipment he needed to use.

"Going scruffy today, is that it?" my father asked me.

"I just didn't feel like shaving," I said. He scooted out again, asked for a wrench, and I pulled one from his rollaway tool chest. He'd kept the same organization system all these years. *Thank the baby Jesus.*

"You're never going to hang onto that pretty Jeannine Gonzalez if you don't look tidy," he said from under the car. Three different colors on the body parts meant that this was not a project near completion.

"I think it'll be okay," I said, trying to figure out how to turn the conversation over to Mom. *Wait, what about Jeannine?*

"Well, it doesn't matter. You could date anyone you wanted."

I blinked. I was pretty sure the girls had opinions about who they wanted to date, too.

"So Dad, can we talk about Mom?"

He rolled out again and stood up, then held onto the work counter, facing away from me. "What do you want talk about?"

"I don't like these new pills," I said. I needed to make sure I didn't reveal my ignorance of what was wrong with her. "She's kind of spaced out."

He turned around, frowning. "She's been spaced out for two years, Jackson. Where the hell have you been?"

"I just—"

"Don't 'just' me. We've tried one therapy after another, and I can't afford to put her in some fancy clinic while they find something that works for her. What do you want me to do?"

I floundered, not finding words. But he waited for me to speak; inside he had more patience for me.

"I miss her. I want her back, all of her. I mean, you must miss her, too."

"Jack, sometimes medicine wears out, or people adjust. You were lucky."

"Lucky?" I was missing something big here.

"Yes, lucky, and you better be thankful! Your epilepsy is gone. And hers will always be with her."

What?

* * *

I stormed out of the garage, down to the sidewalk, figuring it was time to catch the bus to school, when Jeannine saw me. She had grown taller and uh, curvier, in a way that Jacqueline, who was more straight up and down, hadn't acquired. She still had her long hair, but it had a bouncy curliness instead of the straight locks she'd worn our freshman year. She gave me a big smile and waved; it was large enough that I thought she'd heard my father yelling. I trotted across the street to her.

"You look like you're waiting for the bus," she said, and then she touched my collarbone. *Well aren't we touchy feely today?* And then as she curled around me, kissing me full on the lips, my father's comment made a lot more sense.

Holy shit, Jeannine and I are an item.

"Do I not wait for the bus?" I asked, impressed by my sudden ability to distract. She tasted like Scope and strawberries.

"You're silly. We all drive now." I looked over toward Sanjay's house, but didn't see anything other than his mother's crusty Impala in the driveway. Jeannine caught my glance and patted me on the shoulder.

"It's okay for friends to drift apart," she said. She played with a coil of my hair and I did my best not to flinch. I'd crushed on Jeannine for years, but now it felt off. I don't know if it was because we were different people, or because of Lucas, or all my time-hopping, but I wasn't ready to be sucking face with her just yet.

I had to figure another relationship out now, too? With the stench of the burning house still in my nose, the screams of people scrambling to get out still ringing in my ears? It was like lugging ghosts around all day.

"Honey bear, are you all right?"

"I'm okay," I said, forcing what I hoped was easiness into my voice. "Do you mind driving today?"

"Oh, sure," she said. Of course I had surprised her. For one, I should be ecstatic about driving epilepsy-free, never needing to bum a ride. I should act like some manly guy who would never let his girlfriend drive him around. But also I wasn't sure if we attended the same school.

I'd wanted to come home for so long, but now that I was here? Now I just missed them. *Him. Oh, Lucas. I wish you'd believed me. I wish we had more time.* Except, wait. We could have time, maybe. If I could jump back the next time I went to Dr. Dorfpoodle's…I stopped my pondering because I wasn't in the study anymore, was I?

"Would you like to get in the car with me, Jack, or were you planning on jogging behind me?"

She stood with the car door open, her gorgeous hair shining in the sun, and I was still at the edge of our driveway, my father tinkering in fantasyland under a Camaro and my mother probably still in the kitchen caressing a mug like it was a cat. Everything around me was a complete disaster, and all I could think about was some boy I made up in my head? Or from another time? *What the helling hell? I have lost my mind.*

"Coming!" I trotted over to her, stopping suddenly so I wouldn't get hit by a sedan.

"Seriously, honey, where are you this morning?"

"I didn't sleep well last night," I said, climbing into the passenger seat of her Firebird. Everything inside was vinyl and gray or red or cheap chrome and the whole interior smelled like janked-up steering fluid.

She tousled my hair again, cooing at me. Was this how Lucas expected Jacqueline to act? She was sweet, but where had the whip-smart girl I'd known gone?

"I can make you feel better," she said, leaning in. And before I could say anything, she was kissing me, pushing through my lips with her tongue.

"Jeannine, Jeannine, stop." This was not what I wanted or needed right now.

"What is the issue with you? Shit, Jack."

"I just... I don't feel well. Can you just take us to school?"

She stabbed the key into the ignition and turned on the radio.

"If you're that sick you should just stay home." She pulled away from the curb and I looked out the window, trying to pick out what was new to me in the neighborhood.

If I wasn't going to jump back through my erratic brainwaves, maybe I'd never see Marion again. Though all I'd wanted was to come back to my reality, now I worried about not helping Jacqueline, Lucas, and the Underground.

Maybe there was something I could do about it.

Chapter Ten

HOPPING INTO JEANNINE'S CAR was my best decision of the morning. After our rough start, I put my hand on her knee and she started talking to me again. It was weird to be on the other end of the knee touch but it seemed rude to be so cold to someone who wasn't expecting it. In the twenty minutes it took us to get to school—it was in fact the same high school—I learned that we were now seniors, that my brainwaves had turned normal my sophomore year and I'd tapered off my medication over several months. But Jay and I had stopped speaking around then, and now the three of us never hung out anymore.

Jeannine was definitely more grown up. And once she was done playing kissyface with me, I saw she was full of self-confidence and had big plans for her future.

"So tell me again which colleges you applied to," I said.

She ticked them off: Wellesley, Vassar, Smith, Sarah Lawrence, and Syracuse. All of them were women's colleges except Syracuse.

"You like, hate men or something?" I asked.

Jeannine laughed. "Please. I wouldn't hang out with you if I did."

"Uh, yeah. Good point."

"Are you feeling any better?" she asked.

"I'm fine, I'm just a little tired and out of it is all. So anyway, why the girl-only colleges?" I didn't want to be obvious but I was curious.

"Vassar and Wellesley are co-ed now," she said. "But I think it's easier to learn with fewer distractions. They're not about football programs or MRS degrees. You men take up a lot of space! Or maybe you've missed the whole women's movement."

"No, I think it's great." I wondered what Jacqueline would do if she had the chance to go to college. She'd probably thumb her nose at it and call them a bunch of snobs.

Jeannine turned into the parking lot at school. At some point since I'd last been here they'd restriped the spaces. Seniors had assigned parking spots. I had no idea which was mine.

We walked into the lobby and I stood next to the huge statue of Saint Francis. He was stepping on a snake, because that was some nod to his ability to fight evil even as he was like, rescuing baby sheep and puppies from the clutches of Satan. I had stared at the snake before. Like, years before.

I walked down the hall with the seniors' lockers, and kept expecting people to be shocked at my appearance. But it was I who had to keep from marveling at my classmates. The boys had grown several inches and many of them had filled out. A lot of them weren't paying any particular attention to how they smelled. The girls were taller too, less gangly than they'd been in ninth grade. Some of the teachers were new. Senior lockers were the biggest in the school, as if we needed more space. Freshmen lockers were slender, with a cubbyhole we could spring open once we'd opened the thin door. These lockers were humongous, and I couldn't think of why we were granted so much more space. Maybe it was for the heavy wool varsity jackets.

Like my assigned parking space, I also had no clue which locker was mine. Not only that, but as I looked down the row of locks that dangled from each one, I realized I didn't know my combination. Why couldn't I at least have my own memories? This time traveling stuff left something to be desired.

Jeannine noticed my hesitation, as I hadn't made it past the third foot of the corridor.

"Jack?"

"You know, I'm just going to hit the rest room," I said. "Catch you later in—" I stopped, not having any clue what classes I attended.

"Calculus?" She was starting to look worried.

"Yes. See you then." I smiled, probably more broadly than I should have. Jeannine saw another friend, waved, and walked away shaking her head at me. *Yes, enjoy your cockadoodle friend, Jackson. Also known as Jacqueline. From fifty-five years ago.*

In the middle of the hallway I saw Mr. Christenson, who I'd had first year for Spanish. Maybe he could help me.

"Excuse me, Mr. Christenson," I said, coming up behind him.

"Yes?" He looked at my scraggly appearance, and frowned. "Mr. Inman, good hygiene is more than just a catch phrase in health class. You should have shaved this morning. And where is your tie? You know that's a uniform requirement."

"My apologies, sir." This was not going well.

He stood back and crossed his arms over his broad chest.

"Are you being disingenuous with me, young man?" I didn't know what that meant, but it sounded bad.

"No, Mr. Christenson, I just have a small problem."

"And what might that be?"

"I don't remember which is my locker."

He studied me, looking in my eyes for something.

"I thought you were finished with that terrible disease."

"I–it's not a seizure, sir. I just don't remember which is mine." *Maybe I should just turn and run.*

"For good measure, let's go to the nurse." He clamped a hand on my shoulder and pointed us toward the nurse's office. I squirmed and broke free.

"Just playing a joke, Mr. C. Senior prank! I'm totally fine." I jogged away and waved at him to like, keep it light, and then I cut down the stairs next to the gymnasium. I turned a corner so fast on my way to the library that a few of the posters announcing the next school dance flapped against the green cinder block walls. The librarian was the same as when I was a first year.

"Hello, Jack," she said when she noticed me, "Why aren't you in homeroom?"

"I have a project for first period from Sister Phadelus," I said, hoping I looked self-assured. "She wanted me to get started on it early."

Sister Phadelus had a bad reputation, or to put it bluntly, she got pissed and yelled a lot. Nobody would ever use her in a scheme. There weren't enough chalkboard erasers in the world to clap clean to satisfy an angry nun like her.

The librarian, Miss Radise, was a tired older woman who seemed much happier to have her nose in a book than to speak to another human being. She must have figured I was either crazy to lie or pitiful for having any kind of project for Sr. Phadelus, so she waved me on. I knew what I wanted. I was there to find proof, either way, that I was really jumping through time, or totally lost in a seizure. Was Lucas real or not? Marion? If it was a dream I could let it go, sink into this life and get back on track, epilepsy-free. But if those people really existed and I somehow had any ability to fix what was going on with them, then I wanted to help. I had to help.

I looked at the signs hanging from the ceiling to find the right section. *Cartography,* there it was. Narrow drawers held all kinds of maps, organized by place alphabetically. I wasn't sure if I should look for United States or Kentucky, but I yanked open the K drawer. A city map of Kalamazoo, wherever that was. Kansas. There it was—Kentucky. I stuck my index finger on the paper and started looking for the town.

There it was. Marion, near the western border with Illinois. *Wow I do not know my geography at all,* I thought. Marion was a real place after all, and I was sure I hadn't come across it in my real life.

It's time to believe. No more doubts. I really went there.

Now that I'd found Marion, I started looking for Black Mountain. It was in the southeast clear across the state. I found the scale for figuring out miles and made a little gasp when I realized the two points were three hundred and fifty miles apart. That would have been a long way to hold people hostage, but if someone's intent was to kill them far away from town, it made more sense.

The back of my neck tingled, and not in a good way. If my school had these maps, maybe I could find newspapers from the 20s? I put the papers back in order in the drawer and went over to the microfiche section. Bells rang. End of first period. Second period would start in four minutes, and who knows when someone would come looking for me, or call my parents at home. But I had no idea what room I'd be in, what class I was in, and I was three years behind and would be clueless about the material.

Even if I wanted to stay here, in my time, I need to help Lucas and the others first. And figure out how to get back here at the right spot.

I looked for newspapers, and found a big box of microfilm in spools held together with rubber bands. Great library system we have here. The box was marked "Regional Newspapers." I found the

Bowling Green Daily Times on three spools and put the first one in the machine, fumbling with the clips that were supposed to hold the film. Bells clanged again. The first roll of film went from 1890 to 1891. Oh no. What if there wasn't anything from the time period I'd visited? Second spool, also random, from 1915 to 1916. My hands shook as I clipped in the last spool.

1926. I exhaled. It was the break I needed. I scoured the headlines and less prominent articles. Pictures of people, old-fashioned cars and overcoats with fedoras, it was like an old movie reel, but uh, with less movement. Nothing I saw jumped out at me, until I came across a story on page three from September 18.

ABANDONED FARM HOUSE FIRE KILLS 8—Sept. 18 Terry McHutchen, Daily Times Staff Writer — The Bishop farm house in Marion, abandoned last year after years of disuse and neglect, collapsed in the overnight hours of September 17 after a fire consumed the structure. Eight people had apparently been meeting in some organized fashion. Dr. Melvin Traver, a vocal Temperance supporter, leader of the New Life Church, and mayor-elect of Marion, called "The Prophet" by his congregation, proclaimed the loss of life "terrible, but not unexpected, as many of these souls were engaged in the Devil's businesses of gambling, drinking, and bootlegging." Comparing them to notorious figures like Al Capone and Bonnie and Clyde, Dr. Traver promised he and his associates would pray for their spirits and that the town be healed from its troubled past. Sheriff Peter Townsend promised a full investigation, but remarked that as so many of the people involved had been badly crushed, that identifying their remains may take quite some time. People who have missing loved ones or who believe they may know anyone involved in the calamity should contact the Sheriff's office.

I tore the microfiche out of the machine and tucked it in my pocket. Nothing in the article mentioned who was involved, but maybe there was something else in there or in the newspaper around that date. Had anyone survived after the fire at my mother's farm house? How organized was Dr. Traver's gang, if they could pull off an inferno? Was he behind it? What was I supposed to do with this information? Without any seizures, which had been my way back to then, how was I supposed to get there again to stop this from happening?

The puzzles swirled around in my head. Two dark brown orthopedic-looking shoes appeared on the floor, and I knew I was in trouble. I looked up at Miss Radise.

"I spoke with Sr. Phadelus," said the librarian, her hands on her hips, "and she has not given you any kind of special assignment. Although after we talked, she said she could think of a very long and involved project for the likes of you."

"That's strange," I said, shooting out of my chair and heading for the door. "I'm sure it was for Sr. Phadelus, wasn't it? Now then, maybe I'll go see her and check, although I suppose it could have been for Brother Thomas. You know sometimes I just get the two of them confused!" By this point I'd wiggled my way past her astonished face, thanking her repeatedly and then I was close enough to duck out of the library and back into the hallway.

The bells rang again, and a burst of talking filled the hall, so even though Miss Radice was onto me, I lost myself in the sea of blue and green uniforms. *Hooray for plaid.* That was the only time I'd ever been happy we all wore the same ugly outfits.

It was the senior's lunch period, the second lunch of the day. I hoped I'd find Jeannine, because of all the people I knew, I could most likely share this with her and trust that she wouldn't tell anyone else. She'd helped me with the coffee label, after all.

Seeing the cafeteria, I suddenly realized how much time I'd lost. Years were gone, years I'd lived through but had no memory of. *This really sucks,* I thought. My life was disappearing into these snaps back in time. It wasn't fair. I told myself to calm down. Maybe I could jump back to the first clinical study and refuse to go, avoiding all of this mess. And another thought popped up: until this jump back, my time loss in my own time was a lot smaller than what I "lived through" back in time. But this go-around I'd come back two years later. Why?

Scanning the seniors for Jeannine, I found her over at the soda machines buying a can of Tab. She saw me and came over.

"Hey, I haven't seen you in the hallway this morning. You feeling better?" She ran her fingers through my hair, and my back tingled, but in an awful way, not a sexy way.

"I've been working on a project in the library." Okay, this phony project thing was getting old. Even the orthopedic shoe set was on to me.

She flipped her hair behind her shoulder and gave me a longer look. "You've got something going on."

"Maybe."

"What is it, Jack?"

"I'd like to talk to you about it, but not here."

"What, you're a secret agent now? We're in school, where else are we going to talk?"

Before I could answer, Jasmin Carlyle, cheerleader extraordinaire, dashed over to her, giving her an air kiss.

"See you at practice today," she said through an enormous smile. "You did great yesterday, Jeannie."

"Thanks, Jazz. Yeah, see you at four."

Jasmin flitted away like a lightning bug.

"Jeannie?"

"Shh," she whispered to me. "No making fun in front of everyone."

"Me, make fun? Of tiny people who climb on each other but think the rest of us are losers? Nah."

"I needed another extracurricular, you know, and they cut field hockey. So give me a break, it's just for this year."

"I know, I know." Except I didn't know. It sounded like a ridiculous excuse, but I didn't want to piss her off.

"I can't sit with you today, sweetie," she said, and she touched my collarbone. *She has a thing for collarbones, what is that about?* "Because the yearbook club is meeting this period. But I'll meet you at your locker before next period."

"Okay," I said. At least I would see where my stupid locker was. She leaned in for a kiss and I gave her a quick peck, which made her frown.

"What is up with the granny kissing today?"

"I think my breath is really bad."

She nodded, perhaps horrified at my complete lack of hygiene. Whatever, it worked. I watched her walk away and sit down with what I presumed was the yearbook staff. I wondered what clubs I'd joined in the last three years. Did I give a shit about anything?

I felt in my pockets and came up with a couple of crumpled dollar bills. The food smelled semi-rancid, but my stomach growled anyway. Either I was used to eating breakfast in the morning, which I'd skipped, or I was an eating maniac, because even the cafeteria tables looked appetizing. I looked at the school clock and saw it was a bit past noon. Lunches were only thirty minutes long. I got in line and asked for the lasagna. I didn't know where to sit; most of the students had taken up at the long tables already, and nobody was waving me over. Nobody waved me over or said hello to me. Was I a loner? After having close friends through middle school, the possibility seemed depressing. Who was I?

In the corner, near a window, I saw Sanjay, who was sitting by himself. I walked over and set down my tray.

"Hi," I said.

"Uh, hello." He went back to eating.

"The lasagna sucks," I said.

"So don't order it and you won't be disappointed."

"You're really angry with me."

He stopped chewing, swallowed, and looked straight at me. "You know how I feel, so give it up. Why don't you go sit somewhere else?" His hair was longer, he already had a shadow on his face where his beard was growing in, but unlike me, he was still stick-thin. It would have been nice to know what had pissed him off so much.

"Can't we talk?"

He paused again, probably not sure how to size me up. "What are you, a girl? Do you need to process? I don't want to talk." He made air quotes with his fingers around "talk." *Thanks for the emphasis, asshole.*

I picked up my tray, gripping it too hard, and walked over to a small, empty table. Why did he need to go and say that to me? I ate a few small bites of lunch, crunching on the overcooked noodles and blackened tomato sauce. *I'm not a girl. But I don't think there's anything wrong with girls, either. Girls. Jacqueline. I have to figure out how to get back so I can warn them about the fire. Oh God, Lucas. I don't even know who or where I am anymore but I miss Lucas so much.* I had to see Lucas again.

I needed a plan. Jay could screw himself for all I cared. I stuck my tray on the conveyer belt behind the cafeteria, wiping my hands on my jeans. I bounded up the stairs from the cafeteria and half-trotted past the giant statue of St. Francis. As always he stared off in the distance, possibly looking on the horizon for other small animals who needed saving, since that was like, his thing. *There oughta be a Catholic saint for people lost in time.*

I wandered around the school building for ten minutes, waiting for the end of the lunch period. I'm sure I looked like I'd lost my mind, staring at every little piece of modern technology. PA systems had never looked so interesting before.

Jeannine came down the hall with the yearbook crew, a nerdy tiny girl with oversized black glasses, two guys who looked like they'd just as soon be playing chess, and some gal who had on the absolute limit of makeup allowed by the principal. They waved to me and continued down the hall, and Jeannine curled her arm into mine. I was starting to get used to her affection, but I didn't feel anything toward her.

"Why are you standing over here?" she asked. "Your locker is down there."

"Sure. Let's go." Locker A179 was in the middle of the row of lockers, and apparently mine. It seemed perfectly fine, mostly undented, with a lovely combination lock attached. And which I didn't know how to open.

Jeannine sighed, then twisted the knob a few times and unclicked the lock.

Of course she knew my combination. I resisted rolling my eyes.

I opened the door and looked at a neat stack of textbooks and two three-ring binders. I was organized? On the inside of the door were seven or eight photos of Jeannine.

"See anything new?" she asked. Jesus, one of these must be recent. I honed in on the cheerleading photo.

"Aw honey, you look great," I said, lying through my teeth.

"You think so? I was skeptical at first but you know, cheering is growing on me."

"Like a fungus," I said, and the bell rang.

"Come on, we've got Mr. Marshall's class." She tugged at my sleeve and I grabbed a binder, hoping I'd picked the right one. I hated to shut my lock but I couldn't leave everything open.

Mr. Marshall was a new teacher, or well, new since I'd jumped out of time. He taught physics. *Terrific. I don't know anything about physics.* Although maybe he knew about time travel. Wasn't that a physics thing?

Maybe this was just the sort of class that could help me. Unless like, the teacher called on me. I sat in the chair behind Kevin Hunter, because he was usually right in front of me. Catholic school was always good for alphabetized seating.

Taped to the inside of the cover was my combination and schedule. At least that's solved. I had three tabs set up: Physics, Honors English, European History. I flipped to the physics tab. Maybe if I studied my own notes I wouldn't be lost in class. *Nah, I don't get a lick of it.* Mr. Marshall had a way of droning as he talked that made everything a ton more boring.

I kept reading. Scribbled notes, crude diagrams, lots of things about special relativity theory, whatever that was. And then on one page, a note.

Is this how time travel happens?

Ah, so this is why I took physics. I was looking for a way back. And here I'd thought I'd only stopped doubting myself during my last trip back.

Time travel was so freaking confusing.

* * *

After school I ditched into a park behind the high school and watched Jeannine's car, waiting for her to come over for her drive home. I would have preferred to go back to the library, where I could read my notebook in private, but there was only the one entrance, and Miss Radise would be watching for hooligans, if not me specifically, to enter. And so far I'd eluded Sister Phadelus, so I didn't want to press my luck. In front of me was a rusty red merry go round, and some kind of worn out animal on an enormous spring stuck in the ground. If it was ever a happy place, it had long ago lost that feeling and settled into creepy forlornness. To top it off clouds started clumping up overhead, making the already old park equipment look even more tired.

I found a spot on a half-splintered bench that sagged a few inches when I sat down, and thought about what I'd been through—a simple neurology test, a hallucination that wasn't, thrown into some other world that actually had a name and a place on a map. I played with the paper in my binder, clutching it to me like it was some kind of plastic shield. But what I really needed was a way back. To stop the fire. To see Lucas. To be Jacqueline again.

Chapter Eleven

THROUGH THE THIN LINE OF TREES, none of which were as robust as anything from Marion, I saw Jeannine come back out to her car after cheerleading practice. I braced myself for her touchy-feely stuff. Three or four other cheerleaders walked with her, lots of hair bouncing around them and skimpy cheerleading uniforms looking bright and uh, cheery. People in Marion would have laughed their asses off over these costumes. They waved at each other and made beelines for their cars.

I carried an enormous secret with me now, no matter what I did, and there was no way to tell people what I was really going through without them thinking I'd come unhinged. I wasn't just sitting by myself in an unused children's park. I was alone.

Looking up again, I saw Jeannine start her engine. I was going to miss her and then not have a way home, twenty miles away.

I leaped up and raced into the parking lot, waving my arms, and saw the flash of Jeannine's brake lights. She backed up and reached over to unlock the passenger door. A rumble of thunder sounded.

"What the hell, Jack?"

"Can I get a ride?" Each word came out with a gasp of breath in between.

"Of course, get in." I leaned over and flicked on the radio, turning the knob to find an alternative rock station.

Music has gotten so weird, I thought. The radio wasn't familiar anymore.

"So Jack, what is up with you? Did you cut class all day today?"

"I was in the library in the morning, until Miss Radise kicked me out. But I went to my afternoon classes." Not that I'd understood any of it. Apparently physics was one of those classes you needed to kind of get in on at the start.

"Are you a hall monitor now?"

"What? Why were you in the library?" she asked.

I waited for her to stop at a traffic light. The sky had opened up and we were in a downpour, sheets of water drenching the Sunbird. The windshield wipers whipped over the glass.

"Remember when I asked you to go to the public library with me?"

"Back when we were freshmen," she said, nodding. The light turned green and she accelerated slowly, as if we could hydroplane at ten miles per hour.

"I went back there again. It's not a hallucination." I knew she knew where "back there" was.

Silence. We crept along, the rain winning the battle against the wiper motor, and then Jeannine put on her blinker and pulled to the curb. "I can't concentrate and have this conversation at the same time," she said. She turned to me.

"Jack, you know how this sounds?"

I nodded. "I know, but I can tell you things I just shouldn't know."

"Can you?" I couldn't tell if she was exasperated with me, but she was still listening. I really needed her to listen, at the very least.

I explained, as the engine idled gruffly. She needed to flush it. Jeannine switched off the radio in the middle of a song. The windshield had become a waterfall, where the world on the other side of the glass lost its edges.

"Who was that?" I asked. Music. We could talk about music. Maybe she'd forget that her old friend was completely loony tunes.

"It's called R.E.M."

"Rapid eye movement? Why name yourself after something so boring?"

"I don't know, Jack." She looked exasperated with me. "Can we get back to this time travel stuff?"

I was taking up her time, spewing nonsense. I needed to get her to understand. I told her the whole story of the Underground and Dr. Traver.

Jeannine stared into space.

"Let's say this is real. You're not lying, mistaken, or nuts."

"I'm okay with that."

She smiled at me, but only for a moment. "When do you think you left last? This month?"

I hung my head a little, as if being gone for years was my fault. "I went away in the fall of freshman year, and woke up this morning."

"Holy shit," she said. Her hands on the steering wheel turned white as she gripped it harder. "That's three years, Jack."

"Oh, it gets even better," I said.

"I can't wait."

I told her about being in the body of Jacqueline, of going back multiple times at different points in her life. Of Lucas, the tree, the growth of the sleepy town, the threats from Dr. Traver and his merry band of Prohibitionists who set Jacqueline's house on fire. She listened, and eventually the rain let up and we began driving again.

"What I worry about is my mother, here. My real mother. She's sick and the doctors can't help her."

"You've lost time with her, too," Jeannine said, making me think about that all over again. I had a knot the size of a Whitney-Pratt engine stuck in my stomach. Talking about it with someone was supposed to be a relief, but instead it was anything but.

We pulled into her driveway, my house down and across the street from us.

"Look, you need to get started on learning how to figure out how to manage when and how you travel. I also think you have to put today's technology to work for you. If the group back then could communicate better, like maybe with HAM radios or something, they'd have an advantage over Dr. Traver."

Why hadn't I thought of any of this? She was so much smarter than me. Of all the people to be jumping back, why wasn't it someone more impressive than me? What a let-down it would be if the planet found out I'd successfully traveled through time. *Dumbass Goes to Prohibition-era Kentucky, news at eleven.*

"I suppose I also should read up on the history of the town, and that Dr. Traver."

"You have the date from the article," said Jeannine. "That's your goal for getting back, so you can stop the fire. Too bad the microfiche is back in the library."

"Heh, I snuck it out with me," I said, and I patted my shirt pocket.

"See Jack, you are clever," she said. We agreed to do our own research and meet back on the weekend to go over what we'd discovered.

I left her car and shuffled away to my house. I was happy to have a friend in all of this, but I couldn't shake the feeling that she didn't believe me one hundred percent. But hey, even I only bought my own story about halfway.

* * *

Six-fifteen and my father wasn't home yet, so I combed through the books in the garage that sat above his workbench. I knew it was in the pile somewhere, but all I found were mechanic's guides to engines, electrical systems, and suspensions. I grabbed those, and right before I went inside to the kitchen, I found a dog-eared box in the corner. Crouching down, I opened the flap, and crammed in the middle, there it was, the book I'd remembered: *The Boy's Book of Amateur Radio.* I snatched it up with the others I'd taken, and thumped up the stairs to my room. I heard my mother's soft snoring from her bedroom.

"Hi, Mom," I said, sitting on the edge of the bed. She opened her eyes and pulled one arm out from under the covers. "Can I get you anything?" I stroked her hair; it needed washing.

"Hi, Jacky," she said in a hoarse tone. She gripped my hand. She was warm.

"Do you need a drink?" I looked at the night table and saw that Dad had brought her a mug of coffee, which as usual sat full and cold.

"No, honey. You're my sweetheart." She sounded far away, as if she were at the end of one of Mr. Rushman's long underground tunnels. I squeezed her hand and was a little surprised when she sat up.

She looked at me, the corners of her mouth climbing up to form a small smile.

"You're my big boy now," she said. "And I don't want you to worry about me. You're almost a man now. You're outgrowing us."

My words caught up inside me. I tried not to gawk at her.

"Oh Mom, I love you and I love Dad. I just want you to be well and to make you proud." *Also, I'm not ready to be an adult yet. I want my time back. I don't know what I want.*

Mom went back to staring blankly at the wall behind me, though she had a faint smile. I laid her back in the bed and pulled the covers over her. I sat on my bed, in the room that felt like anyone's but mine, and cried for a while, until I heard my father shut the front door. Then I washed my face in the bathroom, feeling and hating the stubble under my fingers. There was so much to catch up on. Somehow I had all the time in the world and no time at all.

* * *

I brought the books with me into the woods at the edge of the tract. It was a lot harder to squeeze through the gap in the fence, and to prove I'd gotten bigger I ripped the bottom of my t-shirt passing against the metal. I was so behind at school I started skipping class entirely, waiting for Dad to go to the shop and then carting off a couple of books, a small notebook, a sack lunch, and a pen. I sat in the small clearing every day for a week, and shockingly, nobody from school called my parents. Maybe they didn't care.

It was weird being in the woods without being chased. These were tame trees, where no wolves would howl near me and no mobs of angry men would intimidate me or attack. Worried I was only just holding it all together, I focused on the HAM radio book. I flipped past all of the chapters on getting an operator's license and jumped straight into how to make one. I redrew all of the illustrations in the book, hoping to imprint it on my mind, and when I thought I couldn't possibly remember another detail, I switched to the book on engines and read about pistons and horsepower and improvements in fuel injection. Swapping books back and forth all day, I crammed as if for a final.

In the middle of week two of my "independent study" in the woods, my calves started cramping up. I decided to take a short walk. It was then that I heard them, a couple of people kissing and moaning. I didn't mean to see who they were, but I stumbled on a tree root and snapped several twigs in a loud mess as my feet went out from under me and I face planted. I could jump through time, but I couldn't walk without tripping.

"Who's there?" I heard. Sanjay's voice. I scrambled to my feet and ran off, through the trees and back to my clearing, not sure if he'd laid eyes on me or not. But I'd seen him, just for a moment—

He'd been kissing another boy.

Chapter Twelve

I REACHED THE CLEARING QUICKLY, wondering how stupid I looked running away from my old friend. I grabbed my books and tried to put the pieces together. Did this have anything to do with our fight, whenever we'd had it?

I jogged out of the woods and onto my block, puffing only a little. *Great. I bet I've become a gym rat.* My own body felt like someone else's.

"Hey, Jack," said Sanjay from behind me, breathing hard. He must have run to catch up.

"Are you going to yell at me again?" I asked.

"I didn't yell at you," he said.

"In the cafeteria."

Jay threw his arms up in the air. "Look, what do you want from me, man?"

I sighed. "Talk."

"I just want to know, do I have to worry?" He buried his hands in his pockets.

"Do you have to worry about what?"

"Do I have to worry about you blabbing about what you saw?"

He meant the kissing. *Pick up the clue phone, dumbass. The clue phone is ringing…*

"Jay, I miss our friendship. You don't even trust me anymore. I'd never get you in trouble." I caught myself. What if I'd already gotten him in trouble? Why couldn't I watch what I said? Why did the words have to tumble out before I'd thought about what to say?

He stepped closer and pressed his finger to my chest.

"You were the one who said we couldn't be friends, that you didn't really know me, that I was sick. Why would I trust you?" He looked close to spitting on me.

"I'm sorry. I was wrong."

The wind went out of his sails. Bingo. I'd been an asshole who needed to apologize. I just wasn't sure why.

"I'm sorry too," he said, backing away. "I'm sorry I thought you felt the same way as me. But now you're Mr. Macho, and I'm just a, what did you call me? Oh, a "little Indian fairy.'"

Now it was his turn to land a blow. He didn't give me a chance to say anything but instead started heading back down the block to his house.

"I'm sorry," I said again, knowing he was too far away to hear me. Why had I been such a jerk to an old friend?

* * *

Jeannine called just in time before I reached a breaking point. Holy crap I cried a lot. I sobbed into the phone that between my mother, Jay, all the years I'd missed, and the people I'd left behind, I didn't know what to do anymore. If she still doubted my story, she didn't show it. We agreed to meet for pizza at seven, a couple of miles away off the highway at a joint called Aljohn's. I needed to catch up to my life at some point.

"Dad, I'm going to get some pizza with Jeannine, okay?"

He sat in a checkered recliner, watching some sporting event.

"Sure, kiddo," he said, not looking away from the screen. "Keys are on the table in the foyer." I could hear him smiling. How he could smile, I didn't know. Mom was like a zombie. Didn't he care?

"Hey, Jack," he called out.

"What?"

"Can you pick up some milk on the way home? I'm out for your Mom's coffee."

The coffee she never drank?

"Sure, Dad." *The family that deludes itself together, stays deluded together!*

The steering wheel was cold where I gripped it. I thought about how I'd driven Lucas's pieced-together ride and what kinds of improvements I could make to it. I took off in the direction of the pizza parlor, hoping that I'd remember where it was.

The pizza joint came into view as I turned the corner, and I parked next to Jeannine's car. As soon as I could smell the fresh red sauce and yeasty dough, my stomach rumbled. I bought two slices and sat down across from her. She had stacked several books and magazines on the table.

"First things first," she said, taking my free hand, "let's talk about you and Sanjay."

I nodded. "What do you know?"

"Nothing. He wouldn't talk to me about whatever latest fight you two had. And neither of you will talk to me about what ended your friendship. So I can't help you." Some fight ended our friendship. Figured. I wondered when our tight group had fallen apart. Jeannine must have felt pushed away by both of us. I sat back, loosening myself from her grip and taking a big bite of pepperoni pizza. For a moment I pondered when pizza had come to America, since there wasn't exactly a pie shop in Jacqueline's town. Pizza was great.

"Well, I think it has to do with him liking other boys."

"You're saying he's gay? I'm surprised."

"Why? I'm not. But I think I was mean to him when it happened. I should have been kinder."

"Wow."

"What?"

"That's just very emotionally astute of you," she said.

"I'm not an idiot."

"I'm not saying you are," she said, covering her mouth as she spoke and chewed. "You're just not like other teenage boys."

I thought about that for a minute.

"Not anymore, I suppose."

"Well, Jay's family is very old fashioned. I'm sure they only want him marrying another Indian girl, and if he's gay they won't deal with that well."

I thought about it. They'd even told him he couldn't date Jeannine, the actual girl next door, because she was Cuban. Of course they'd go off a cliff if he said he wasn't straight.

"It must be lonely and scary for him," I said.

"For you, too, with all that you have going on."

"I'll try to talk to him later," I said, remembering how angry he'd been with me earlier today. "Let's talk about how to get me back to 1926. I have got to warn those people, help them get rid of Dr. Traver."

"I've done some research on that," she said, and she pulled a thin book out of her pile. "It's a history of central Kentucky."

"Oh? And what does it say?"

"Bad things."

"Well, okay,"

"No, Jack. Very bad things. This Prophet Traver character, he gets his whole congregation to commit mass suicide in 1930."

* * *

I figured I needed to go see Dr. Dorfman, because his study set all of this time-jumping in motion. Even though I wasn't participating in his experiment anymore, I wondered if I could use his equipment to send me back again. And it was possible that I'd talked to him at some point in the past three years, but I was ready to play dumb and pretend I'd forgotten in some major memory lapse.

The hospital, even after all this time, was familiar, down to the odor of ammonia and latex. I walked in, remembering the string of turns and doorways, over to the neurology wing. I smiled at the woman sitting at the reception desk. She looked at me curiously.

"Can I help you, young man?"

"I'm looking for Dr. Dorfman," I said. Two rooms away I'd sat in a plush chair for his study. I could see a slice of the waiting room from the nurses' station here.

"He no longer works at this hospital."

"He, he doesn't?" I should have called first. "Do you know where he is?"

"No, I'm certain I don't." She folded her arms across her chest. It was like I was asking for the codes to the missile silos so I could bomb Russia.

"Is there anyone here who would know where he went?"

"Well, I'm not going to walk around and ask everyone," she said. This was going nowhere fast.

"But I need to find him!"

She stood up, and on a raised platform, stood much taller than me. "Don't make me call security, young man."

In the hallway I noticed Cindy, the nurse who had assisted Dr. Dorfpoodle for the study. I ran over to her, against the shouts of the woman at reception. I hoped she'd recognize me.

"Hi there," Cindy said, her smile dissolving as the receptionist rushed over and clamped her hand around my arm. She began pulling me away, but I resisted.

"Mrs. Finney, what's going on?" asked Cindy. I yanked my arm free. "Let me see what he needs and I'll send him away."

The woman named Mrs. Finney gave me a hard stare. "One minute," she said in a low growl, "he doesn't have any business here." She huffed away.

"You look all grown up," said Cindy.

"Thanks." I got right to the point. "I'm looking for Dr. Dorfman."

Now she looked sad. "Well, he doesn't work here anymore."

This whole trip was a waste of time.

"Does anyone know where he is? Can I call someone?"

She looked around to see who could hear us. "The other nurses are very protective of him. Everybody liked him."

I couldn't understand what he would need protection from, exactly. Certainly not me.

"I just want to talk to him about his study. I don't even have seizures anymore."

"I know," she said, her face brightening. "That's wonderful."

"So where can I find him? I have questions only he can answer."

She sighed, and noted that Mrs. Finney was watching us, telling her to hurry it up.

"Dr. Dorfman isn't well."

"Okay," said Mrs. Finney from across the ward. "Move along, young man."

"What do you mean, not well?" Sounds of Mrs. Finney dialing security, the rotor on the phone whirring as it sprang back into position for the next number. Thank god she didn't have a push button phone.

"He had a nervous breakdown, I'm afraid to say."

"A what?"

"He's ill. Mentally, Jack. I'm sorry." Mrs. Finney, still speaking loudly, told security she needed a removal from neurology, right away.

"Can he talk?" I tried to process this information before anyone hauled me off.

"He can talk. He's just—he has delusions. He'll be better at some point, I'm sure."

"Delusions?" I remembered the psychology class I took my first year of high school. "You mean he believes things that aren't true?"

"Yes." Behind me, the double doors to the ward pounded open, and an enormous man, nearly bursting out of his security uniform, bounded over to Mrs. Finney. She pointed straight at me. *Great.* I was no match for this steroid-puffed rent-a-cop.

"Where is he?"

"Oh, he's here, in the mental wellness ward." As the guard approached, I held up my hands in surrender. I wanted no fight with the giant.

"So he can hold a conversation, he's just crazy?"

"Shh, don't say 'crazy.'" More large hands set on my frame. And Cindy leaned in to whisper to me just before I was hauled away: "He just had this idea that he was sending people back in time."

Chapter Thirteen

IN THREE WEEKS I had studied up on everything I could think of that would help me, if I could only get back to Jacqueline's time. I continued to wake up damp in my own cold sweat, smelling the house fire. Not much was improving in this time, either, although I'd succeeded in my battle to get my father to take Mom to a different doctor. I'd organized all of her pills and done some research to find out which ones had side effects and which ones could make her so spacey. I was prepped for the doctor visit when I would march in and order him to change her medication.

Jeannine and I met on a regular basis, and it was like she believed my ridiculous story. I still hadn't gotten Jay to talk to me, even though I'd knocked on his door a few times. At those points his mother would look at me with sadness in her eyes, saying he was busy or not at home. And although I still went to the woods—which were especially serene when they were snow-covered—I didn't see him there again. I presumed that with his hiding place blown, he'd found a new space that I wouldn't know about. Jeannine agreed that if I just kept trying, eventually he would reconnect with me.

I'd gotten Mom to come down to the kitchen, and she was willing to eat scrambled eggs. I whisked two in a bowl and she turned to face me from her seat at the table.

"How did my baby grow up so fast?" she asked. She clearly didn't recall that we had this conversation every week or so.

"Oh Mom, I'll always be your baby." I poured some milk into the bowl and whisked it.

"I hope so," she said, fingering her coffee mug. "I'm sorry I've been in such a fog."

I poured the eggs into the pan, silencing the sizzling butter.

"I just want you to be healthy. And safe."

"You're not supposed to mother your own mother." She lapsed into a long silence, but she ate her eggs and a little toast before heading to the patio to rest. On the windowsill over the sink I saw my old pill box. Because it was transparent I could tell it didn't have my old medication in it; Mom's pills were in there now.

I was cleaning up when Jeannine knocked at the door.

"Time to study," she said when I let her in. She always had a stack of reading material for me. I'd started keeping her favorite soda in the house, so I poured her a glass.

"Thanks," said Jeannine, taking a sip of Tab.

"So what's on our lesson plan today?" I asked. I read through whatever I could on my own time, but when we were together we followed whatever Jeannine had set up for us that day. Most days I had my head in a book since I still had to catch up on all the high school I'd missed.

"Evasion systems," she said, pulling a beat-up book from the top of the stack. I chuckled.

"What is it?" she asked, suspicious.

"Nothing, just that I have my very own Q, it seems."

"Q?"

"From James Bond. The spy movies? Q makes all of the gadgets."

She nodded, not as gleeful as me about it.

"Well, I'm counting on you to learn how to make them. I just do the research." She thought for a second. "Does James Bond have a librarian?"

"Probably," I said.

We read through the mechanics presented in the book, taking notes. Jeannine looked at the calendar on the kitchen wall.

"Nine more days?" she asked.

I nodded, still reading. Her fingers were sitting on the center where the pages came together in the book, holding it open for us to read. They were slender and tapered, and I glanced at my own hands, almost against my will. My knuckles were becoming more like my father's—big knobby hinges joining thickening fingers together as my hands spread out wider. I was supposed to get used to having no control over the changes in my body, but so far, it still pissed me off. I slid my hands under the textbook to hide them.

"Are you going to celebrate?" she asked.

"Oh, probably not. I think it would be too depressing."

"Turning eighteen is never depressing, silly," said Jeannine, and she sat back, taking stock of me.

"Well, I'm excited I can go to the hospital." Adult visitors were allowed to see some patients on the mental ward, and I planned to talk to Dr. Dorfman as soon as I could.

I found a way to change the subject and we went back to reading. Jeannine opened up another book and I sensed I'd read this book before. But where? I closed the cover enough to read it: *A History of Law Enforcement, 1880-1939.* It was familiar somehow, but maybe I'd just poured through too many navy blue hardbound books in the last month.

After an hour, it was time to get on with our actual homework. I stood up from the table and stretched, and my shirt came untucked.

"You're sure getting furry," Jeannine said. She grinned on one side of her face, and with quick movements pet my stomach. I pulled back, sucking in air and pulling down my shirt. A warm feeling spread out from the bottom of my torso and I blushed.

"Geez, Jack, try not to act like I'm repulsive. I'm just teasing you."

"No, it's okay," I said.

"It clearly isn't okay," she said. "I'm sorry. I have no right and I don't want you to get the wrong idea." She had pulled back her affection since realizing I had missed the whole hooking up thing last year. I felt bad for disappointing her. So we hadn't really broken up, but we weren't the item we had been, either.

"Don't worry about it, I'm fine," I said, standing behind a kitchen chair. Even if my heart wasn't in it, my body had a way of reacting all on its own.

She was kind enough not to insist on a hug before leaving, and I was relieved to gather up the library books from the table that I'd been assigned to read for our next meeting. Maybe none of this made any sense, but I was out of ideas for what else to do until I could talk to Dr. Dorfman. I worried he wouldn't make any sense.

When I finally got to see him during visiting hours, we had a much different conversation than I'd anticipated.

* * *

The morning was chilly enough that I had to spend ten minutes scraping frost off the windows of my car. The freaking scraper sucked, peeling back a quarter inch of frost even though the blade was like five inches wide. Down the street, I saw Jay trying and failing to get his engine to turn over. I hopped in and drove up beside him, my heater blowing near-freezing air at the glass. Leaning over to the passenger side, I rolled down my window.

"Do you need a jump?" I asked. He considered ignoring me but then sighed.

"My father says it's the alternator, not the battery." He looked defeated.

"So get in, I'll drive you to school."

"I don't think so." He held the steering wheel hard.

"Jay, the bus left already, and Jeannine's gone. Just get in so you can get to class."

"Fine." He grabbed his backpack and clambered in, the window vibrating after he shut the door. I headed off.

"So look," I said, but he cut me off.

"How about you don't talk while I'm here?"

"Jay, come on, we used to be friends. Good friends."

Sanjay gritted his teeth and talked through them. I could see his chest puffing quickly in and out as he tried to control his breathing.

"You made it clear you don't want to be friends anymore."

At a stop sign, I hesitated. "I can only say I'm sorry and try to make amends, man. I was an ass."

"Boy, were you ever," said Jay. I hoped he would smile.

"I miss you."

"I miss you too, but in a different way, Jack. And you're not ever going to feel the same way."

My first thought was *Oh my God I blew him off after a flirt or something.* That was bad enough. My second thought was a thousand times more depressing.

If only you knew, buddy.

"Can we just see if we can take it a day at a time? I think we can both use a friend to help us deal with our families, at least."

"Well, that's the truth," he said, sounding like he was trying to keep from choking. "If my family found out, they would disown me. Literally."

"If you ever want to talk, I'll listen."

"You've sure worked on getting in touch with your feminine side," he said as we pulled away. He rubbed his eyes.

"It's something I picked up at the gym," I said. That brought a laugh out of him, and we drove the last few blocks to school. Puffs of frost appeared before our faces as we crossed the parking lot. Dang this heater took a long time to get going.

Jay headed off to his locker with only a small wave.

I hadn't seen any need to stay in school except that the truancy officer had finally called my father after a month of skipping class. I didn't need to worry my parents, and I acknowledged that it helped me feel rooted in this time, which was my time, after all. But my grades were ass.

* * *

This part of the hospital had a long window that ran along a colorful garden and patio so that from anywhere in the communal room, people could gaze at the outdoors. A little dustiness on the glass reminded everyone that really, they were locked in, at the end of a building that could be entered only through a series of double doors and a guard who buzzed in visitors in thirty-minute increments.

I left my license with the guard and got a colored visitor's badge that I wore clipped to my shirt. Wednesday was yellow, apparently. Past the guard's desk an orderly pointed out Dr. Dorfman, who was sitting listless in front of a television mounted high on the wall. He was watching *The Price Is Right.* As I got closer, he noticed me, squinting as if he couldn't see me clearly. He looked disheveled, a little dirty, his teeth yellow in a way I hadn't noticed during the study. His perm days were over, and now his hair was a little too long, a little matted, the fluffy sideburns shaved off. I noticed a crumpled pack of Winston cigarettes on the end table and figured out why his teeth were so ugly. The ashtray overflowed with crushed butts.

"You." His eyes were unfocused, glassy.

"Do you remember me, doctor?" It was only then that I clued in to the fact that I didn't really have a plan for talking with him. Sure, I'd played the conversation I wanted to have with him over and over in my own head, but that wasn't an actual conversation.

I grabbed an orange plastic scoop chair and pulled it over to face him.

"Showcase Showdown. They always try to get a dollar and lose. No, no, no, don't spin again," he said to the television.

An orderly noticed how animated Dr. Dorfman had become.

"He loves that show," she said, and then she walked away, over to a patient who was refusing to take some pills. I saw her and another orderly, who was trying not to argue over an older man's medication. She coaxed him into submission. The patient swallowed the pills and then on command showed them the space under his tongue.

"Do you remember the epilepsy study, doctor?" I asked him.

He just stared at the TV.

"Now she, this woman here, needs to spin the wheel twice. You can't stop at forty cents. Don't stop at forty cents!"

Cindy had warned me about this. This was a mistake, coming here.

Another orderly came over, a squat woman with silver hair. "Son, I think you'll have to leave. You're getting him too riled up. It's not good for him."

"Wait, we can talk about something else," I said. *No, don't make me leave now. I need him, he knows how to help me jump back.* After all this time waiting and preparing, filled with memories of people in pain and dying, I couldn't just leave.

"Maybe we could turn off the show," I suggested.

"No, I don't think so. Come on, don't give me trouble now." She got up close to me, like I was one of her patients. She wrapped a hand around my wrist, pulling me away from him.

"You'll win the showcase," said Dr. Dorfman, who kept his eyes to the television.

I was figuring out how to get back to see him. I couldn't wait any longer. I mean, I could come back later, maybe, but I needed to know who else was traveling through time, and where they went, and if I could get back there. So many questions.

"I forgot something," I said, squirming out of her grip. I ran over to Dorfman.

"Please, just help me get back. Tell me how to get back."

Our eyes connected. He looked at me, really looked, finally uninterested in the game show.

"It's inside you," he said. "You just need the notebook, is all. I wrote it all down. About all of you." He strained for words, and I was pulled back to the door by the tall orderly who knew how to get pills into people. He gave me one last look.

"Bye-bye, my time traveler." He waved at me like a toddler.

Chapter Fourteen

JEANNINE SAID OUTRIGHT that she was frustrated, at least as much as I was over my non-conversation with Dr. Dorfman. She held my hand, a spot of warmth on my skin against the chill outside. I felt bad about taking her affection, and I found myself wishing she was Lucas, which of course made me feel even worse. I was in a cycle of lonely assholeness.

"Sounds like they're all so spaced out on drugs that none of them know if they're coming or going," she said. We were back in the woods, off the edge of our neighborhood, but it was too cold to stay long. A branch snapped not far in the distance. Before I knew it, I was standing and ready for an attack.

"Settle down. Unless you didn't mean it about being friends again," said Sanjay, toeing carefully through the trees. He sat down on an old metal chair.

"Sorry, guess I'm on edge," I said. "What are you doing out here?"

"Not what you think," he said, giggling a little.

"I'm glad to see you two are talking again," she said. "It's been a long time since we all hung out back here together."

"Ain't that the truth," said Jay. He brushed a brittle dusting of snow off a fallen tree and sat down. "So why don't you tell me what you two lovebirds have been up to?"

Jeannine and I looked at each other, neither of us ready for his question.

"I don't think you'd understand," I said. *That was weak.*

Sanjay bristled and crossed his arms over his chest. "Oh, here we go, I see."

"It's not like that," Jeannine said. She dropped my hand and sat down on a log next to Jay.

Dr. Dorfman had told me the answers were in "the notebook." Where would I find it? Did it still exist? I had no idea where he lived, or how I'd get inside or what it looked like, or anything. Then a light bulb went off over my head. I jumped up.

"Where the hell are you going?" called Sanjay after me. I stopped, twenty yards away from them.

"I have to go talk to someone," I said, checking my watch. "Jeannine, fill him in."

"Really?"

"I have a better GPA than both of you clowns," said Sanjay, as if we were questioning his abilities. I burst out of the woods and ran down the sidewalk to my car, then jumped in and sped to the hospital. If I hit all the traffic lights just right, I could get there before Cindy left at the end of her shift.

Maybe Dr. Dorfman's notebook was at the hospital in the clinical study office.

* * *

This time, I knew better than to try to get past Mrs. Finney, so I stayed in the parking lot, crossing my fingers that I'd picked the right outer doors to catch Cindy. I leaned on my car even though it was warmer in the vehicle, but I wanted to make sure I could talk to her before she drove away. *Please let her get out here before the frostbite sinks in,* I thought.

A cluster of nurses, some still wearing their uniforms, came out together as the evening shift began. I saw Cindy walking with two other women. Thank god Nurse Ratchet—I mean, Mrs. Finney—wasn't with her. I trotted over, waving when she noticed me.

"Jack, you sure hang around the hospital a lot for a boy who's well now." She looked at me sideways, like I was suspicious.

"I went to see Dr. Dorfman."

She stopped groping for her car keys in her purse and looked at me. She drove a run-down Ford Escort that had a lot of rust along the left rear fender where it had been struck at some point. Maybe nurses didn't make as much as I thought they did.

"Oh, honey, he's not fit to talk to anyone. Did he say anything?"

I thought about the once-famous neurologist, now close to drooling on himself and obsessed with a game show.

"Not much, I'm afraid."

"You shouldn't go over there again," she said. "Those people are working on getting better, and they don't respond well to changes in their routine."

"Are mental patients always on that much medication? Is that how it is?"

"We don't call them 'mental patients,' Jack. But unfortunately, often it is. It can take a while to find a balance of medicine that helps people."

I thought of my mother. She was a lot like Dr. Dorfman.

"I don't remember a lot from the end of the study," I said, changing gears. "Is there a record of my lab sessions? I'm eighteen now." Hopefully that was helpful to add, since being a legal adult and all was a big deal.

"Well, as a clinical study those sessions are put into a blind panel," she said.

"Um, I don't know what that means." So much for instant adulthood. *Just add water!*

"Who receives the treatment is kept confidential, even from the doctors. And I don't really remember their names anymore." She shrugged. "I'm sorry to give you bad news, hon, but I couldn't go back and even tell which sessions were yours. And you're better now, so why do you want to know?"

I didn't know what to tell her. If Dr. Dorfman was locked up and drugged because he insisted I and possibly others had traveled through time, what would happen to me if I told the same story? I was just a nobody kid from the suburbs, and he was a prestigious doctor, and still nobody bought his story.

"I'm having some memory problems from that time. Some false memories. I wanted to see if there was anything in there that would help explain it to me."

She looked really upset for a moment, then nodded. Maybe she was trying to think of a way to help me fix my problem. *Because time travel and loves from another time, totally easy to fix!*

"There are other doctors on the ward, I suppose, who you could see to get some understanding. What kind of memories do you have that you know aren't real?"

"I keep seeing a burning house," I said, going for something that was true but not crazy-sounding. "A white farm house at the top of a hill."

She frowned. "I see. That does seem pretty specific, but I've heard of those things happening before. The human brain, it's so complicated." *Wow.* Cindy was blowing me away with her scientific knowledge of brains.

"Wasn't there a time when Dr. Dorfman reversed the EEG machine and sent electricity to my brain?"

"Well, it was a different machine, since EEG machines can only read brain waves, not produce current. But yes. Do you have a specific memory from that?"

Lucas, smashing through the branches and crying out in pain. Meeting Dr. Traver as a full-fledged drunk, scouring the back office for coffee to sober him up. Kissing Lucas, tasting him, feeling my heart pound, running through the tunnels of the Underground Railroad. I'd say it was a specific memory in the extreme.

"Yes."

"I can try and find another doctor to talk to you, Jack, if you really need to explore this."

"That's okay," I said. I had hit yet another dead end. "I just wanted to look at my records if I can't talk to Dr. Dorfman. And I'm glad the study cured me, I guess." Did I mean that? Even if I couldn't go back and save everyone? Or see Lucas again?

"The study didn't cure you, Jack. You just grew out of it. Many people, when they hit puberty, their brain waves just correct all on their own." *Fucking hormones. It's nuts that some stupid chemical from south of my junk can totally change the electricity of my brain. But there you have it. Enjoy testosterone!*

I walked back to my car after thanking Cindy. She wasn't the Cheshire Cat she used to be. Which made me trust her more than when I'd been in the study. But now she only gave me bad news.

* * *

I turned into the driveway after dark, battling the winter fog with my headlights. If only Dr. Dorfman or Cindy could explain the study, or what they thought had happened to me. Instead I had to settle for knowing a bunch of people were going to die horrible, fiery deaths. It was too much.

The engine cut out in a gruff as the key slid out from the steering column. The key's millings were so worn sometimes it fell right out of the car. My chest felt tight and the cold air bit me through my light jacket. I wondered idly why the foyer lamp wasn't on, because my parents usually let it burn through the night like a tiny lighthouse. Maybe the bulb had died.

"Surprise," shouted the group gathered around the kitchen table. My parents—Mom looking better than usual—Jeannine, Kiernan, and Sanjay, stood next to each other, each singing their own version of "Happy Birthday." On the table sat a cake with my name on it.

Oh right, my birthday.

For the next couple of hours, I was distracted from all the crap about time travel and Jacqueline. We stuffed ourselves on take-out Italian food and a chocolate cake from A&P. I thought back to my wish as I'd blown out the candles: *Please save them. All of them.* I didn't really know where my wish was going, though, or who gave a shit about it.

"You're blushing," said Jay, taking a bright paper plate with a square of cake from my mother.

"What of it?" I asked, making an attempt to be coy, "don't you ever blush?"

"Nope, Kashmiris don't blush, silly." He fake batted his eyes at me.

We cleaned the kitchen and moved to the family room. I took stock of my presents—a boom box with a dual cassette rack, a pair of jeans, a gift certificate to Sam Goody, and a HAM radio, assembled by my father, who had noticed I'd been reading up on amateur radio.

"I'm going to say goodnight to Jeannine," I told Jay, who looked nowhere near ready to leave. He grunted at me and thumbed through a copy of *Rolling Stone.*

In the foyer, Jeannine gave me a peck on the cheek. She smelled like birthday cake and icing, and I wished it was Lucas's hands around my waist.

"Happy Birthday, Jackson," she said softly.

"Thank you, Jeannine. That was fun."

"Were you really surprised?"

"I was really surprised."

She nodded a little, agreeing with I don't know, the truth of my statement or something.

"Onto bigger and better things," she said. I raised an eyebrow.

"What do you mean?"

"I mean, we have to figure out how to help those people in Marion. Tomorrow is a new day."

"It is," I said, but I was relieved. Any help I could get, anything. I leaned in to give her a thank you hug, and she pushed me away.

"What?" I asked.

"I know you're not into me. You haven't been since you came back. It's okay. But we have to stay friends forever."

"Oh, Jeanne, you are amazing."

"Yeah, yeah, I know," she said, and her smile faded fast. And then she was bounding down the front stoop steps, across the street to her house. I watched the door shut behind her, and then closed my front door, sighing. I shuffled off to the family room to find Jay still reading about *U2* and Bono.

"I suppose you think you've changed," he said.

I considered his statement. "I think I have. It kind of happened without me noticing."

Jay kicked his feet up on the coffee table in front of the couch. "Jeannine told me quite a wild story this afternoon."

"I know, you think I'm crazy."

"It's impossible." He paused, watching with disinterest a hockey game on the TV. "But if it could be true, it's amazing."

"I spent a long time telling myself it was all in my head, Jay, but I know it's real." He laughed.

"What's so freaking funny?" Was he mocking me?

"It's just—that's what I said to myself about being gay."

I gave him a soft punch in his shoulder. "See, we still have so much in common."

"Watch the fine wool, buddy."

"Oh, excuse me."

We relaxed, partly because we needed to in the midst of our stress, and partly because we didn't know how to begin talking about my bizarre story. Eventually I told him about going to see Dr. Dorfman, and later, Cindy, and what dead ends I'd reached. But I still felt a little vindicated that any other person believed what was happening to me, much less two.

"I wish we could get him out of there," I said.

"Well, we can," said Jay.

I stared at him.

He came up with a wild but weirdly sensible plan. At least, the plan for getting the doctor out of the hospital made sense. It was after we freed the doctor that we didn't have much of a blueprint, so we put our heads together and figured it out. We reckoned that once we got him off his medication, he would be able to talk to us. And once he could talk, Dr. Dorfman would put the missing pieces together for us. Jay and I agreed to talk to Jeannine about it in the morning and see if she had any ideas.

But maybe a rescue of Dorfpoodle could work.

That night I tossed and turned in my bed. I couldn't settle down. What if people said I was becoming delusional or commit me like they'd done to Dr. Dorfman? At some point I nodded off, but like had become my habit, I woke up in a panic, the smell of smoke and charred wood burning my sinuses. I remembered something, but what was it? *The picture, the picture from the newspaper.*

I fumbled for the light on my nightstand, and shielded my eyes with one hand as I groped on my desk for the microfiche I'd snagged. I'd created a whole filing system for this information. I dug through my folders labeled "Marion history," "HAM radios," and the like and yanked out a file. I stared at the microfiche, but I couldn't read the tiny inverted print on my own, so I picked up a magnifying glass from the back of my desk, a leftover part of my "detective kit" I played with when I was little. Yanking open the top drawer of my desk, I found a flashlight. I stuck the microfiche in the wax of a half-burned candle, and aimed the flashlight through the magnifying glass. The image glowed on my wall.

There, in the background of the Temperance Union meeting photo, was Jacob Van Doren.

It was right there in the article. Lucas's father was a traitor.

I clapped a hand over my heart and turned off the flashlight.

CHAPTER FIFTEEN

SANJAY LOOKED MUCH OLDER IN SCRUBS.

"Green's a good color on you," I said, sitting in my car. I kept the engine running so the heater could warm us up a little.

"Oh shut up." He clipped his brother's hospital badge on his shirt and said, "Wish me luck."

"You know, this is your brother's badge, and he doesn't really look like you," I said, holding it out and examining it.

"Please, Jack. Ain't no hospital doctor gonna be looking at my badge to see if I'm different from the other brown men in the building. I'll be fine." He seemed sure about this.

The plan was for Sanjay to say Dr. Dorfman needed to go to respiratory therapy, and he was the orderly to remove him. With all the smoking the doctor did, we hoped it wouldn't look suspicious. According to Jay's brother Prabal, lots of patients on the mental wellness ward smoked a lot and it was common for them to get checkups from the respiratory therapy staff when they inevitably had problems breathing. Class A medical service.

"Well," I said, "just be convincing."

"Nobody looks closely at us Indians," he said, and he walked off, giving me the finger behind his back as he walked into the hospital. I smiled because there was nothing like getting the bird from him to show that we really were back on good terms.

Now I had to wait. I continued to think about Mr. Van Doren, wondering why and how he could turn on his friends that way. It wasn't like Dr. Traver was nice to him, destroying his business and forcing him out of his home. I was pissed that Van Doren would put Mother's life in danger like that, not to mention his own son's. *How could you kill your own son?*

I didn't believe for a second that Lucas could also be a turncoat, because he could have just waited for the thugs to come into Mr. Rushman's farmhouse, and take me away. He'd protected me, smuggled me past them, helped me and the others plan. I supposed it was possible that all of that was done to build my confidence, but Lucas didn't strike me as that kind of a long-game person.

The passenger door opened, and Sanjay told me to help him. Dr. Dorfman looked as out of it as he had two weeks ago when I'd gone to see him.

"Hoo, it's time traveling boy Jack," he said in a loud voice.

"Won't you sit down, doctor?" I asked him. We needed to hurry but we also needed him to be cooperative.

"Don't stop on sixty cents!" *Fucking Price is Right, I hate you.*

"Okay, let's go to the show, doctor," I said, leaning over the seat so I could help pull him into the car. He snatched his arm away from me.

"Don't make me catch it," he said. Sanjay put the doctor's feet in the car and shut the door. At the hospital entrance, I saw the security guards assembling, the tall orderly from the ward pointing at Jay and the now-empty wheelchair.

"We have to go," I said. Jay jumped into the car.

"I know! So go!"

I sped off. When we were sure we'd made it away alone, I changed direction to our destination.

I read Jeannine's directions and drove out to a house at the edge of a country club. This was her friend Aimée's parents' house, and they were away for the holidays, skiing somewhere in Europe. Most of our classmates lived in the suburbs, like us, but there were a few who came from money, like Aimée. I'd have thought she'd attend an expensive prep school, but getting a Catholic education where her father had attended was more important to her dad. Plus hey, it came in handy for sudden subterfuge.

I pulled into a long driveway that ended in a courtyard, long rows of pruned shrubs lining the gravel road. The house was almost as big as a block of homes in my neighborhood, with thick columns holding up an extension of the roof that sheltered the massive front doors. We got out of the car and propped up Dr. Dorfman, who kept talking about the television he watched and time travel.

Jeannine met us at the bottom of the white front steps, surrounded by expensive architecture. She helped us get him out of the car, grunting as she pulled at him.

It had occurred to us that technically, we were kidnapping him. We hoped that Dr. Dorfman wouldn't press charges once he was off his medication.

"Okay, you get back home," Jeannine told Sanjay, who had to return his brother's badge before Prabel noticed it was missing. I watched him drive off in Jeannine's car, and then I took in the grand entry of this house. I should have been paying attention to Dr. Dorfman, but the house distracted me.

Marble floors and life-sized portraits in gold-gilded frames set up the edges of the room, and at the far end a double stairway curled up high to the next floor. In the entry, all of the furniture was oversized, as if they were made for giants. At the middle of the round room stood a stone table with three thick, swooping legs. I imagined that when the occupants were here it held some fresh flower arrangement, but today it was bare and lonely. I'd known that there were rich people in the world; I just hadn't dreamed they lived in houses of this size. The rooms could have doubled as basketball courts. They were echo chambers; acoustics came in handy when Jeannine called out to me to help her with the doctor.

"Where did you go?" I asked the foyer/ampitheater.

"Come through the living room," she said.

I picked which room could possibly be the living room, and saw a doorway at the other end, after a long line of bookshelves. Down a few steps, I saw her and Dr. Dorfman, sitting on a plush couch in front of a projection television.

"Behind the couch is the Betamax," she said, pointing. "I taped the show earlier."

I walked up to the machine, pressed the power button and then play, hoping I wouldn't have to do anything else to get the video on the TV. In seconds Bob Barker was introducing the people in Contestant's Row.

"*The Price is Right,*" said Dr. Dorfman, clapping his hands.

"How long is it going to take him to come out of this?" I asked. Jeannine had read up on anti-psychotics, or so she'd said.

"It could be anywhere from a few days to a week."

"A week? What are we supposed to do with him for a week? We can't baby sit him around the clock. And the hospital will be looking for him!"

"Relax," she said. "It could be sooner than that. We just have to take it one day at a time. We have two weeks off before we have to go back to school. Aimeé's parents won't be back until the third week of January."

Dr. Dorfman was engrossed in the show.

"You sure do find that interesting," I said.

"The show is easier," he said.

"How do you mean?" I grasped at whatever else the man would say.

"Life, so precarious, dangerous. Showcase Showdown is safer." He let out a big sigh and slumped into the plush couch.

"Maybe he really is crazy," said Jeannine to me, whispering.

"Actually, now I'm convinced he isn't crazy."

On the couch, Dr. Dorfman rolled his eyes at us. "I wish I had my notebook."

* * *

Around dinner time, Sanjay showed up in his car.

"The hospital is going nuts," he said. "When my brother showed up everyone was checking badges. It's like Checkpoint Charlie, and there are police all over the place."

"Maybe this was a bad idea," I said.

"Nonsense, it's fine," said Jeannine. "Nobody's hurting Dr. Dorfman, and when he gets off these anti-psychotics, he'll be happy we rescued him. He didn't commit himself, after all."

We looked at the doctor, who was sleeping, still on the couch. He hadn't been cared for very well at the hospital, judging from the smell of him.

"At least you two are underage," I said. I understood that he would be better off with us, or at least I hoped he would. But I wasn't sure how he would reintegrate. Wouldn't he just be committed again once he went back into the world?

"It's going to be fine," Jeannine insisted, and she sounded final about it. "Did you bring any supper?" she asked Jay.

"Yeah, it's in the kitchen. I scarfed stuff out of the fridge. There's lamb stew and some rice. This is a hell of a house. I bet there's a swimming pool here somewhere."

"Why have a swimming pool when you can have a whole country club," I said. "There's a putting green out back."

"What? You're kidding!" He rushed to the windows, which ran all the way to the twenty-foot ceiling. When he walked back to us he was shaking his head. *What would Lucas think of this place*? I wondered.

"Holy crap, there's a putting green out there. What the hell, rich people?"

We went into the kitchen and heated up the food in the largest microwave I had ever seen. Sanjay's mother was a great cook. Jeannine suggested between bites that we ought to be invited over for supper at his place much more often. I sat between them, relieved to be with friends, but full of thoughts about Lucas, Jacqueline, and her mother, worrying about how they'd been betrayed by Mr. Van Doren.

Our heads turned together as we noticed a shuffling sound at the edge of the kitchen. Dr. Dorfman stood there, rubbing his hand over his scruffy face.

"You must really want to talk to me." His voice was scratchy, but didn't have that frantic quality like when he was talking about the game show.

Jeannine dropped her fork.

It was Sanjay who stood up and helped walk him over to us. "Would you like some dinner?"

"Yes. It smells great."

I leaned in to Jeannine.

"This is not three days."

She nodded.

"I stopped taking my pills a week ago," Dr. Dorfman said, obviously overhearing us. "I knew I had to get off the meds after you came to see me, I just had to figure out how, since they check our mouths."

He'd palmed his pills, using sleight of hand to trick the orderlies. Dr. Dorfman explained that since he was such a model patient, they didn't pay enough attention to him to notice that he'd gone off his medicine.

We offered him what was left of Jay's mom's cooking and he scarfed it down.

"This is the best food I've had in six months."

"Yeah, it's great even when you're not comparing it to hospital food," said Jeannine, and Dr. Dorfman laughed. After talking with him for a while, I was ready to ask my nagging question.

"So are these hallucinations I'm having or am I really traveling through time?"

"Jack, you're really time traveling. Well, kind of. As far as I can figure, your consciousness is jumping. But I'm still a little fuzzy upstairs," he said, poking with a fork at the remains of food on his plate. "I tried to draw things out in the other room."

He was much more cognizant than I would have been after months in his condition. It hadn't occurred to him right away that my mutterings were anything other than disorientation, but my brainwaves were unlike anything he'd ever seen, with aftereffect trails that weren't supposed to happen after an epileptic seizure. And then he saw it with two other people, during only the sessions in which he induced seizures in a certain area of their brains, near the visual cortex. They also returned talking of traveling back in time, but in their cases they'd visited some point earlier in the day or week, well away from where they were in real time, places they'd never visited. He started fact-checking people's visions and decided they were really encountering these earlier times. He made a note in his lab work, meant only for himself, but a supervisor responsible for the study read it and called him in to a meeting.

He'd been told to take the day off to rest. Instead he spent it confirming his hypothesis. When he came to work the next day, he learned his wife had agreed to admit him for observation. By the time we'd stolen him away, she'd sent his lawyer divorce papers.

We went into the den to see what he'd drawn up. On the screen of the projection TV, he'd written a lot of squiggly lines.

"Uh, what is this?" I asked, walking around the couch to get a better look. It looked vaguely familiar but I didn't know what it depicted.

"It's how the EEG and the fourth dimension interact," he said. "This part of Einstein's theory of relativity, that time flows backwards as well as forwards, has never been proven. Everything else has been shown scientifically except that.

"Einstein said time travel was possible?"

"In a way, he did. Einstein said that time does not travel in only one direction. That makes time travel theoretically possible. I think your brain waves are predisposed to catching that reverse flow."

"Which is why I'm not myself going back in time?"

"Right," he said, pointing at his diagram. "It's like your brain waves are an extension of your consciousness, not just an effect of it. And they can skip across the time flow, like a stone."

"Or a HAM radio signal," I said.

"Yes, sort of." He looked surprised.

"Well, but one time I just jumped by myself, not in your lab."

"By that point I think your epileptic brain was capable of 'jumping,' as you call it, all on its own."

"Okay. But I don't have epilepsy anymore," I said, shrugging as if I'd done something wrong.

"Oh, that's not a problem. We can make you seize."

Jeannine's eyes narrowed. "Isn't that like, against your oath as a doctor or something?"

"Yes, if there's no medical benefit to it, sure. But my license to practice has been suspended anyway," said the doctor. He flashed a sad smile. "I suppose I sounded pretty crazy, didn't I?"

"A little," I said.

"I could really use a shower."

Sanjay had to head back home. I'd told my parents I'd be out late, which was fine with them, and Jeannine's father worked the third shift at the firehouse, so her mother took this as downtime until she turned in for the night. We decided to keep Dr. Dorfman company since he hadn't actually talked to anyone after he'd been committed, and since we needed his information.

I filled him in on the story about the people in Kentucky.

"Doctor?" asked Jeannine, who'd been lost in thought.

"Yes?"

"If Jack is in someone else's body when he's in another time, could he die there?"

"Well, I don't know. Our conscious selves respond to the signals they receive from the brain, which gets its input from the body. If the body has suffered catastrophic damage, I suppose Jack's consciousness could fade, but then I don't know what happens."

It was a question I didn't want answered.

Chapter Sixteen

WHILE DR. DORFMAN WORKED on building a crude EEG machine, I drove out to Marion, Kentucky for more information on the town and who lived there now. Whatever town square I'd seen was gone, absorbed into a street grid. Farm lands hugged the outlying areas, but the vast majority of the area had been developed. I pulled over, seeing a yellowed sign in the window of a storefront: Marion Historical Society. I fumbled for dimes in my pocket and filled the meter, then headed inside. An older lady with curly white hair greeted me.

"The suggested donation is one dollar," she told me, "but you can see if that's worth paying after you walk through." *It's not a good sign when the volunteers at the museum aren't real excited about the place.* I smiled and put a bill in her metal box. I was the only visitor there.

The museum was once a home. Two rooms in the front were lined with glass cases filled with pictures and trinkets of earlier times. I asked the greeter where the oldest items were. She pointed me to the next room.

Founded in 1804, the town didn't expand past eight hundred residents until the twentieth century, when it found itself between an increasingly busy highway and a major waterway. It was formally incorporated before the Civil War, the last bastion for slave owners before the free states of Ohio and Michigan picked up in the north. Several hundred slaves moved through central Kentucky as they fled toward Canada. Only a few pictures of abolitionists sat pinned inside the jewelry cases. I searched but didn't find any information on the Underground Railroad. Wouldn't it have been something a little museum would tout, if they'd brag about being a refuge for ex-slaves?

I worked my way up to the 1880s, and found a faded photo of Mr. Rushman's farm: the house, the stables behind, a small granary, and the long rows for planting. It must have been taken around the turn of the century, because there was a Model T Ford parked at the front of the house, next to the porch.

Pushing my face closer down to the glass, I strained to read the hand-written caption in white ink beneath the photo:

ORIGINAL FARM HOUSE OF WILHELM FOLK

Somehow Mr. Rushman had come to acquire the house, I gathered. Maybe Mr. Folk was richer.

Further along, in a case at the corner of the once-dining room, was a plastic model of the original layout of the town. I stifled a gasp, looking at it. I could see the view from the trail on the hill, the one I walked up in my first two jumps. Why had I started out here? Was it random? *Work, damn brain, work!*

"Can I explain anything?" asked the old woman from behind me. I jumped a little in surprise.

"I'm sorry, young man," she said.

"No, it's fine," I said. "I've seen this farm house before." I pointed at Mr. Rushman's house on the map.

"You couldn't possibly have seen that house," she said, smiling and the hair on my forearms stood at attention. She was definitely creepy. She walked over to me. "That burned down well before you were born. 1927 or so."

"Really? How did that happen?" I hoped I sounded nonchalant. *But let's face it, you don't really do nonchalant, Captain Obvious.*

"Hmm, I'm not sure. I was just a little girl when it happened. Electrical system? A lot of these houses were retrofitted because they were built before electricity."

That was plausible, certainly, but something about her story unsettled me.

"Are you from the area, son?"

"I'm just doing a school project." *I should have thought of an excuse before,* I thought. *That sounds pathetic.*

"Well, if you'd like me to point anything out, I will help if I can."

"Thanks, Mrs.—" I glanced at her nametag. "Griffith." I'd heard that name before. The horse I stole. "Are you related to a Lucille Griffith?"

She inhaled sharply and smiled. "Why, she's my aunt. I'm the daughter of her younger brother, Alexander. "So you are local."

"Not anymore," I said, hoping I didn't look like a total fraud. I really wasn't spy material. "We moved away a while back." *A while back? What the hell are you saying?*

"Well, do let me know if I can help." She left me alone again, and I studied the miniature model of the town. Where Mr. Van Dorn's tavern had once stood, the model showed a squat hotel. I scanned the top of the hill but didn't see my mother's house. Finally I turned back to the pictures for 1910–1930. And right there, he glowered at me, looking cruel with his weasel eyes: Dr. Traver. He'd grown a white beard in the years since I knew him, but it did nothing to warm him up. This photo must have been taken in the winter.

He had his arm wrapped around a smaller figure, a young woman or girl, and then I gaped at the faded photo because Holy Hostage Batman, it was Jacqueline Bishop being smothered in his arms. I read the caption:

MAYOR MELVIN TRAVER AND HIS WIFE JACQUELINE, DECEMBER 26, 1926

I stood there for a time, shaking, trying to get a grip. Jacqueline looked miserable. And holy wedding bells here was something else I needed to prevent from happening.

I thanked Mrs. Griffin and asked when the museum closed.

"Four o'clock sharp," she said, making it clear that she didn't intend to wait for me or anybody else to return to browse more, potential dollar donations be damned. I thanked her and left through the front, the door jingling quietly as it shut behind me.

I drove down Main Street slowly, trying to orient where I was in relation to the model. Rushman Farm was my first stop. Driving into the valley was ridiculous. I was stuck in some kind of traffic jam. A construction worker held up a sign that read "Slow," so naturally I thought about yelling that he should change it to "Screw You Drivers You're Never Getting Anywhere," but whatever, that was probably too long for a sign. The engine idled and I thought about Jacqueline bound up in Dr. Traver's arms. Lucas would never have allowed such a thing. If Jacqueline was married to Dr. Traver, who somehow became mayor, and Mr. Van Doren had betrayed the cause, did it mean Lucas had died in the fire? There were only two months, give or take, between the events.

In any case, I had to change history so that this didn't happen, especially because I worried I'd already changed history to make them happen. But who knew? Time was like molasses, sticky and messy as hell. I might not have asked for the ability to jump time, but if I could do it, then I had to try to make things better for people. And I really wanted to be with Lucas again, feel him next to me, hear his voice and wipe his stupid bangs out of his face. I had to save him.

And I had to face it that I was in love with him, whatever that meant.

* * *

The big farm house was definitely gone, surrendered at some point to a suburban neighborhood that looked a lot like mine, ninety minutes away, but this one didn't have any sidewalks. It seemed rude to walk on the lawns of strangers so I kept to the edge of the street. I mean, the last thing I'd want to be when trying to rescue friends from a time before I was born, in a totally different person's life, was to forget my manners. I stared at the block of houses, trying to assess which one was closest to the old spot, based on where the ground began to rise. Even if the house had burned down, what became of the basement tunnel?

I checked around the street, always afraid Dr. Traver or one of his cronies would show up to stop me by force, even though that wasn't possible. Why pretend time had any stability, after all?

No lights on in the house, and no cars in the driveway, so I hoped that meant the house was empty. I skirted along the side, which was covered in dingy, light blue vinyl siding. Maybe it had looked nice for a few years, but now it was chipped and looked like garbage. In the back yard tall evergreen trees ran the length of the property. *There must be a door around here that I can jimmy,* I thought. Since I'd already abducted someone, breaking and entering was small potatoes for a criminal mastermind like me. I found a sliding glass door that was held in place by a metal bracket, and I couldn't budge that, and the rear door that led to a laundry room was locked shut. Lex Luther I was not.

Looking for windows, I tripped over something hard in the grass. I tapped it with my toe and saw that there was a round piece of concrete under a light layer of grass, kind of like the well caps at some of the older houses in my town. The grass pulled up like ribbons, which I tried to stack so that I could pat them back in place later. I worried the slab would be too heavy for me to move by myself, but I was able to get some leverage on it, and with a thick grating sound, it slid over, revealing a vertical shaft lined with rusty ladder rungs, leading down into the blackness. Totally inviting.

No time like the present! I tested the top ring with most of my weight before I let go of the top of the shaft.

Down in the dim column, memories flooded me of creeping through the tunnels with Lucas, kissing him while on the run from Traver's thugs. I wondered what Jay would think of my eagerness to be back with Lucas. Shit, maybe that was why Jay and I had fought in the first place. Leave it to me to be all ridiculous about having sex feelings I couldn't deal with.

My feet hit the ground, and my thoughts evaporated when I saw an old lantern, long since dried out of oil. It had created its own rust ring where it sat on the cement. I wasn't sure if it was the same lantern Lucas and I had used, but it looked similar. I didn't touch it.

A line of light streaming in from the top of the shaft hit the concrete floor in a tight sliver. My eyes adjusted a little more to the darkness, and I made out a door about twenty feet away. A few paces in front of it, I hit an object on the ground and stumbled forward. Crouching down, I patted it. I couldn't figure out what it was except that it had thin rods of metal and some floppier pieces stuck to it.

I walked over to the rungs I'd climbed down and held it up to the tiny ray of light. It was a leg brace, the kind that strap around the calf and have a knee pivot joint. Was it Lucas's? It looked mangled, little stiff wires poking out of it in places that would slash someone if they tried to strap it on. Why was it here?

I'd come all this way, and that door taunted me. *Next time, bring a freaking screwdriver.* I wanted to explore what was beyond it, but I admit I was scared down there all by myself. This was definitely part of the tunnel structure I'd been in with Lucas. I could blink and see him back with me. Almost.

I climbed the rungs and was halfway up when my left foot crashed through the bar, which had rusted out. I hung from my hands, bits of metal digging into my skin, and scrabbled against the damp sides of the shaft. I pulled my right leg up high and found the next bar and quickly climbed up the rest of the way. I dragged the concrete cap back into place and wiped my hands on my jeans.

I walked back to my car and climbed in, looking around to measure up my surroundings again, but everything seemed the same until I got to the end of the road. Turning right would have taken me back the way I'd come. That was when I noticed the older woman from the museum sitting in the passenger seat of a brown Impala parked along the curb. In the driver's seat was a middle-aged man, talking to her and waving his hands around a lot, but when they saw me, they stopped talking. His engine raced and he shot across the road toward me. I hammered the gas pedal to the floor and turned left, getting as much speed as I could. My transmission screeched in anger. A small sign along the side of the road pointed to the highway, and I turned sharply, nearly tipping over. The driver chasing me was forced to slow down a lot more—*thank you, Chevrolet engineers, for such a crappy wheelbase*—giving me some distance. I took a fork in the road, heading deeper into the valley, not wanting to stay in his field of view. I could feel the adrenaline flooding my bloodstream, and I nearly wiped out because I was looking in my rear view window and didn't see the huge pothole until the last moment. My squat car teetered around as I yanked hard on the steering wheel. Behind me, the Impala careened along the road, hitting the hole hard, and then he stopped pursuing me. A thin twirl of gray smoke wound out from under his hood.

I made a quick turn and saw another sign for the interstate. Finally, on the entrance ramp with no Impala in sight, I relaxed a little. Why were they after me?

* * *

I walked into the mansion, feeling tingles at the back of my neck because the parking area was empty and the lights were out inside. I found the front door unlocked, and I didn't know what to make of that. I tried not to make any noise as I nudged inside.

Creeping along the wall toward the back of the house, I saw strings of wires lying across the floor in the den. I looked for a weapon of some kind, hoping nobody had planted a bomb. What if the three of them were strung up in the corner, or dead already? I picked up a heavy stone planter from a table in the hallway, holding it in front of me to use as a shield or a bludgeon. In all likelihood I would just drop it on my feet but whatever, it looked intimidating.

"What on earth are you doing?" asked Sanjay, who stood next to the video machine, loading in a tape. "Redecorating or a sudden interest in floral arrangements?"

"I'm sorry, I thought, uh," I said, taking in the scene. The mess scattered around the room started making sense to me: a sound equalizer had been pulled from the electronics behind the couch, a peg board, probably from the garage, set against the coffee table, and a clump of different colored wires leading from one to the other.

"That's one smart fellow I rescued from the hospital," said Jay, walking over and looking at the homemade EEG machine with me. He hefted the vase out of my hands and gently put it back in the hallway.

"You're so tense, Jack. What happened to you?" He put one hand on my shoulder and I was embarrassed at how knotty my muscles had gotten. I told him the story about the tunnel and showed him the screwdriverish tool. Then I told him about being chased by the Impala.

"Wow," he said, his eyes wide. "Weird. I'm glad you're okay."

"So that's why I thought I was in for more trouble."

"I don't know what to make of that."

"I don't, either. Like, were they just super territorial about their town? They're not going to come all the way back here, right?"

"You say you lost them before the highway?"

"Yeah." I'd checked my rearview mirror at least a hundred times.

"Then I think you're okay. You need to relax, man. Being alert is good, being paranoid, bad. Between you and me I'm not too sure about this contraption here." We looked at Dr. Dorfman's handiwork.

"I mean, what do I know? Does it look anything like a regular EEG?" For emphasis Jay scratched his right temple.

"Kind of," I said, crouching down to get a better look. "I never got very close to these things." All of the reading about HAM radio had paid off, and I understood more about the assemblage and wiring.

"I think he needs a screen or a print out," I said, standing back. "Where is he? Where's Jeannine?"

"Off in search of a printer," said Jay. "The people who live here are rich, right? Jeannine says her friend has her own Apple computer and dot matrix printer upstairs."

"Has it settled down at the hospital yet?" I asked him, still not comfortable with the idea that we'd kidnapped him, even if he was happy to be free from there. We'd probably broken a gazillion laws. But also, I had brought other people into this situation, and it seemed like a lot more danger than we'd bargained for. If one of them got hurt, how would I live with myself?

"It's still under a lot more security," he said. "There was a headline about it in the paper today."

Dr. Dorfman was going to attract attention, and we needed a plan about what to do next. I also didn't know what he thought about all of this.

"They haven't traced anything back to your brother, have they?"

"Fortunately for us, there are a lot of men from India who work at the hospital." He smiled at me. "It's getting easier to spend time with you again."

"Is it?"

"Yeah. I'm remembering why we were friends in the first place, before you were such an asshole."

I dropped my head. I'd been mean to him because he was gay, and here I was pining away over Lucas. *I should tell him.*

"It's just that I don't know, in some ways I think I'm different, too."

His forehead scrunched up. "What are you saying?"

"I'm not sure. It's so hard to know what's real in all of this crap." I tried to tell him about being Jacqueline, about loving Lucas, but the words were crowding up on my tongue.

"Sure," he said, cutting me off before I could start. And then Jeannine and the doctor came downstairs, holding beige computer parts in their arms.

"Okay," said Jeannine as they set down the equipment next to the makeshift EEG machine, "Dr. Dorfman thinks this is about all we need."

"How can we help?" I asked.

He looked at me directly, his face seeming surer than I'd seen him since the neurology study.

"I really would like a glass of water, thanks," was all he said. We left him to work on his own while we went to the kitchen to get lunch and a drink for him.

I asked Jeannine, "Is he really all back?"

"I think he's kind of damaged, or haunted, by his experience. His fellow doctors think he lost his mind. His wife left him and took their two kids."

"It's my fault," I said. I ran my fingers along the beveled edge of the white Formica countertop. It was a lot nicer than the counter we had at home, which had metal strips along the edges that caught dirt and were impossible to clean. All the houses in our subdivision had the same shitty countertops.

"Look at me," she said, and I obliged. "This is not your fault. You didn't create the study, you were told to be part of it. You have to believe it isn't your fault."

"I'll try."

"Seriously, Jack. It's not." She paused. "But it may be your calling."

Chapter Seventeen

CLOSING MY EYES made the experience feel more familiar, even if I knew I was sitting back on Jeannine's rich friend's couch and not in a lab. Dr. Dorfman's voice was strangely comforting even with all of the guilt because of everything I'd put him through. Without seizures anymore, he wasn't sure if this would work. Sitting still made me almost miss all the years of pills and needles and brain scans, but not really. Maybe I should have been more nervous about the hand-built EEG machine than my own capacity for out of control neuron activity, but I didn't think the doctor would have subjected me to anything that could hurt me. Even as revenge.

We'd had a long discussion about trying to send me somewhere. Dorfpoodle wanted to have witnesses present who agreed that time travel was at least a possibility. I wanted to see if I could time jump without my own seizures, and I was desperate to see Lucas again. Alive. I prayed to nobody in particular. *Please give me time to fix what was so screwed up back there.*

"Relax, Jack," he said. It occurred to me that I didn't know why he cared to do all of this for us. Was he interested in inventing a time machine? Wanting to prove himself correct? Was he actually delusional? Why were these questions only now just popping into my head?

I considered ripping off the wires, held to my scalp with some kind of hair product instead of the medical putty I was used to. This was crazy. What was I thinking? *I should get out of here, explain to my parents that I've been stupid and desperate. They'll have to get over it at some point. Maybe I'll super enjoy juvenile detention.*

I felt an uncomfortable tingle all over my body and heard a low hum in my ears, and then figured I was getting a shock. *Oh no.*

I opened my eyes but was no longer in the posh living room. I coughed, waving at the dust in the air. Something was in my hands, warm where I held it but colder just a couple of inches away, where I hadn't heated it with my touch. I tried to get my bearings.

"Hey, Jacqueline, where did you go just then?"

Lucas. It was Lucas talking to me, holding himself up on one brace while he held a small metal box in his other hand. He had a small splotch of grease on his cheek, and his jagged bangs shook as he opened the box, revealing a pile of virgin rivets.

"I was just thinking," I said, lying. *Which I was getting good at, shazam!*

"About what?" he asked. We were in the abandoned bank. The car I'd driven away to my mother's farm house sat in the middle of the room, the hybrid frame sitting on cinder blocks, surrounded by lots of smaller pieces and scraps. I looked at the assortment of metal and understood how it all fit together. I'd drawn much of this configuration down in my bedroom in Ohio, playing around with car ideas. I hadn't realized it was a kind of training for the time when I could put it to use.

My moment had come.

Lucas stepped closer to me, putting his free hand on mine, which rested on the counter. "What's going on in there?" he asked again, quietly, in a sexy tone.

I leaned into him and kissed him, inhaling car grease, the nutty smell of old dust, and the soap he used when he bathed. The same soap I'd used when his father had discovered me in the compost pile.

I caught him off guard at first, and then he returned the kiss to me. A blast of warmth went through me, much nicer than electricity, and I pushed harder into him. He tasted delicious and warm. I dropped the screwdriver and ignored the clatter as it hit the floor. Finally we pulled away to get a breath. I wiped the smudge of grease off his cheek with a rag from the workbench.

"I didn't think you'd ever do that," he said. He looked straight at me, still up close to my face. Was this our first kiss? I needed to figure out the date, or at least the season, but the windows were shuttered.

"I wanted to," I said. "I want to again." I was lightheaded.

We drew together and kissed deeper this time, and I didn't think about anything except how his lips felt, the sense of him holding me, and the burning inside me. The world nudged its way back into my consciousness, whatever consciousness meant at that point. We were in a fight over the town and people's lives. *Right.* We needed to make progress, and this was a distraction. *Stop it with the kissing.*

"We have to get back to this," I said, staggering over to the car. I looked again at the screwdriver I'd dropped. It was the strange tool from the box in the sewer. I picked it up and turned it around to get a better look at it. Was this another one or the same from before? *I mean, later? Oh my god, Time, you're ridiculous.*

"I know," he said, handing me a curved piece of metal. The blankness in my brain fell away, replaced by knowledge. This was my design, and I knew where it went. I crouched down and screwed it into place under the carriage. Its sister hung on the other side. I was grateful that all I could see from down here were his shoes.

"Are you hiding under there?" I heard him ask.

"I'm working," I said. But yes, I was hiding, and that was my business. I asked Lucas for a few more of my devices, and he obliged. *Tubing for a smokescreen, wiring for a HAM radio. Set a scrape plate underneath to protect the nonstandard wires.* Under the car, I cried without noise, thinking about what only I knew would happen to him and the other underground members. My body betrayed me, and my nose filled up. I sniffled and gave myself away. I'd been planning to come back, I'd convinced myself all of this was real, and now here I was and I had to make everything better. *I really, really was here.*

"Okay, come out from under there," Lucas said.

"Don't tell me what to do." *It was a reflex, I'm sorry I snapped at you.*

"You are so headstrong. I just want to talk to you."

"You can talk to me fine from there." So what if I was childish? I focused on tightening bolts and screws with a pair of pliers on the ground. They were heavy, and my arms started shaking with muscle failure. In so many ways I was different as Jacqueline, and I liked that. But okay, I wasn't a big fan of muscle fatigue.

I heard a clatter, and Lucas crashed to the ground, his face in an odd half-grimace, half-smile.

"I like seeing you when I talk to you." His hair fell over his face, and I saw he'd torn his shirt at the elbow.

"You are a ridiculous person," I said.

"Are you calling me a cripple?"

"Most certainly not. I'm saying you're ridiculous. I think that's self-explanatory."

"First you kiss me and then you won't look at me," he said. "What's going on, Jacqueline?"

"Can we please discuss this later? I need the oil pan."

He lay there, continuing to look at me. *I'm not ready. I thought I was ready but I'm not.*

"Do you need help getting up?"

Lucas frowned.

"Sometimes you really are insufferable, Jacqueline." And then he stood up, slid the hunk of metal over to me, and left out the back door of the bank. *Well, let's just add being a jackass to the list of reasons to sob.*

At least he'd given me some space to cry. I didn't want to be in someone else's body, after months readjusting to mine. But I did, too. I wasn't sure what any of this made me, even as I felt such a strong pull to fix situations that I suspected were at least partly my doing. I was drawn to Lucas but I also worried that what we were doing was wrong. Sanjay would disagree with me, but he wasn't here to talk about it, either.

I crawled out from under the car, wiped my eyes, and looked around the room. The last time I was here the car had tires and was ready to use, but didn't have a HAM radio, for sure. So was I earlier or later than the day we roared out of here to Jacqueline's mother's house? But more weird, if I was only just now coming back to put in a radio, how were the wires already in place? That didn't make any sense.

I went in search of Lucas. I whispered his name instead of shouting in case one of Traver's people was nearby. He called back to me, and I followed the sound.

He was up in a tree, maybe thirty feet off the ground. His crutches were propped against the roots. He clearly had not learned his lesson from the last go-round.

"What are you doing up there?"

"What do I ever do up here?" he asked. "Come up."

He had much better upper body strength than I did, but I was light and apparently nimble. I made sure my feet and hands were well planted before taking any new step, but I winced as the sharp bark broke through the skin on my forearms.

"So sensitive," Lucas said, inspecting me. He leaned in to kiss me.

"Wait," I said.

"Must you do everything backwards?" he asked.

"What do you mean?"

"The man is supposed to lead, like in dancing."

"Well, that's an old-fashioned way to see it," I said, before I remembered we weren't in the 1980s. Of course this was his opinion. "Look, I like you. I just have fears."

"Because of our predicament?"

No.

"Exactly," I said, lying. *Because I'm really a boy like you, or at least I used to be, or I am when I'm in another place and time but here I am from the frigging future and oh by the way I've completely fallen for you and I don't understand a bit about any of it.*

"Well, that's a good point. But I fancy you and I can't change that."

"I wouldn't want my own space if I didn't really like you." At least this was mostly true.

This time when he leaned in to kiss me, I didn't push him away. But it was less intense than before, mostly because I had to put some of my energy into balancing myself on a knobby branch. He sat back, staring intently at me.

"I better quit before I fall out of a tree again."

* * *

We worked on the automobile for a few more hours, until the sun got too low in the sky for us to see well. Neither of us wanted to use any lights because they could give us away. Lucas had put in a radio himself because he'd seen the sheriff and deputies using them in their patrol cars.

"I'm an Amateur Second Class," he announced to me and the car. "Which just means that I had to take the radio test by mail since there's no Radio Commission office anywhere near here."

"Such accomplishment," I said, pretending to swoon.

"I acknowledge that you are in the presence of greatness," he said. "Remember to find me at 100 kiloHertz after twilight."

"Why then?"

"Because I'm busy all day, of course."

"Of course."

"Do you fancy another kiss?" he asked me, tilting his head.

"I do."

I fell into him a little, breaking away only when my need for fresh oxygen took priority. *I could do this all night.* After basically making out with him for I don't know how long, he stood back and looked at me.

"We must meet the others."

"We must," I said.

"Are you mocking me?"

"Never." My giggle gave me away. He took my hand and we locked up the door, walking back into the woods. We found the horses I supposed we'd ridden in on earlier in the day. I watched him lash himself to the saddle, and I tucked my feet into the stirrups and pet the horse's mane as he got ready to ride. It was the same horse I'd had in the other time jumps. We were familiar with each other somehow, even through my strange time jumps and in and out existence.

"I need to ask you a question," I said.

"What is it?"

"How long have we been working on this car? I'm having some memory problems."

"I know, Jacqueline," he said; I wasn't expecting that. "It's been a month or so, I imagine."

"Okay," I said, trying to figure out the time line, the real time line, including jumps and all. Judging from the buds still on the trees, it was early spring. "Can you remind me what year it is again?"

"It's March 20, 1926," he said. "You know, you should procure a calendar for yourself."

"What great advice you have."

"It's rather banal advice, I'm afraid," he said, but I didn't know what banal meant so I let it go.

We turned onto a trail, still covered by woods, and trotted over fallen logs. A buck with enormous antlers off to our left watched us from fifty yards away, and behind him, a herd of forty deer waited for us to pass.

"I want to, but it's unbelievable. You'll think I'm crazy." Now we cleared the edge of the forest and galloped off to the Rushman Farm, where the downstairs was lit but looked empty. Puffs of warm air blew out from the horses' nostrils and mouths but they seemed to enjoy the downhill slope, an easy challenge for the end of the day. Reaching the porch, we walked around to the stables at the back, where we unsaddled the horses and latched them into their stalls. Lucas took my hand and held it to his lips.

"I care for you, Jacqueline. You are clearly your own woman, and I admire that. When you want to tell me your story, I'm sure you will."

I wanted to fall into his strong arms, but I saw several pairs of eyes of the underground members watching us from the kitchen. We went inside to update them instead.

Walking into the warm kitchen, Darling handed me a mug steaming with liquid. She said it was her family's tea blend. Earthy and soothing, I took a long first sip, trying to cool it while I drank. Arnold Dawkins, his hair in a messy crown around his head, stepped aside so we could sit around the long wooden table just off of the kitchen. I noticed grease on my fingers and begged off to wash my hands. Mr. Van Doren lingered while the others took their seats. Lucille Griffin stood next to the windows and clutched a beat up leather notebook. Her hair had a few gray streaks in it that I didn't remember. She was in a tailored green tweed jacket and her skirt reached exactly the middle of her knees.

I lathered up, fighting the car fluid that wouldn't let go of my skin.

"I've got a nail brush if you want one," said Mr. Van Doren.

"I'm all right, thanks."

"How did it go today?" He was trying to sound casual, but I knew better. I thought about him in the picture with Dr. Traver's gang of merry Prohibitionists. When would he sell us out? Had it happened already? Was he why my mother's house was burned to the ground? If so, why had he tried to help us get out? If he was a traitor, I hoped I had time to stop him. I wasn't sure what to do about it. Jeannine, Sanjay and I had never figured out a plan. I should have stuck around before jumping so that we could have worked out a strategy, but I'd pushed so hard to get back here, and I'd been so afraid of getting found out by the cops after we took Dr. Dorfman out of the hospital. Jeannine was wrong. This was all on me.

"It went well," I said, trying to avoid giving any details until at least I could provide them to the others.

I thought such bad things about Mr. Van Doren, and he was Lucas's father. What an awful person I was—kissing him while plotting against his father.

"I'm glad," said Mr. Van Doren.

"I'm glad, too."

"Jackie, is everything okay? You seem distant."

I seem distant because I am, I thought. Why state the obvious?

"It's been a long day, Mr. Van Doren. I'm tired, is all."

"Well, there's a bit of food on the table if you're peckish," he said, patting me on my shoulder. I did my best not to recoil.

"Thank you." I moved to the table as fast as I could without making him notice my discomfort. I had to figure out what his angle was, and soon. By my reckoning, we had six months until the fire at my mother's house. I'd wanted to get back earlier and somehow, here I was. But what to do next? Get information on what Dr. Traver's people were doing? Find out if there were any more turncoats in our midst? Telling everybody that I was a time traveler and knew what was going to happen in the future didn't seem like a workable strategy. I settled in at the table to give myself more time to like, assess or something.

I sat down next to Lucas, who pretended to be busy in conversation, but in one short second I caught him noticing me, and I felt heat in my cheeks. A big part of me wanted to be kissing him again, but as soon as I felt lusty for him I got guilty. We had way more important issues to deal with than my time-trotting love life. I brought my attention back to the group, which unfortunately was in the middle of a sentence from Darling.

"So I knew I had to come and tell everyone what Miss Kleinman said." Miss Kleinman was her employer, Lucas explained to me in a whisper. *I must not have a good poker face for covering up when I'm confused,* I figured. She owned the town's only hotel, and Darling worked there part-time as a housekeeper.

"What should we do about it?" asked Darling. Her hands were folded neatly in front of her, and she had the best posture of everyone in the room. She reminded me of the teachers at St. Francis: her back straight, perched directly under a carefully tied hair bun.

I leaned over to Lucas and asked what Mrs. Kleinman's news was.

"Dr. Traver had lunch with a state senator today."

"So? Why does that matter?" I asked Lucas.

Lucas seemed unflustered.

"Just that he may have stronger connections than we realized. We're looking for allies at the state level, not influenced by his people in town, but if he knows powerful officials in Frankfort, then we need to double check that Mr. Dawkins's friend will stand up for us if we find any evidence of Traver's criminal acts." *Of course, they haven't found any bodies or evidence yet. No wonder Traver burned the farm house down—they had tracked down his secret cabin on Black Mountain. That's what they don't know about yet.*

Mr. Dawkins cleared his throat, a sign that we should stop whispering. I apologized. *Everything is just like school.*

They sure had a lot of people around town to pick up gossip—Mr. Dawkins, Lucille, Darling, and Mr. Van Doren all regularly gathered information from folks who either considered them friends or who underestimated their importance to a collection of people like us. Because we had formed with a common interest instead of a known central relationship, we had not come to Dr. Traver's attention, at least not yet.

Lucas took his turn at the meeting, speaking in glowing terms about the creative ideas I had for our defense against the stockpile of weapons Mr. Dawkins said our enemies had acquired. I offered that he was overstating my contribution, but he wouldn't hear of it, and the others nodded their heads, as if they were used to hearing me be too modest. I needed to get some time alone with Lucas again, though not because of my affection for him. I was floundering, trying to sort out who knew what, and it was beginning to exhaust me. I wanted to share the truth about my situation with him, even if it was a risk.

What if he wanted nothing to do with me after I told him I was Jack Inman, born in 1964 in Cleveland, Ohio? How could he continue to put any faith in me after such a revelation? I'd only been back for twelve hours but already my life as a teenage boy seemed like a lie, some tall tale I'd made up to look more interesting. I'd done so much research about the 1920s that I wasn't sure anymore what was familiar because of a book and what I'd laid eyes on here myself.

I stopped listening to them talk, trying to replay what I'd done and seen the last time I was here, anything that could help us now. I could figure out later how I'd gotten back at this earlier time. Now that we had a kind of head start, I should help us make the most of it.

The cousin. Darling's cousin, the one she'd told me to go see on the west end of the state. I was supposed to sneak out in the middle of the night and go find him. She'd packed the horse up for me, she'd said. What if I went to see him six months early? *Couldn't hurt, right?*

I stood up from the table. Conversation stopped, and all the people gathered stared at me.

"I have to. . .powder my nose," I said, running off to the bathroom. It was a terrible excuse, but it was the best I could come up with.

I shut the door and set the lock in place. From the other room, I heard chairs squeaking against the hardwood floor as people pushed back from the table. A few minutes passed, and a soft knock rapped at the door. It was Lucas's quiet voice asking for me to come out so we could talk.

I put my back to the door and looked at the room. A bar of soap next to the sink. A pull chain hanging from the tank over the toilet, with a soft gold fringe attached to the bulb of wood. A frayed, but still serviceable rug next to the iron tub. And there it was—a window, half-hidden by a lacy curtain.

I pushed opened the window and climbed out, crash landing on the hard ground. The stable was close. I threw a blanket on the back of my horse and set the saddle behind her withers, then checked that it was tight. Were there supplies in here? *There must be.* I found an ice chest and there were a few cans of beans inside. I took those and from another chest door, grabbed a box of crackers and a can of hash, whatever that was. I put three scoops of grain into a feeder sack and tucked it all into a leather pack that hooked on to the saddle.

I led the horse out through the back of the stables, figuring someone would come after me any second. Pressing my heels into her, she knew I was looking for speed, and gave it to me. *This is better than throwing a transmission into gear,* I thought. We galloped off toward the other side of the valley following the last bit of sunrise. My last thought before getting some distance from Mother's house: *Someday I'll have to actually plan the shit I do before I do it.*

Chapter Eighteen

MY HORSE NEEDED A REST, even as she pounded across a long stretch of grass and weeds, shelling out every ounce of energy she had to take me as far as possible. I sat back in the saddle to slow her down, telling her it was okay, she was a good, good horse, and petting her on her mane. The leather squeaked quietly as we walked along, blending with the clicks from bats hunting in the trees around us. I'd run off without paying attention to how cold it was out here, and although the horse gave off a lot of heat from her run, I was shivering. At some point numbness had crawled into my hands, nose and ears. I should have at least taken an extra horse blanket from the stables. *Or a can opener. Oops.*

So far I was full of crappy ideas and I hoped my cousin would be an energetic genius. Where would Darling's cousin live? *I better find his home fast or I could be wandering around Kentucky the whole six months before the fire.*

As I came to the top of a rolling hill, I could see the fringe of another town. There certainly was a lot of farmland out here. I wondered how often people went from one small town to another. Hopefully this place was outside of Dr. Traver's reach. We walked slowly to where a dirt road shifted into pavement, and from where we stood I could see a gathering in a small, white wood house. Beyond the front porch, in what looked like a living room, one man stood in the middle of a crowd of about twenty-five people. *Shit, it's Dr. Traver. So much for a better town out here.* He held a small black book in one hand;

his other palm was raised to the sky. He appeared to be shouting, although I was too far away to hear him. The others were animated, too, raising their own arms up and swaying to some rhythm.

My horse lowered her head and picked at a sprig of something on the ground, the only food she'd had in hours. I tried to figure out the layout of the town—the house full of people stood at the end of a long row of homes. Faded paint but otherwise tidy. Off to their left was a strip of store fronts: a cobbler, grocer, butcher, bank, barber shop, and trading post. Past the strip was a school house not unlike the one I'd been in before. This school though, was missing glass in its windows and instead of a proud bell out front there was a broken post. Who would let a school look like that?

I had an answer, perhaps, as I saw a line of dirty children walking toward the town, covered in black dust, a few of them wearing headlamps, most of them carrying small metal…lunch pails, I guessed. Were these children miners? When did we stop making children mine stuff? I didn't know.

I clicked my tongue to get the horse to move, trying to stay out of view. We trotted along the periphery of the town until we were behind and then past the school. I was thankful that I had a dark brown horse.

Past the vacant playground were a few other empty buildings, so I headed there hoping we could rest and the horse could find something to eat. My own stomach was grumbling; I hadn't helped myself to any food at the underground meeting. *Just another instance of pure brilliance from the wonder nugget.* I dismounted and tied the horse to a tree. She nuzzled me with her head, a small streak of white running between her eyes. I pet her and tugged gently at her fuzzy ear.

"I'm sorry I don't know your name. I need to find you some water, huh?" She gave me a soft whinny.

I pulled out her grain sack and tied it around her head and she seemed happy for some kind of sustenance.

Leaning against the side of the building, I pushed hard against a large door that slid over and a line of cobwebs burst open. I brushed off the spiders that descended on me, and walked inside. Faint light beams streamed in from holes in the rafters, and old, moldy straw crunched under my boots. It felt a little warmer in here, but I had lost feeling in my lower legs so hey, who knew anymore what temperature it was.

I crept further in, expecting to be startled by someone else who had taken refuge, maybe through another opening. In the far corner, a low pile of blankets sat folded and stacked, maybe once used for livestock. Good enough.

Little clouds of dust collapsed onto the ground.

I hunted around in the barn for tools that a horse groom might use so I could bust open a can of my provisions. I might actually have gasped when I came across a can opener, but nobody was around to notice. And I found a can of sardines, but my hash seemed more palatable. I went back to the horse, untied her grain sack, and saw a water pump not too far from the barn. I cleaned out an old trough that was next to the pump, digging through a pile of mushy leaves and at least two pounds of worms, The horse figured out what I was up to right away. She even nudged me with her nose.

"I'm working on it, okay? Everybody's in a damn hurry." I crossed my fingers that the pump would work and was relieved to see clear water spurt out from the end of the pipe. I tied her to the pump and then tried to wash off my hands before using them as a cup to drink from. Whatever, it tasted magnificent.

I grabbed some food from the pack and went into the barn to hunker under a mound of scratchy blankets. There was something else Darling had mentioned about traveling to see her cousin, but I couldn't quite remember it. I dozed off.

*   *   *

I had no one to take watch while I slept, or make sure I woke before dawn, so I told myself I'd sleep with one eye open. I'm not sure what that one eye was supposed to do if I was sleeping, anyway. I didn't feel rested when I woke up.

It was the morning sun streaming onto my face that got me up, not the mad crowing of some nearby rooster. Sunlight had just begun peeking over the eastern ridge. I was out of time. I grabbed the top blanket and ran out to the horse, who looked at me nervously. She huffed and brayed, and I turned to look at what was in her field of view.

A sheriff's deputy stood in front of his car, smoking a cigarette. He busied himself by scraping mud off of one knee-high boot against the running board of the vehicle. I tiptoed to the horse, shushing her and strapping the blanket in to the back of the saddle, and then quickly untied her from the water pump. Planting my foot in the stirrup, I bounded up, snapping a branch, and this alerted the officer to my presence.

"Hey," he called out to me, "stop!"

His shouting startled the horse, and she burst into a gallop, with me not quite in the saddle.

"Whoa, horse! Whoa, horse!" She carried on at her full speed.

Okay, so this is where cars are easier to use.

Behind me the police siren wailed, and a jury-rigged blue light on the roof did its best to alert the world that it was shining. From my crooked position, half-lying across the saddle, I saw that he was chasing us through the grass and would soon overtake us. I managed to pull my right leg around and sit upright. I hunkered down over the horse's neck and leaned hard to the left, over toward a stream. The car roared after us.

"Halt! Halt! Tresspasser, or I'll shoot!" he yelled.

Just as a big moment of concern hit me, the horse bounded over a thick log that crossed the stream, and in a second we were on the other bank. I craned my neck around and saw the sheriff out of his car, now stopped, taking aim at us with a shotgun propped up on the open driver door. I yanked hard to the right and we ducked behind a small crop of trees, heading in a direction I thought would provide some cover. How could sleeping in an old barn justify shooting a person?

After a time, the horse slowed down, too tired to keep running.

"I don't blame you," I said in her ear. She snorted, like she agreed with me.

We meandered through another wooded area and I saw a small clearing up a ways. I unbridled the horse and stroked her cheek a few times. She cupped her muzzle in my hand, then wandered a few yards away to graze and drink some water at a creek that marked the edge of the clearing. Above us the sun provided as much warmth as it could muster on a mid-spring day. There were still patches of snow here and there, wherever they found sanctuary out of the sunlight.

I thought about calling Lucas with all of my buckets of new information before I realized I'd have to ask for the Rushman farm house, and the operator would rat us out. Too bad we couldn't talk directly.

Wait. The HAM radio. I'd installed most of one into the car in the abandoned bank. I'd studied those amateur radio manuals for so many hours, sitting at the edge of my subdivision, writing out installation instructions and specifications. Maybe I'd written all that shit down here, too. Only the speakers and speaker wiring were left to finish in the car I was building with Lucas. Really, speakers were the simplest part of the whole assembly. Lucas was at least as handy in the workroom as I was. I didn't know if we'd talked about transmitting on short wave radio, or how familiar he was with building a radio, though. But if I could get to a radio, maybe I could communicate with him. We didn't have a license but we could probably get a message through to each other.

So now I'd run away but I wanted to talk to him. *My first sentence should be, "Hello, it's me, the dumbass."*

Maybe he thought I was never coming back. He and his father had been shocked when I'd shown up later this year. The whole town had thought I was dead. Why had they assumed that again?

A telegram sent to my mother. That was it, yes. But what had it said? I didn't know what the cause of my death had been, because my mother became too distraught to speak that part, even as she could see I was alive and well. But without knowing, I was less able to see danger coming. I would have to keep using my cruddy wits and cruddier instincts.

* * *

After resting for a couple of hours and letting the horse graze, I grabbed the saddle off of a fallen tree and hitched up again. Following the sun we headed north-northwest, taking a slow trot. I appreciated not having boy junk to deal with as I bounced along toward Michigan. We walked along a narrow highway the whole afternoon, the shadows from our bodies growing longer and darker, and finally, we approached another town after a series of farms. It looked larger than Jacqueline's hometown but not any more modern or wealthy. I hadn't gotten any attention since my run-in with the deputy from the morning. Still, I refused to let down my guard. An attack could come when I was least expecting it. That made me start thinking about horror movies. I wished I'd gotten to see *Halloween*.

I almost ran down a man who called out my name as I rode by his house.

"Stop, stop," he said, holding up his arms in defense. It was the same thing the deputy had said to me, but he seemed more urgent and less homicidal.

"Jacqueline, wait!"

My horse also seemed disinclined to bear down on him. She held back, sidestepping away from him, not wanting to follow my instructions on where she should go. The man was short, with a crown of brown hair hugging his temples, and a tight-cropped beard hiding most of his face. He had wide-set eyes, and a hawk-like nose. His black boots had red clay all over them, but the rest of his clothing was spotless. I stopped the horse but remained mounted.

"How do you know me?" I asked him, spitting the words out like they had a bad taste.

"Darling, I know you from Darling. I'm her cousin."

"But you're white," I said. *Here comes Captain Obvious again!*

"So I am," he said, shaking his head like I was a fool. "You ever hear of slavery, girl? Come bring that horse inside before someone sees you." He took the reins and led us to a clean stable. *Hopefully this isn't where he slaughters young women from out of town,* I thought.

I checked out his row house, which looked like something I'd have seen in Cleveland, except the ones in Ohio came in clumps, and this stood alone, with the next house a stadium-length away. It was narrow but long, light blue with a porch that boasted its own swing, screwed into the ceiling. Incandescent lights inside gave everything a warm glow.

"So how do I know you're Darling's cousin?" I asked.

"She said you would ask that. Come on inside and we'll talk. I know you ain't had a decent meal in at least a day." He looked around at the street, like he was some kind of bank robbing lookout.

It could be a trap, I thought. But it was worth figuring out what his story was. I pulled the horse into the front stall and took off her gear. He put a loose rope bridle on her and walked her back out of the stables.

"Of course I've heard of slavery," I said to him. I had to walk faster to keep up with him.

"Well then, my great-grandfather Buford owned slaves, right here in Kentucky, and he is Darling's great grandfather, too. It's a shameful history, but I don't have better family than Darling." He and the horse walked over to a fence.

"Uh-huh."

"Ain't no 'uh-huh' about it, girl. You need to meet up with some manners. That woman lives up to her name." He opened a gate so my horse could move into the large pen. He took off the bridle and gave her a pat on her neck. She needed no further prompting, and ran into the yard with several other horses.

"Good Pie," he said.

"Pie?"

"Girl, are you stupid? That's your horse's name."

"Who would name a horse Pie?"

"She's Award Winning Pie, and you named her when you were ten," he said, frowning. "I am running out of patience with you. Act like you know your own story."

"How do you know my story, then?"

He sighed and waved at me to follow him into the storm cellar next to his house. I had no horse now and he wanted me to follow him into the ground?

"Jacqueline, I am only going to say this once. I am Jackson Hartle. In seventeen years my wife will bring Katherine Hartle, your mother, into the world. I have been waiting for years until I could talk to you about your time travel ability."

I was related to Darling. *Distant cousins. This man was my grandfather, Jack's grandfather, who I'd never met as Jack. But who knew me here. Before I even knew. Holy Christ. And he KNEW about my time travel?*

It was too much for me. I fainted.

Chapter Nineteen

I CAME TO IN A DARK ROOM, smelling cedar. Great, I was in a hamster's cage or something. I rubbed my eyes and pushed aside heavy blankets. There was some geometric pattern on them—handmade quilts. The mattress was lumpy and scratchy.

I sat up. Once again, I resided in a different body. I pulled back the waist of my pants. Boy body. *Well, isn't this just peachy?*

I moved around the room in short darts because I'd expected my limbs to require more energy. Running fast was probably the sole advantage this kid had. Looking over the objects in the room, I guessed at the story of this person. Two toys—a beat-up metal soldier and a caboose of a wooden train that was missing two wheels, caddy-corner from each other so it couldn't stand up on its own. On the nightstand was a small black bible with faded red edges. I picked it up and saw that someone had filled it with notes, scribbled in the margins; words circled, more in the first half than the second. A small cabinet with a few worn clothes, but patched and mended.

After I'd assessed my surroundings, I thought about what I'd just learned from Jackson Hartle. My namesake. I'd found him and now I was somewhere else. And he knew about me. *Finally someone with answers in this freaking world!* I couldn't believe that once again I was stuck on my own.

I needed to find out where I'd gotten to this time.

The window, on the far side of the room. I walked on the balls of my feet so I could be quiet, and pressed my face to the glass. I was only able to look out of the lowest pane. That would make me what, five or six?

Outside, I saw a city in summer. Smokestacks in the distance puffed out gray and black plumes, but the city streets were lined with trees. Not a car in sight, but plenty of horses and maybe mules or donkeys, most of them hitched to dark carriages. There seemed to be two kinds of women—ones who looked like Jacqueline's mother in their faded house dresses, doing some kind of heavy-duty outdoor work, and others in much nicer clothes. Most of the rich-looking women wore wide-brimmed hats, some with bits of lace trailing around the sides. There were few men to be found, and no children anywhere I could see.

My bedroom door burst open, and a large woman came in, wearing a dirty apron over the bottom half of her dress. Her dark blond hair was braided in the back, the top of her head covered with a tight linen cap. She skittered across the room like a waterbug and had clamped onto my ear before I could blink. *Note to self: ears are sensitive little body parts.*

"Edgar, why are you standing about? You know I need your help today!"

"My apologies, ma'am."

Apparently this was the wrong thing to say.

"Ma'am? Ma'am? I'm your mother, and don't you forget it!" *I need to stop making this same mistake.*

I wasn't sure I could handle another mother. *Three is a charm or something, right?* Especially one who would pull me across a room by part of my head. It hurt like whoa.

"I'm sorry, Mother! Stop, please."

She released me, and I fell down with a thud on the thin area rug. This was when I noticed that my ass was particularly bony.

She wiped a tear off the side of her face. "You are aware how important this party is, and I need you to help us prep in the kitchen. It's not every day a young lady turns sixteen."

Sweet cheeks, where am I?

"You're right, of course. What should I wear?" I didn't want to make any more grievous errors.

She beckoned me to stand up and come to her, to see if I was feverish. "You do have a quick pulse," she said, her hand clamped around my wrist. I stood and waited for her to speak again. First she put her fingers under my chin and lifted my head to look at her.

"Don't bring your illness on anyone today, Edgar. If you are weak of stomach, come up here and manage it by yourself."

"Yes, Mother."

"Now prepare yourself and put on your work clothes," she said, pulling out a nondescript pair of short trousers and a cotton shirt from the wardrobe and laying them on the bed. "And wash behind your ears, do you hear me?"

"Yes, Mother." She nodded at me and shut the door behind her. Whatever was downstairs, I figured today was going to suck ass.

I dressed, finding a basin and a water pitcher in the hallway outside my room. The door to the next room was open a crack, so I peeked inside. A carefully made, small bed was pushed close to the one window. There was another open wardrobe like the one in my room, with a few housedresses and one black dress fringed with white lace hanging from hooks. A chest sat at the foot of the bed with no padlock. In high snooping mode, I slipped into the room, tiptoed to the check, and opened the creaky lid to see what was in there. Shoes, lye soap, nothing valuable. A yellow envelope, discolored at the edges.

I checked the hallway again. *I wonder how long Edgar takes to wash behind his ears,* I thought as I slipped my fingers under the flap. Inside, there were two birth certificates—Janet MacComb, whose mother was Frances Hammond and father was Peter MacComb. And there was mine; Janet was my mother, but a big "UNKNOWN" sat on the page for my father.

What the hell does this mean? Great, now I have a new mystery to unravel? No more mysteries, universe!

Stairs down the hall squeaked that someone was coming, so I stuffed the papers back in the envelope and shut the locker. I made it just to the other side of the door when I saw a boy, maybe ten or eleven, jump onto the landing. He wore black shorts and a jacket, with a crisply ironed shirt and a thin black tie that crossed under the middle of his collar. He stood broad-chested and squat, looking like a junior wrestler who'd somehow gotten his pants cut off while managing to keep his legs intact. He seemed like a total asshole.

"MacComb, get downstairs already. Why do you dawdle?"

"I'm coming," I said, rushing to the stairs and letting the lid slam shut.

Before I could get to the stairs, he punched me in the nose. I landed back on the floor for the second time that morning.

"That's not how you talk to me, you stupid dog. Now get to the kitchen, runt."

I scrambled to my feet, pinching my nose to stop it from gushing, even while I tasted metal in my mouth from my blood. I was around him and down the stairs as fast as my tiny legs could carry me. His laughter chased after me. *Yup, he's an asshole.*

The stairwell ended at a short corridor lined with doors, and from there I smelled the kitchen. Chopping and clanging cutlery banged all around the room, each implement handled by a chef or assistant, in a blur of activity. It was quite a contrast with how food prep happened in our kitchen at home. *We're a bit more complicated than toaster ovens here,* I thought, eyeing the large room. Three women worked diligently: my mother, chopping a huge pile of onions, more tears streaming down her cheeks, a very large woman who stood as tall and wide as a Christmas tree, mixing some sort of batter in a bowl, and an older woman who stood over the large brick fireplace, where two kettles boiled away, steaming up the windows even though they were twenty feet away. The scents of the food traveled past my nostrils and my stomach rumbled in response. They noticed me as I entered, and my mother gasped when she saw me. She dropped her knife and came over to me, crouching down to examine me.

"Child, what became of you?" So much for getting any concern out of her.

"I . . . ran into the door upstairs," I said.

"Hardly likely," said the old woman at the hearth, but she kept stirring. "Master Traver at it again."

Traver?

"We shall talk about this later. Now go kill three chickens for us from the coop."

"What?" I knew I wouldn't like her response, but I wasn't ready to process her command just yet. Was that jackass on the landing Melvyn Traver?

"You heard me. Three. No daydreaming, Edgar."

How was I freaking supposed to kill a chicken? She stood up and pushed me toward a back door, telling me the axe was outside. *Sure, because we just leave implements of murder hanging around for anyone to use.* Before the door shut behind me I heard the old lady mutter, "Those chickens will peck him to death before he catches a one of them." She and Christmas Tree laughed, but I caught the eyes of my so-called mother through the glass in the door, and she wasn't smiling.

I took stock; there were chickens picking whatever they could find out of the ground, clucking quietly, and just outside their wire fence, an axe half-buried in an old tree stump. As I got closer I could see that the stump was stained dark brown. *This must be the final destination for the birds.* I yanked hard to get the axe out of the stump, stumbling backward a few paces once I freed it of the wood. Jack or Jacqueline's body would have been much better for this, but I had to work with what I had.

So much for gathering information on Master Traver over there. I couldn't get back to anything until I'd satisfied the cooks. Catching a chicken turned out to be next to impossible. Once their guards were up, they stayed the hell away from me, fluttering around, clucking and crowding together so that I couldn't tell what I was grabbing for. It was also apparently a stupid way of collecting dirty feathers. At one point I cornered a bird and got ahold of its wing, but it just banged against me with its other wing until I let go. *Stupid reflexes.* I cursed a lot, and wound up with a checkerboard of scratches on my arms. No wonder this kid had holes in his clothes.

Master Traver stood behind me outside the fence laughing his ass off at me. I thought about throwing the axe at him but didn't want to give him a weapon, as my own blood was just starting to dry in my nose.

"You have to catch their feet, you stupid bastard," he said, continuing to giggle at me.

"Isn't there something else you should be doing, Master Traver?" I asked, diving for another fowl. Finally I had a decent hold of it. I let it hang from its neck and kept my grip tight. It flapped its wings and screamed. Who knew chickens could scream?

"Everything else around here is boring," he said. He clapped at the bird's capture.

"At long last, you have one."

"I'd thank you but I don't think you're sincere."

"You better watch how you speak to me," he said in a growl.

"Why, or you'll punch me again? I might drop this chicken and then you'll have to explain why your sister's party didn't go the way it was planned."

"Well, I'll just blame that on you, you little prat."

"Blame me, I don't care," I said, and I perched the bird on the stump. *I'm sorry, birdie,* I thought. *If not you, me.* The axe dropped through the air and made a dull thunk onto the wood as the chicken's head rolled off, freed from the rest of the body. The wings kept fluttering and in my shock, I let go. It ran, headless, in a curving arc, over toward Traver, thick blood still pumping out of its neck to where its brain ought to have been. He was a terrible mess almost instantly.

"You did that on purpose!" He ran toward the house.

"You should have stayed inside, bored," I said, to his retreating figure.

The fight seemed to have gone out of the chickens when I re-entered the coop; I caught and killed two more in short order, and brought them all into the kitchen.

"Well, look at him," said the boiler. "He managed quite well. Miss MacComb, I told you he was ready to begin helping."

"So he is," my mother said. "But you're a right mess. Go wash yourself upstairs and then come back here. Get those feathers out of your hair."

Christmas Tree chuckled. "He looks like a Thanksgiving turkey."

* * *

I squeezed many thoughts into the time I had while cleaning up. Chickens smelled worse than wet dogs. I missed my family and friends from Ohio, and now also from Jacqueline's time. But first I needed to learn whatever there was to learn about the infamous someday Dr. Traver.

Back downstairs, my mother put me to work peeling potatoes. I saw one chicken simmering in a boiling pot, while the old lady plucked another clean of feathers, depositing them in a burlap sack on the floor.

Christmas Tree came up to me and bent over. She extended a finger, and I saw that she'd dipped it into white frosting. "I know I shouldn't, but here, you can take a taste."

I glanced at my mother. If she were as horrified as I was, she didn't show it. I opened my mouth and the baker rammed her finger in my mouth, giggling as I licked off the frosting while trying not to gag. I pulled back, attempting a smile, and while the frosting tasted delicious, it had mixed with her own scent—something between sour and salty milk. I thanked her and asked to be excused. My mother gave me a knowing look, nodding. "Two minutes, Edgar. There's a lot left to prepare."

I clomped back up the servant steps, throwing open the door to my room. I was crestfallen to see Melvyn Traver on my bed, sprawled out in a new outfit, claiming my space because after all it was his to let me use or not. I didn't have anything to myself here, not even a half-inch of space in front of my nose.

"Haven't you harassed me enough today?"

"Oh you're rich," he said, sitting up, gripping the edge of the bed. Now looking at me straight on, I could see that his right eye was bruised. "You think you can tell me what to do? You're the servant!"

I stood there, for the moment taller than him because he remained seated. He could yell but I could tell he had no energy for another fight. He must have gotten in real trouble for dirtying his suit.

"I'm sorry you got hit," I said.

"What business is it of yours? Don't pretend to care. I'm sure you'll run downstairs and tell your whore mother all about it."

"Can you stand not to be mean for one minute?" I reckoned I could run faster than him if he lunged for me, but he continued to sit there, defeated.

"Just because my father produced you with a housemaid does not mean you can address me this way!"

Terrific, we're half-brothers! Of course that would be why I had no listed father on my birth record. It would have been a scandal or something.

Other than the bruise, which was growing redder around the edges as I watched him, he was perfect-looking: incredibly strong for his age, with piercing blue eyes and ruddy blond hair. Then it hit me.

Blue eyes. Dr. Traver didn't have blue eyes.

I bolted back out to the hall, stood in front of the basin and mirror that hung over the vanity.

Traver bounded up after me, hulking over me from the doorway of my room.

"What on earth is wrong with you today, Edgar?"

I trembled as I looked at my reflection. Those hazel, almond-shaped eyes. I knew those eyes.

I was Dr. Traver.

Chapter Twenty

MELVYN—OR WHOEVER HE WAS—shouted after me as I ran down the stairs. I flew through the front of the house, like I was blowing past the evil bus driver again. I ran past two servants hanging decorations in the front living room. The front door, made of carved wood, was large and heavy but I pushed it open and made it into the street. I hoped I could lose myself in all of the activity outside. I was at the top of a long slope, and I could see that the street several blocks down had plenty of people and carriages; I'd just burst out of the biggest house around. At the bottom of the hill homes didn't have so much as a small front yard, but up here vast plots of land were dedicated to each home.

Melvyn stood in the doorway, calling out after me as I huffed down the hill. His voice grew fainter with each step.

"Leave! Nobody wants you, Edgar! Not even your good-for-nothing whore mother!" He really got all gravely on the word "whore," like it could be the last insult he could hurl my way. *Whatever, little monster, fuck off. I don't know where I'm going, but I can run my ass away from you.*

I let gravity give me a little extra speed, but this turned out to be to my disadvantage, because it made stopping more difficult. I careened broadside into a peanut truck, spilling nuts all over the street. The vendor was not happy with me.

"Lookee what you did there, son," he said, pulling his cart upright and scrambling after his indigo umbrella that was rolling away from him in the breeze. I helped him reinsert it into the cart.

"That's a lot of product you just ruined." He rubbed a handkerchief over his forehead.

"I'm sorry, sir," I said, picking up peanuts and realizing they were covered with road dirt. *Nutty and delicious!*

"Apologies don't earn me any money, you know," he said, puffing. He looked down at me and I was reminded again how small I was.

"You need to pay for all of this damage."

"I don't have any money." I felt in my pockets just in case but I already knew I wouldn't find anything in there.

"I see," he said. He looked at me with intensity, making me feel even smaller than I already was. "Didn't you just come from the Traver house? At the top of the hill?"

"I-I'm a servant's child. My mother doesn't have any money, sir." *I should just run,* I thought. *He won't catch me, either. I'm the Gingerbread Man, shazam!*

He seemed to guess my thoughts, because he plucked at my shirt on the shoulder, and began walking with me over to a small green house with a front picture window. It sat in the middle of the block, two other tiny houses up close on either side. I could have tried to make a break for it, but his hand was a clamp around my arm.

He pushed open a low gate and then we were marching up a few wooden steps to the front door. The man didn't bother knocking before he pulled open the screen door.

"Darling! Come here." His deep voice bellowed through the tiny house. It was clean enough inside, but all of the furniture seemed fragile. Like the outside paint, most everything in there was green.

From beyond the next room a woman emerged, wiping her hands on a kitchen towel. I gasped seeing a much younger version of the woman I knew from Kentucky. Still small, she stood as tall as her bones could make her, her hands free from the gnarls of arthritis that would later deform them, but her eyes flashed the same careful wisdom she had in her older years. Knowledge crashed over me: *Darling knew Melvyn Traver?*

I turned the revelation over in my head. Couldn't I just kill this body? Then there would be no Dr. Traver to terrorize a town and pull Jacqueline into his web. Of course, I wasn't sure what would happen to me, Jack, if I did that. What if my life, or my grandfather's, was dependent on Dr. Traver's existence somehow?

"Papa, who did you bring me here?" She assessed me, pulling at my other arm in some kind of hand off or hostage exchange. Darling knelt down to me.

"I know what you're thinking," she said, "and it is a terrible idea."

"What, what am I thinking?"

"If Papa brought you in here, you are full of bad thoughts, little boy. What is your name?"

"Edgar," I said. It was as true as anything else. She stood up.

"What happened?"

Darling's father answered for me.

"He knocked over the cart, and everything fell in the street. Now he says he has no money. So he needs to work off what he cost me."

She stared down at me again. I wanted to know how much she understood. It was impossible, right, for her to know anything about later. Right?

"Look here, Edgar. You are going to sit on that couch, and keep your feet off of it. Don't you move one inch. We are going to have a little chat. Go on, now."

I walked to the couch, looking back at Darling and her father. They moved into the dining room, which came nowhere near the size or opulence of the Traver house's formal dining room. They spoke in low whispers and I couldn't hear them. It seemed they were arguing, and then the old man pounded across the room to me, rattling the dishes in the dining room cabinet.

"If I could chain you up in the backyard until you worked off your debt to me I sure would," he said through gritted teeth. "But my daughter tells me there are better ways of dealing with you. You mind her, boy. If you disappoint her, you will disappoint me. Understand?"

I nodded.

"Yes, sir."

"Sir," he repeated, shaking his head. "Lord have mercy."

He slammed the screen door behind him. I stayed seated.

"All right, come here, child," she said, waving me over. I slid down until my feet touched the floor, then walked over to her. *Young Darling.* Again she crouched down to me. Her forehead was smooth and her dress was mended at the shoulder.

"What happened to you today? You ran away for a reason?"

"Yes, ma'am." She looked at my swollen nose and the dried blood that clung to my nostrils. I looked at the morning sunlight filtering through the lime green curtains in the kitchen. They were pretty.

"Did you misbehave today?"

"No, ma'am. I mean, I didn't mean to knock the wagon over." We stared at each other for a moment. I wondered why she was pausing.

"Edgar, every bad person has some good in them."

"Yes, ma'am."

She flashed me a smile. I could see how tired she was already at this point in the day, barely scratching noon. "Come with me."

She led me out into the tiny back yard, mostly dirt instead of grass. At the end was a small wooden tool shed. I tried not to gasp because it resembled the burning shed in my fake memory—from a seizure I'd had years before Dr. Dorfman walked into my life. Maybe all sheds were similar. *That must be it.*

She opened the door and motioned for me to go in first. My heart slammed itself against my chest. It was probably pure curiosity that got me to step past her and into the shack.

There, in the corner, was a decrepit barber's chair, and strapped to the top, an aluminum helmet with a series of wires soldered to it. It looked like a freaking electric chair for executing murderers. I screamed and turned to run, but Darling caught me on my elbow and reeled me in. I ran in place, screaming through one of her hands as her free arm wrapped around me. She was a ton stronger than she appeared.

"Just hush, boy," she said, but she didn't sound gruff. "I'm going to send you back now before you hurt this body, because that is not the answer. You hear me? Don't make a mistake you can't fix."

I quit fighting. *Back where?*

"You're going to kill me."

Darling shushed me. "I have no plans to do that. Now sit down."

"But, how do you know who I am?"

"Promise not to run off."

I nodded.

"Say it, boy."

"I promise not to run."

She released me in the direction of the chair, still blocking my path out of the shed. I saw that the wires led to a wooden box, and from there, to a hand crank.

"Explain this, please," I said. My voice squeaked and I really wanted not to be in a kindergartener's body right then. Actually never again would I want to be five years old.

"You're a Traveler, a person who can move through time."

"It's like, a thing?" I wanted to understand, but I was distracted by the stream of *HOLY SHIT* repeating in my head.

"It's a 'thing' as you say. A class of people who can shift from time to time. It's hard to control and carefully guarded by people. Like me." She relaxed the littlest bit.

"Guarded? What do you mean? Why? How do you even join up? This doesn't make any sense!"

"Hush, settle down now. We don't know how Travelers are born, they just are. Most of the Guardians are related to each other in some way, but we are all sworn to secrecy. We can feel it when a Traveler comes through the time current. We are here to help you and keep your ability secret."

"Secrets are bad," I said, almost like a reflex.

"Oh, you think it would go well for you for everyone to know you can move through time at will?"

"I can't control it, though."

"You can't yet," she corrected me. "You will learn."

"How am I supposed to learn?"

Darling sighed, putting her hands on her hips. *Come on! I have questions! Don't be pissed at me.*

"You will learn from your Guardians, and with practice."

"But I can't tell anyone? How am I supposed to find a Guardian? And why don't I have one in my real time?"

"You have a Guardian in your own time, but perhaps they haven't made themselves known to you. They must have a good reason."

"What good reason could there be for watching a kid worry he's crazy? It would have been a big help two years ago!" I curled my hands into fists and wished there was something I could hit. Even though I wasn't much of a boxer.

"Maybe your Guardian wanted to learn about you as a person first, see how you used your ability. I may only guess at their intentions."

I wondered what it could be. Did they think I wasn't a real Traveler, like it was just an effect of the epilepsy study? Was I not good enough for a Guardian? *What the hell am I thinking! This is bizarre!* I considered running past Darling, but remembered my promise.

"Well, I want a Guardian. I have so many questions. Like why did you tell me you're a Guardian? Are you my Guardian, or are you here for someone else?"

"Little boy, not all of the answers are your business." She squatted down so we were eye to eye. She sighed.

"I had to step in before you did something to this boy. And I suspect you learned something important in the Traver house. Is that true?"

I nodded, hoping she would just continue.

"I am from this time, not your time, so I am only a kind of temporary Guardian for you. Your Guardian will reveal himself or herself to you at some point. Use your instincts and do right, never ill, toward anyone."

"How can I find this Guardian if they don't come forward? How can I figure out what I need to do if I don't tell anyone about the time travel?" And uh, I'd already told three other people—Jeannine, Sanjay, and Dr. Dorfman. No harm had come to me. In fact, they'd all tried to help me as much as they could.

Then it hit me we probably didn't need to destroy Aimée's parents' television screen. *Oops.*

"Some Travelers have told others—outsiders—and they are instantly a threat." She ticked off the reasons on her fingers.

"You cannot confer your ability on anyone else. You cannot bring anyone else with you. You cannot carry even the smallest object with you as you cross through time. You are of no help to any government or powerful man. All you can do is act as a spy, yet you have every ability to run away from your stated allegiances. So in all likelihood, once word gets out you are a Traveler, you will be killed and the truth of your life covered up by your enemies. That is why we Guardians are your protectors."

"Well, way to burst my bubble."

"Beg pardon?"

"I just mean, that's a lot to take in."

"You are more than capable of it."

I nodded, to get to move on, not because I agreed with Darling.

"So how many Travelers are there? How many Guardians?"

"Nobody knows how many Travelers there are. Many. They are born all the time, and we try to help them over the course of their lives."

"Don't they like, have a lot of power?"

"Do you feel like you have power?"

"I mean, I must. It feels awkward, winding up in new places when I don't expect it. But like, I could just find a time I like and…"

"And what? Do something you wouldn't do in your own time?"

"Well, no. But like, I have knowledge. From like, the future."

"Have you intentionally hurt anyone with that knowledge?"

"Of course not."

"Mmm hmm. You have a strong ethical center. You should rely on it. Well now, you need to let this little boy get back to his life." She guided me to the metal chair.

"Where do these people go when I'm uh, inside them?"

"So many questions. Your Guardian can explain that to you."

"I've been jumping around for long enough," I protested. "I want to know what's happening, and how to stop Dr. Traver and get back to my own life."

She stood up and stopped fiddling with the connections.

"I don't know what your goal is or with whom you've been interacting. You will have to speak with your Guardian. Although truth be told I wouldn't be surprised if you and I meet up again. Travelers and Guardians tend to meet several times if they meet even once."

Well, if this isn't a completely frustrating conversation. She's freaking talking in riddles now. She noticed my frown and patted me on my knee.

"I can tell my Papa liked you," she continued, pressing the cap into place on my head. She leaned over the box and began cranking. It whirred as she made it turn, becoming louder and higher pitched.

"How could you tell?" I asked.

"He let you in his house," she said. "You're the first white person he ever willingly let come inside."

"I recall that he yanked me in," I said.

"Don't be splitting hairs, child," she said, "See you around." And then she pushed a button on the crankbox and I was gone.

* * *

Nighttime, back in the woods. This felt familiar. The quality of the moonlight through the trees. The humid summer air. My scratchy, tailored clothing. I was Jacqueline. That made me grateful; I knew this body at least as well as I knew Jack's. I appreciated her surefootedness. I enjoyed her gait and the way she cut through space. I felt more centered, as if I was better able to be me.

A flicker off in the distance knocked me out of my thoughts, and I reached for a knife I knew I'd sheathed to my belt. The wolves. Maybe I'd arrived back at the same point as before. His howling preceded his movement, and I quietly tracked back to where I knew Pie was hitched.

After some time stalking through the trees I whistled out for Pie and in the distance heard her bray back at me. I'd gotten closer at least. The back and forth howling had let up some. The pack sounded further away. Finally I saw the horse, strapped to the tree the same way as last time.

"Hello, buddy," I said, finding the sugar cube in my pocket and feeding it to her. *This replaying stuff comes in handy.* She sucked it down and pushed her head against me softly. I gave her a pet and then we were off at a canter, away again from the forest. I wanted no part of that place.

I took a direct route to the Rushman farm, knowing the grid of country roads between the flank of the woods and the fields. I'd dozed on my last ride to the Rushman farm. This way was faster, although not any better. Because I traveled out in the open, I caught the attention of two men in a car who were on the lookout for anything suspicious.

Body-changing time traveler? I most indeededly fit the bill.

Chapter Twenty-One

AWARD WINNING PIE made me aware of the car with a snort and a head pull to the side, veering us away from the road that led to the front of Rushman Farm. I turned to look as we galloped, and seeing them track me by turning their heads—two men, wearing suits and hats, following the line Pie and I made—confirmed for me they aimed to apprehend me or worse. I clicked my tongue and changed course suddenly, away from any paved surface. *Thank the baby Jesus I'm getting good at this horse riding thing.*

The car jerked off the road, bouncing over the uneven grass on narrow tires not made for rocks and dirt. It was a black Studebaker Roadster, a popular bootlegger's car because it was reliable and seated four, so the illegal alcohol could fit in the backseat, or so my research back home had said.

These guys weren't smugglers, though. Except maybe of people. Dead people.

Pie pounded over the ground, grunting, while I looked back to see how the men were responding. If we could just lose them, I could double back later and alert Lucas and the others. There was no way we could outrun a 40-horsepower engine, though, so I tried to find terrain that would stop the car.

I was about to jump a rocky stream when the car blew a tire behind us. The sound ricocheted off the edge of the woods. Pie reared up, braying in surprise. I held on to her neck, staying in the saddle, but in the process I pulled a muscle on the underside of my leg. Fire shot through me and I yelped much like Pie had just done. I pushed the horse on, grimacing and trying to go easy on my muscle, which apparently I needed to keep riding. *Terrific.*

The first shot rang out and a moment later, a bullet smashed into a tree near us, startling the horse again. Pie bucked as she ran into the thick of the forest, and I tried shushing her in her ear. She settled down a little, and after we had made a little more headway, I finally let her slow down.

I needed to find a way back to the farm, to talk to Lucas or his father. I remembered Jackson, my grandfather, someone who knew about time travel. I'd only just started talking to him when I jumped into Edgar. Because I'd totally fainted in front of him.

I'd never met my grandfather in my real life—he was a two pack-a-day smoker and had a huge heart attack delivering Wonder bread when my mother was still a young woman. But he was alive in this time, and Darling had told me to see him. His cousin, Darling. And thus related to me, Darling. Guardian Darling, who had introduced him to Jacqueline when Jacqueline was still a girl, before I'd ever jumped into her life. I had to figure out what these connections meant. Was he also a Guardian? Or just clued into the whole thing by Darling?

I let Pie drink for a while until she picked up her head and huffed at me. I fished around and found a small apple in my pack, which she gobbled up in two bites.

I headed off to find Jackson Hartle.

* * *

We had quite a ways to go before we'd show up at his row house at the edge of the field. As the sun prepared to set, I sniffed around an abandoned strip of train cargo cars. Judging from the height of the weeds and the rusty state of the tracks, no trains had passed through here for a long while.

I slept in fits, Pie tied to a crumbling handle on the open cargo door. The wood was rotted in places and my nose filled up from the smell of mold and old piss. I hoped the horse would alert me if I were in any danger.

People came to me in my dreams. People I missed, which seemed like everyone. But at least now I knew that I wasn't alone, even if I felt alone a lot of the time. And I had at least some pieces of a plan—find Jackson, bring him to the Underground folks, get evidence on Dr. Traver, and stop all the potential awful things from happening, like the house fire and Jacqueline marrying Dr. Evil. And back in my world, help my mother get better, and get Dr. Dorfman's life back on track. Okay, so it was a long list, but at least I wasn't hopeless about it. At least, not in that exact minute. *Whew.*

Light broke and I fed Pie the last bag of barley that I had in the pack, and an apple I'd hoped to eat myself. I was sure she was still really hungry. We needed to find some hay bales or something. I looked toward the horizon and checked that the saddle was the right tightness for riding. I hopped up and we set off.

The train tracks crossed a gravel road, and as it seemed familiar for some reason, I switched off and we walked along. An hour later, there was the house, looking a little better tended than the last time I was here.

I knocked on the door. "Mr. Hartle?" No response, or sound of anyone approaching. "It's Jaqueline." I waited, listening to a few birds chirping from a bush next to the porch. I put my face up to the window at the side of the door and cupped my hands over my eyes. It was empty inside. Walking down the front steps I remembered the garage at the rear of the house. I stood in the doorway.

He was bent over the hood of the car I'd been building with Lucas, and he twitched when he heard me come in.

"Geez, girl, you should announce yourself."

"I didn't know you were back here. I tried finding you in your house," I said, not intending to defend myself.

"Well, I don't have time to lay about my house," he said. He stood up and looked me over. "There's a bit of bread and butter over there on the table. You need to eat something."

Instead of following his directions I walked over to him to see what he was doing. He'd removed the carburetor, which was sitting on a green workbench. He looked to be installing a turbo charger. From the crude appearance of the metal, I guessed he'd made it himself. He didn't seem very confident about installing it.

"So are you a Guardian too?"

He jumped again, this time hitting his head on the underside of the hood.

"Jackie, you sure have imperfect timing," he said, bending up straight and rubbing the crown of his skull.

"And charm. Don't forget my charm."

"That too. No, I'm not a Guardian. Not yet, anyway."

"What do you mean, not yet?"

"It's a long story. You came all the way out here. Did Darling send you?" He looked out past the driveway toward the street, like he'd done the last time I'd ridden over here. Then he wiped grease off his hands onto a rag, and started walking out of the barn. I ran my hand over the driver's door, checking to see if this was the same vehicle as in the abandoned bank in Marion. This one was a Model T Ford with the roof cut off, and it was much more bare bones than the Auburn Beauty I'd been customizing with Lucas. My Dad had taught me a lot more about engines than anyone seemed to have taught Jackson Hartle. *But I'm a car snob like that.*

"She did, only not yet. She sent me to you in the late summer. I mean, is it 1926?"

"Sure is," he said, still cleaning his hands. The paradox didn't seem to bother him.

"It's only May. But I suppose we can take a road trip out to see my favorite cousin."

"Do you think that's a good idea? It's okay to change it up like that?"

"Oh, you think you're an expert now?"

"No, I'm just asking a question."

"Well, it's a stupid question," he said, and he dropped the rag on the bench and walked out of the barn. I trotted after him.

"There's no such thing as a stupid question," I said.

"Of course there's such a thing as a stupid question! And that was one of 'em. If Darling told you to come out here, she's not going to care if I show up three months early. Now mind me, girl. I need to fetch a few things from the house. Keep yourself inside here."

My grandfather is an asshole. I was shocked my mom was so nice to me if that was her dad. I wiped away a tear I didn't want to cry. I'd show him. How was he going to drive anywhere without the frigging carburetor? I rolled up my sleeves and picked it up from the bench, checking to see if it was clean, which it was for the most part. I found the bolts on the bench too, and dug through his toolbox for the right set of socket wrenches. In a couple of minutes I had everything assembled. I hopped in the driver seat and tried the ignition.

It didn't catch. The crank turned over and over, but it wouldn't start. Probably he needed to change the intake and exhaust timing because he'd installed the turbo charger. I was midway through tinkering with the throttle when Jackson came back into the barn.

"Why don't you listen to a thing I say? You were supposed to wait for me." Without waiting for an answer, he shook his head and kept talking. "I sure hope my future children aren't as headstrong as you. But at least you have a brain between those ears."

"I am waiting. I'm just making it so the car will start. While I'm waiting."

"Well aren't you the precocious one?"

"I wonder where I picked that up."

Without realizing it, I started smiling.

"Just what are you grinning at, girl? Wipe that smirk off your face and get in the car. Does it start now?"

I nodded.

"Between your handiwork and mine, I think we've got a lot more horsepower now."

"Well you're a little cocksure, ain't ya?"

In all of this mess, I had to deal with this cranky jackass. Just in case I was going to get bored by time freaking travel, the universe handed me a jerk.

"Pardon me, but do you know what time it is, grandfather?" I asked in my most pitch-perfect singsong.

"Why yes," he said with his head next to the engine block, which I figured meant he was inspecting my work on the carburetor. I heard him sigh and then he dropped the hood back into place, taking care not to mess up his clean hands in the process. He sat in the driver's seat and fumbled for his watch, pulling it from his vest. He pushed a button and the face snapped open, revealing a gorgeous mother of pearl face that reflected back all of the miserable light in the barn. "It's one-forty."

I nodded. "Nice watch."

"Thank you," he said, putting it back. "Well, I reckon this engine will work better for ya." He turned to face me.

"I was in the Navy in the Great War," he said. "Enlisted a few months before the whole brouhaha started and I have now peeled potatoes for America's finest fighting force. Never made it out of that damn mess."

"What mess was that?"

"The mess hall, kid. You don't know hard work, do you? Your cousin Darling sure knows the value of a long working day."

I thought about chasing chickens around a shit-covered coop, just one day in the life of Edgar MacComb. One morning, in fact.

"You're right, we farm folks don't know how to work," I said. He harrumphed at me in response. He opened up the bag he'd brought out of the house and handed me a cheese sandwich wrapped in brown paper.

"Here's some milk from this morning," he said. "Drink up before you blow away in a breeze."

The milk was unlike anything I'd tasted from the grocery store. Rich, almost nutty in flavor. It coated my throat in happy. My stomach growled, almost in delight.

"I suppose it's not your fault, your whole generation is soft," he said. I wondered why we were eating in the car and not his house.

"You're too kind," I said between bites. Holy crap I was hungry.

"Now don't go getting smart with me," he said, poking in my general direction.

What had it been like for my mom to grow up with this guy as her father? My own Dad was about as unlike him as a person could be. It hit me that I'd never thought about my Mom as a regular adult before, someone who had a life before I came along. Maybe she'd actively picked someone completely different from her family to marry. I wondered if Dad got along with Mr. Hartle here.

"You're not paying attention to me, girl."

"You know, you're not that much older than me, so anytime you feel like stopping calling me girl, I'm good with that."

He stood up, brushing off his trousers even though there was nothing on them. "Now I really know you're from another time. You should show your someday grandfather a little respect."

"Yes, sir."

I needed his help. And it seemed I hadn't told him I was his grandson, not his granddaughter.

"I'm sorry."

"It's all right," he said, softening. *Wow, this deference crap really works. But I still don't like it.*

He checked his pocket watch.

"We need to get in the car now."

"We do?"

He nodded.

I put out half a bale of hay in the horse pen, not knowing how much the four horses needed for an afternoon. I met Jackson at the car, which he was fueling from a small can. I jumped over the side and into the driver's seat.

"Just what is it you think you're doing?" he asked me.

"Oh, I'm driving," I said, snatching a pair of goggles off of the floor of the car.

"Women sure have changed in your generation."

"You're darn tootin'," I said, and he clambered into the car, grumbling something about insolent offspring.

I pushed the ignition button and the engine he'd carefully expanded growled awake, sputtering out dark smoke from the tailpipe. I cut into gear and we popped out of the garage before we could be overcome from exhaust. I sized up all of the features I'd inserted into the dashboard—the same set of knobs, buttons, and dials that had confounded me the last time I'd been behind the wheel. This was the same car or a twin.

"So, where to?" I asked.

Jackson didn't speak, instead choosing to point to two sheriff cars that were racing at us from two blocks down the street.

"Away from them," he said. "They musta seen you coming into town. There's wanted posters of you all over the state."

"There are? Why?"

"You done piss off someone with power, girl. Now drive like you know what you're doing."

I floored it, aiming at the road out of town. Our thin tires kicked up a small dust and gravel storm, and then caught some traction.

Jackson whipped his head around to see how close they were to us. I saw the needle on the odometer reach to sixty-seven miles per hour, far faster than this car should have been able to speed. The customized engine was a beauty. At once the cars flicked on their sirens, which wailed at us painfully. We had been running from them for all of ten seconds, but it seemed much longer.

He pulled himself back around and faced forward.

"You didn't tell me everything, you know." He shouted so I could hear him.

"What didn't I tell you?"

He looked at me and yelled again, "That when they come after us, they'll have guns."

"They always have guns! Weren't you in the Navy?"

"I told you," he said, pointing out potholes for me to avoid, "I peeled potatoes."

"All the World War I vets in the country and I have to find the guy who was stuck in the kitchen."

Jackson frowned at me. "What do you mean, World War I?"

"Nothing, I don't mean anything."

We were getting some distance on them, although one of the cars managed to keep up with us better than I'd have thought possible. The cop in the passenger seat propped a shotgun up on the door and fired, tearing through our low windshield. My face stung as small cuts opened up in my skin. *Holy crap! Thank god for goggles.* And then we were out of range.

"Don't tell me there's another goddamn world war," screamed Jackson, as we sped out of town.

Chapter Twenty-Two

WE DROVE UNTIL we reached the other side of three towns, and then pulled up to a general store. I cut the engine. Jackson and I inspected each other.

"Well, you've looked better," he said, lifting my chin.

"You've looked worse," I said. That made him smile for a moment. "So who was that back there?" I asked.

"Deputies of the town," he said, taking the opportunity to look back behind us, where the dust we'd kicked up was settling back on the wide lane. We hadn't seen another car for at least an hour. "So many bootleggers in the news, idiot coppers would love to get some attention for catching an outlaw."

"Right, a kid and some random guy. We must be a big deal."

"Fine, fine, you keep up your jokes. You better be nice to me when I'm an old man."

He caught me downcast at the mention of him as an elderly person.

"What? What do you know?" Jackson grabbed the fabric of my shirt at my arm. "Do I not? Do I not get old?"

I took in his face, trying to imagine how it would look with saggy jowls, wrinkles, bald, a face he would never grow into because he only lived a few years past his fiftieth birthday. I wanted to tell him but I also feared it because if there was such a thing as fate knowing wasn't going to help him. *I can travel through time, but I'm no philosopher, buddy.*

"You're going to be just fine," I told him, giving him a nod. "Think of it this way, you're like an old man already."

I was grateful he changed the subject, by asking about the car and what other modifications I'd done to it. He had only followed my instructions for enhancing the engine by changing the air intake, which was the request I'd made of him.

"Oh, a few other things I thought would come in handy, like the radio?" I asked him for the time, and he shook his head.

"Sorry, Jacqueline, it's three forty-five." He pulled at the cord, sprung open the dial. The watch face was beautiful.

"Let's try anyway." I kicked on the starter and we drove to a parking lot behind a large white church with the tallest steeple in the small town. As long as the engine idled, we would have power for the transmitter, actually far more power than most ham radios had in the 1920s.

I dialed the frequency as before, and gave out a short call: "I don't feel like waiting for twilight."

Jackson shook his head. "What a fool girl you are."

I shot him a wide, fake grin. *Fine, go ahead and think I'm stupid.*

The radio crackled, breaking the static.

"I'm here, I'm here." Lucas's voice. I gasped without meaning to, and punched Jackson after he rolled his eyes at me. He grimaced, as some of the broken windshield had cut his arms.

"We ducked two uh, former friends, about an hour ago. I'm with the old man."

I ignored the glowering stare from my passenger.

"Oh, good. Things here are the same…full of old friends, like for a big party."

Big party? What does that mean?

"Well, we will join you then."

"We're looking forward to your visit."

"We're ready for a blast!" *Nothing like sounding super cheery when we're on the run from men with guns. I bet this is exactly how the CIA works.*

"Well, I have to go," Lucas said. I heard a tinge of nervousness in him, or so I thought. "Good to talk to you."

"You too." The line returned to static.

Coming out of the church, a man dropped a wooden box he'd been carrying when he saw us and our blown-out windshield. He pointed right at us, shouting. "It's the girl!"

Terrific. All this time back in the 20s, and it's like we've been plastered across the evening news.

I threw the shifter into reverse, which pushed back against me. We could hear the gears grinding from under the hood.

"More clutch," said Jackson, who had taken to pressing against the dash. "More clutch!"

"I know!" I slammed my foot on the leftmost pedal, and the stick grabbed into gear. We flew backwards until I had clearance to get out of the small parking lot.

Two more men jumped out from the building; a man in a minister's shirt and collar, and another man in a suit, this one burly with a handlebar mustache. He held a shotgun. "Citizen's arrest," he said, taking aim at us.

"Go, go go," said Jackson. I shifted into first gear and hit the gas, and we kicked dirt into the men's faces. The churchman took a shot at us, blinded from the dust, and missed. We sped out toward the emptiness beyond the town on a narrow highway.

"People sure do like to shoot at you," he said.

"I like to think it's affection." My heart hammered inside me.

"Pull over here for a second," he said.

"What? Why? We have to get out of here!"

"Pull over," he repeated, and this time I did as he asked. He hopped over the passenger door and clambered up a telephone pole like a monkey. A pop of electricity, and the dark wire hung limply in the air. In a manner of seconds, Jackson was back in the car.

"Now drive fast," he said

I obliged.

"What was that about?"

"They have to assume we're headed back to Dr. Traver's town, so I figured they'd find a phone and call to warn him."

"Good thinking."

"Well, thank the Lord her Highness approves," he said, closing up his pocket knife and tucking it away.

"Let's not talk holy, okay? I'm a little over the prophet's friends."

"Anyone claiming to be a prophet isn't," said Jackson. "He's twisted the good word into a monstrosity."

We drove in silence, concentrating on any sudden attacks from Dr. Traver's followers. It had been so good to hear Lucas's voice. I couldn't wait to see him.

A red light flickered on near my left hand. *The gas gauge.* "We need more fuel," I said. Behind us the sun crept toward a ridge; minute by minute the day was fading. I clicked on the headlamps.

"There are a few cans in the trunk," said Jackson. I pulled the car off the road, onto a bolt of grass, and fumbled for the trunk lock. I wrestled the straps open and felt in the dark for a metal can.

I jumped when Jackson started talking to me; he'd come out of the car and I hadn't noticed.

"Settle down, girl. It's just me."

"Are you going to fill up the tank?"

"I wanted to talk," he said.

"Right now?"

"Tell me about your mother."

"What's to tell?" Now I struggled with the gas cap, but Jackson twisted it in a quick yank, and took the can from me, unscrewing the top. I winced at the acrid stench.

"Come on, talk to me. What is she like?"

"She's–she's kind, very kind. She's smart, and observant, and sometimes she gets sad."

I could tell he was scowling, even in the dark. "Kind? Sad? Does she keep a good house, child? Was she married when you were born? When were you born?" *Cripes, talk about old fashioned! Jackson here was a real drag.*

"I told you what was important. She's pretty. Yes, she got married and my parents are good together. We don't have a lot of money–"

"I knew it."

He capped the tank, then tossed the empty gas can onto the ground. I gasped.

"You're littering."

He glowered at me some more. "I'm what?"

"Littering. You can't just throw garbage onto the grass."

"Girl, of course I can. Now let's get going before someone shoots off our asses."

I sighed again. I did that a lot when Jackson was around.

"So, what do you know?" I plopped back in the driver's seat.

"What are you going on about now?"

"You said, 'I knew it.'" I took care to say it all nasally like he had. He looked like he almost enjoyed my mimicking.

"I knew no offspring of mine would ever amount to anything." He sat down next to me, his palms facing the night sky. I gripped the wheel tight.

"My mother takes care the best she can, and she is a terrific person. And I miss her, and you should be grateful you get as much time with her as you will."

"And how much time is that?"

Damn, I had said too much.

"Is it ever enough?" I asked.

"I suppose not," he said, opting to turn silent again. I turned the engine over and the machine sputtered, then caught.

"You just be nice to her, every day," I said, "when you think you're going to say something awful like that, just hug her, or something, instead. Try not to be so snippy with her. And you know, maybe don't smoke so many cigarettes."

"I don't smoke."

"You will."

"You sure have a lot of opinions," he said.

"Unfortunately, I take after you," I said.

* * *

We woke up after sleeping in the car for a few hours, and an itchy sensation on my arms reminded me of having an EEG session with Dr. Dorfman or what I would feel shortly before a seizure. I still hadn't wrapped my mind around living epilepsy-free, never needing to watch a clock to take my next pill, but here I was.

I had several mosquito bites, and so did Jackson. One landed on his neck, too greedy to leave him alone, and I slapped it away. In reflex Jackson grabbed my wrist, then woke up.

"What are you doing?"

"Killing a bug," I said. "You can thank me anytime."

I wrenched my arm out of his clutch.

He sat up, rubbed his eyes. "Let's get some breakfast." He looked himself over and frowned. "I should have brought a change of underclothes."

I cranked over the engine, which sounded rough, probably due to condensation from the morning dew or the new turbocharger. We really needed to install a fuel injection, but for now we were stuck with a carburetor, which at the moment was moist and inefficient. It would clear out soon.

"Maybe they'll have some at a diner," I said.

"A what?"

"Okay, where do you want to get breakfast?" Apparently there weren't any diners in 1926. *Silly 1926.*

"Just drive to the next town and we'll find a food counter," he said. I nodded, since it seemed easier than arguing with him about words. *You're right, a food counter is completely different from a diner.*

"I know of a great breakfast counter," I said.

We drove to my mother's house. I figured it would be okay because we were three months before the fire, and Traver's cronies wouldn't know I was back in town or alive, for that matter. As we drove past fields with bright green crops I worried this was the wrong thing to do, but I hoped that without having found the evidence of Traver's crimes he wouldn't feel the need to kill us quite yet. Clearly I could change history with my behavior, but at least I had a Guardian in training with me.

By the time we pulled up I'd convinced myself this was the best move. Even so I felt my breath catch at seeing it again, standing proudly. I could still picture the fire licking out of the windows, charring the paint, making that rushing sound as it swept through the floors. I kept staring at it, telling myself, "it's still here."

I parked on the side of the house, crushing a few rogue pansies that had bloomed between the concrete slabs of the walkway. The sky was barely blue in the early morning light, but it was enough that the rooster had noticed. I clomped up the porch steps and opened the front door, calling for her.

She came out of the kitchen and gave me a long hug. *No big drama like when you come back from the grave, I guess.*

"It's been so long! I was going to leave you for dead. And who is this?" She quickly untied her apron and smoothed out her dress. "I'm not prepared for company, Jacqueline."

"Mother, this is a friend of mine, Jackson Hartle."

"Pleased to see you again," she said, and I thought she might add a little curtsy, but she refrained. "I think it's been since oh, two summers ago at the state fair?"

"That sounds about right, ma'am." He gave her a short smile. "Pleased to see you, Mrs. Bishop."

"Well, we were looking to have a little breakfast, if you can spare it," I said. She and Jackson continued to look at each other, neither of them responding to me. "Okay, I'll go see what's in the kitchen while you two gawk at each other."

I headed off to the other room, but was still within earshot. She had four eggs, a third of a loaf of bread, and half a cup of milk at the bottom of the ice box. Not the level of hunger she'd reached the last time I was here, but not good, either.

"I apologize for her manners," said Mother.

They joined me as I whipped eggs in a bowl. "I can't use the stove," I said.

"You raised a lovely son here," said Jackson, waving his thumb at me.

"He'd rather you taught me to be completely dependent on men," I said in response.

"Do you enjoy each other's company at all?" she asked, taking the bowl from me and lighting the wood under the burner with a long match. She handed me the bread and a knife and told me to cut slices.

"Sure we do," I said, fighting to make even cuts. Slicing bread was a lot harder than it looked, although not nearly as much as catching a chicken. "Jackson seems to think we'll grow on each other."

"I see," she said. She leaned into my left ear. "You keep your legs together and respect your family name, now."

"Mother!"

But she didn't have anything else to say, turning away from us to work at the stove. Jackson glowered at me and handed me a plate for the bread.

"Well, I thank you for the breakfast, ma'am," he said, and he stepped aside so she could place the bread in the oven for toasting.

We ate quickly, mother and Jackson too uncomfortable to talk much, so I filled in the empty conversational space by blabbing about the beautiful morning and complaining about mosquitoes. Jackson asked where the outhouse was, and I pointed him to the backyard. He shuffled out before I was finished talking.

I rose to clear the table.

"What is going on?" she asked me.

I let her in on what had been going on with Dr. Traver's followers, the false accusations about illegal drinking and bathtub gin, and how the police for several towns over seemed to be part of his organization. She nodded and added her own information.

"He just announced this week that he intends to run for mayor. I'm sure he'll want something else after that. Men like him are never satisfied unless they're grabbing for more power. He even pressured the banker to close my accounts." She scrubbed the plate and handed it to me to dry it. It was heavier than anything in my house in Ohio, with scalloped edges and flowers painted around the border, but there were a few chips around the edge.

"Mother, I need to tell you something."

"You're in love with him," she said without turning around.

"What? No. No, it's nothing like that."

She faced me. "Don't tell me anything that would be the death of me." I pondered what that kind of list looked like. Probably long.

"No, mother, this is about you."

"Well, that's a relief. So, what about me?"

"I think you should build a cellar where you could go in an emergency."

"I don't have money for such frivolous and unnecessary things."

She snatched the cast iron skillet from the stovetop and began scrubbing it hard. I came up next to her and put my hand on her shoulder.

"Mom, Dr. Traver will set his sights on you, and you need to be safe." This got her to stop mauling the pan.

"Jacqueline, I did not fall in on the last drop of rain. I'll be on the lookout for him. All right?"

I gave her a kiss on her cheek, and her hand fluttered to cover the spot as soon as I stood back.

"All right, Mother. I just don't want anything bad to happen to you."

"I appreciate that, my dear. I can't imagine how I ever have taken care of myself all these many years absent your counsel. But you are a sweet girl."

The sound of hard foot falls indicated Jackson had returned to the house. He stood in the doorway.

"Well, kiddo, I think we need to keep to our schedule," he said.

Mother raised her eyebrows, but didn't remark. Jackson wasn't much older than me.

"Well, next time give me a longer visit, and don't take as much time between them," she said. I hurried up and hugged her, whispering in her ear: "Just keep your guard up and be safe."

"Hmph," she said as she stood back, still holding my hands, "It's not I who is off gallivanting all over God's creation."

Jackson gave a little bow and thanks and we were off to the Rushman farm in the valley. We made it about halfway there when six cars rolled up and surrounded us. The drivers got out of their vehicles and pointed shotguns at our heads.

Chapter Twenty-Three

I WATCHED A CAR DOOR OPEN, and out stepped Dr. Traver, who took his time walking over to us. Nobody made a sound except a couple of crows who apparently hadn't gotten the memo.

He put one dirty boot on the running board on my side of the car. "I thought you'd run off, or met a terrible fate somewhere, what with all of your sinning," he said to me. In his hand he held a toothpick, which he twirled through his fingers.

"Let us pass."

"Oh, I don't think so, Miss Bishop. You and your hooligan friend here aren't going anywhere."

"For a religious man, you sure have a lot of guns," said Jackson.

"Don't make this worse," I said to Jackson.

"No, don't make it worse, Jackson. You let a woman talk to you that way?" He leaned on the car door, popped his toothpick in his mouth. Dr. Traver smelled of a high perfumed soap, but underneath there was another odor, something sour that turned my stomach. Now his hands were braced on my door, and I could see dirt under his nails and caught up in his knuckles.

Jackson glowered, but was silent, and he'd curled his two hands into fists.

"Miss Bishop, kindly turn off your engine," demanded Dr. Traver.

"Why should I do that?" I wasn't sure what stalling would get me, but I delayed anyway.

"Because I asked you to," he said. Spit had started to form at the corners of his mouth. "And I'm not going to ask twice."

"Well, you have no authority to demand I do anything," I said, worrying instantly about the words as they popped out of my head.

"To the contrary, I have been deputized by the chief," he said, now smiling. The spaces between his teeth were burnt umber. I imagined little odor lines coming out from his mouth, like I'd seen in comic books for things like rotting meat and onions.

"Don't do it," said Jackson in my ear. Around us we heard the clicks of the men cocking their guns. I laid my finger on the shutoff button, which was one inch away from a covered switch that I knew would get us out of this ambush, but I would need to lift the cover first. I had a decision to make.

"What you fail to understand is the power of the Lord God to repudiate all evil. Sin is not the way to everlasting life, it is death."

Oh boy.

"Hate the sin, love the sinner," said Jackson. "Jacqueline, get us out of here."

He didn't mean it, I figured, since we'd have been blown to bits before I could press the gas pedal. But just in case I was inclined to split, he had another card to play.

"I already have Lucas and his father. So whatever uprising you and your group were planning, is over."

I shut off the car, and the engine quit with a long shudder. That couldn't be true, unless history had shifted from something I'd done in Edgar's body when he was a boy. So now I had to find out what was really going on.

"What are you doing, girl?" asked Jackson.

"It will be all right," I told him. "He's got us, right?"

"You better know what you're doing," he whispered. I gave him as large a nod as I could under the circumstances. We raised our hands in surrender, and Traver's men were upon us, leading us away from the car in the middle of the street as the sun descended from its highest angle of the day. Back in Ohio I never gave a shit about the sun, but here it was like one of the few timepieces I could count on.

"You gave them the car," Jackson said to me in the back of a wagon, where we sat with our hands shackled.

"It's okay."

"Pray tell, why is it okay?" He fumbled with the metal clasps, but they wouldn't spring.

I got close so I could whisper. "I looked under the hood back at your house. We took off with a loose manifold. If they prop the car up to tow it, it'll disconnect and then the engine won't start."

"You're brighter than you look," he said.

"I guess I figured my mechanical knowledge might come in handy at some point."

"Lord help us all." And with that, Jackson looked to the ceiling of the wagon, as if he could still see the sky.

* * *

Instead of heading to the sheriff's office our caravan went out of town, east, by the look of it. Our wagon had only one small, barred window at the rear, about half a foot wide, in the middle of the door. I peered through it to identify where we were headed by looking at where we'd been. Jackson, who had never been this far east before, didn't recognize any of the landscape.

"Well, they're not taking us to jail, because we passed it at least an hour ago," I said. I held onto the bars of the window with a few fingers, but as we hit big bumps or potholes in the road, I had trouble keeping my balance.

"Terrific. So that means where we're going is worse. What's the plan?"

I sat down next to him.

"Meet up with the others, see what they know and go from there."

"Jacqueline, that is not a plan." We bounced on the hard bench as the wagon careened along. The roadway was getting rougher. *Is it too much to ask that a prison vehicle come with decent shocks?*

"The plan is to see what we're dealing with and find a way to escape," I said, in defiance. "Your negativity isn't helping. Anyway, you're the almost Guardian."

"I'm a realist," he said. "We can't escape without a key to these things. Unless you're going to tell me that somehow you're also Houdini."

I burst into a smile. "Or a pick."

"A what?"

"A pick. Something that can act like a key when you don't have the key."

"We don't have anything like that."

"Oh, yes we do," I said.

"You have it?"

"Nope."

"Jacqueline, you are making me insane. Maybe this Guardian thing isn't for me."

"Oh, like Darling will let you out of it?"

He nodded; I was right on that score.

"Lucas will have it," I said.

"Lucas will have what?"

"A pick."

"And you know this, how?"

"Because I know Lucas." This was total bullshit, but whatever, I was going with it.

"You fancy him, don't do?"

We came to screeching halt, and it was all I could do to not go flying across the interior of the wagon. One of Traver's henchmen, who I recognized from his revival at the house that night after I'd run away, opened the door and waved for us to get out.

"I really, really do," I said, and I climbed out, squinting even though the afternoon light had lost its punch from earlier.

We were at some kind of mill, or what had once been a factory of some sort. The gray, flat building stood right at the edge of a broad river; rust from metal siding ran down the wall. From there it stained the ground, and trickled off into the water, ugly orange grooves in the dirt. The air smelled terrible, like rotten eggs or old meat. It got stuck in my nose. *This is what Traver smells like.* Two thugs pulled Jackson along, and though he fought at first, they were prepared for him. I had been assigned the squat man who'd opened up the wagon door to us. I considered kneeing him in the crotch, but I wanted to meet up with the others.

If it stunk outside, it was ten thousand times worse indoors, where there was no good air circulation. Jackson and I coughed. My breakfast tried to make a second appearance in my mouth.

"Over here," said one of the men, shoving Jackson and me toward a flight of metal stairs.

"What is this place?" I asked, not expecting an answer.

"Used to be the tannery," he said, and Jackson stumbled into the wall at the landing between flights. A guard lifted him by his shirt.

"Some soldier you are," he told Jackson.

"Seaman," Jackson corrected. The guard responded by punching him in the face, and Jackson fell down again. He spit out a tooth, and it bounced down the stairs like a tiny Slinky. "See, now you'll just have to pick me up again." Grinning, the guard cocked his hand back for another blow, but Jackson held his arms up.

"Stop, I'm getting up."

They led us into a large room that seemed to be the old loading dock. Now I really did vomit, which only pissed off the man who'd been holding me at my elbow.

"Damn it, girl, them's my good boots." He shoved me into a smaller room inside this one, and I saw that there were iron bars all along the perimeter. Jackson stumbled in next, and a gate closed after us, the lock clicking into place.

"You're not even going to remove my cuffs?" asked Jackson.

"Nope," said the guard, turning on his heel. "May God have mercy on your souls." *Mr. Drama, that guy.*

He closed the tall door, which scraped on the concrete floor.

"Welcome to the gang," said a voice from a dark corner, and we looked over to see Lucas, Mr. Van Doren, Darling, and Arnold Dawkins. They all sat in shadows, and all with their hands bound in shackles like ours, a curved piece of metal hinged onto a straight bar.

"I suppose you brought a key with you?" asked Mr. Dawkins.

"Not that you're not happy to see us," said Jackson, who then spit out another quarter-spot of blood.

I did my best to keep from running into Lucas's arms, but halfway through the cell I stopped caring what other people thought and just wanted to feel him. Despite the stench in the air he smelled sweet and clean, and he was as warm as I remembered.

"I missed you," I whispered.

"And I you," he said. I leaned close to kiss him and then had to calculate if we'd had our first kiss yet. Was this weird for everyone but me? I caught my breath.

"I'm glad you're okay," I said, patting him on the shoulder. And I turned around to face the others. *I have to pull myself together.*

"Other than Jackson, is everyone here okay?" I asked.

Mr. Van Doren spoke for them. "We're okay, just roughed up."

I noticed who was absent. "Did Mother and Lucille get away?" We'd just come from Mother's house, but had been driving a while before we ran into Traver.

Mr. Dawkins spoke up. "We don't know where your mother is, but we think she's safe."

Darling came up to me and had to lift both arms to pat my shoulder, shackled as they were. "If she were dead or captured he would have lorded it over us."

"And Lucille?" The mood in the room shifted around me.

"No one know," said Mr. Dawkins. "I worry she's really double-crossing us."

"But she told us where the cabin was," I said. "Why would she do that?"

"What cabin?" asked Mr. Dawkins."

The cabin discovery hasn't happened yet, idiot. This time travel crap is overrated.

"Darling, can I talk to you?"

Darling gave me a nod, and told Jackson to hush.

"Okay, so how do we get out of this, Guardian?" I asked her quietly, emphasis on "Guardian."

"Good afternoon to you, too," she said. "Traveler." She looked like she was thinking, so I let her take a moment.

"The boy who knocked down Daddy's peanut stand."

"Yes. Sorry about that."

"Oh, it was good for him to have to be nice to a stranger. But that was then." She sighed. "I don't have answers for how to get out of this, Jackie."

"I just came back yesterday."

"From my house?"

"Yes."

She nodded and took five seconds of thinking time again. If the others thought it was strange that we were huddled in the corner together, they didn't tell us that.

"Did Jackson have anything in the car that could help us?"

"I don't know what may be in the trunk, but I don't think so. You mean like guns and stuff?"

"No honey, Travelers are not supposed to use weapons except in self-defense."

"Well, what would you call this? A pre-emptive strike?"

She chuckled a little.

"I don't have magic answers for you, Jacqueline. But I could suggest you rely on the skills you already have."

"What does that even mean?" Mr. Van Doren noticed my tone and came over to us.

"Anything you should share?"

A light bulb went off over my head.

"No, we're okay. Lucas, can I see one of your braces, please?"

"Sure. Why?"

Without answering him I turned the brace upside down and popped off the leather strap where it was riveted to the metal. Underneath that I could get at a stiff wire that held the one side of the brace together, and then I started twisting the ends of the wire.

"Hold up your hands please," I told him, and he thrust his shackled arms at me. It took some tweaking, but then I heard a click inside one handcuff, and it popped open. I did his other wrist, and he was free.

"Well I'll be a monkey's uncle," said Jackson. Mr. Dawkins let out an exhale. In short order we were all unshackled, and then I started to work on the lock to our cage. This was a lot harder though, because I couldn't see the lock from behind the bars.

"What is our plan once we're out of this prison?" asked Mr. Dawkins. "We don't have any weapons."

"Our plan is to get in the car they brought here and drive away," I said. *Once I check that it will start, that is.*

They didn't look convinced. I continued to fiddle with the lock.

Jackson spoke up. "She never has much of a plan. But do any of you have better ideas?"

"I wonder how long they'll let us stew down here." I had no idea how much time I'd need to figure this out.

"Not long," said Darling, "They did say we won't be needing supper."

"Well, we won't bother them about that, then," I could feel two of the pins in the lock moving. I may have loved mechanical devices, but I was probably out of my league.

"Oh, the hell with it," said Jackson, and he ran like a bull at the cage door. It popped open with a screech of old metal.

Jackson shook his head as we gawked at him. "What? It worked, didn't it?"

"It also made significant noise," said Mr. Van Doren, but he didn't seem too worried about it.

I looked at Lucas. "Are you okay on just one brace?"

"I shall manage," he said, wiping his bangs out of his eyes. "Thank you for asking."

He took my hand, leaning on me to half-hop forward. He made eye contact with me, and I couldn't look away. "You're a very impressive woman."

"I try," I said, not knowing what else to say.

"Would that you and I could share a normal day."

"Would that." I hurt inside from not kissing him.

Mr. Van Doren rubbed his wrists and crept over to us. "I think we should head out to the loading dock. I suspect that's where your car is, Jackson."

"Is it drivable?" asked Mr. Dawkins.

"I have to check, but probably," I said.

"We need to get moving," said Jackson. "There's no telling when they'll be back."

Mr. Van Doren still liked his idea of going to the loading dock.

"We need to get the car back," said Darling, caressing her wrists where the cuffs had pinched her. "And our evidence."

This was news to me. How many things had changed between this visit and the last one I'd made to 1926? What evidence was she talking about?

"Uh, what evidence?"

Mr. Van Doren looked at the stairwell from the doorway of the holding room we were in. "Lucille found letters to and from Dr. Traver about the deaths and cover ups of Mr. Rushman and Earl. We think their bodies are somewhere on Black Mountain on the east end of the state."

"Don't we think Lucille is a double-crosser?"

"I worry about that," said Mr. Dawkins. "But the others don't agree with me."

"Why do you think that?"

"Because I can't understand how someone would leave incriminating letters in a church office for the secretary to find. I think they're a decoy to get us to reveal who is in the Underground."

Well, that made sense.

"We don't have time to chit chat, let's get out of here," said Jackson.

Quickly Jackson and Mr. Van Doren split us up into two groups. Lucas, Jackson, and Arnold Dawkins would go to the loading dock as a distraction, while I, Mr. Van Doren, and Darling would sneak back to the front to retake the car, where we could rendezvous with the others. The car wasn't really built to hold six people, but since it had no top and a rumble seat we hoped we could all pile in to escape. And then we would drive to Frankfort to talk to Mr. Dawkins's old law school classmate, the Attorney General, Frank Daugherty. We certainly couldn't go home.

We stood outside the cage, preparing to head off, and Lucas took my hand.

"Soon we won't have to engage in this nonsense anymore."

I smiled a little. "I'm so tired of running."

"Let's go, you two," said Jackson. Darling kicked him in the shin.

"You never were one for sentiment," she said.

Lucas squeezed my hand, and gave me a peck on my cheek. I wanted so much more, and at the same time I couldn't believe I could think about getting to second base with him in the midst of all this trouble. I let him go, watching him hurry away with Jackson and Arnold. He was slower without support on both sides, leaning on Arnold Dawkins, but he was Mr. Capability, and he was only a half-step off his usual speed.

Darling, Mr. Van Doren, and I huddled over at the door that was the entrance to the stairwell. Across the wide room our groups looked at each other and nodded. And then we made our jump into the unknown.

Chapter Twenty-Four

MR. VAN DOREN PUSHED THE DOOR open a few inches, and then we waited for all hell to break loose. Instead there was only silence from the stairwell. No voices, nobody running toward us, no sound of shock that we'd escaped. We crept up the first flight, pausing on the landing where Jackson had fallen earlier. Mr. Van Doren went first, looking up toward the next floor for any activity.

We hunkered down inside the doorframe at the top of the stairs, peeking out into the hall. They had gathered in a room to our right, halfway down the hall. Across from their room was the front door, which Mr. Van Doren pointed to, as if Darling and I needed his help to see the total freaking obvious. I held up my crude lock pick, praying it could work in reverse to set the lock and perhaps slow them down until we could reach the car, which we saw was sitting in the broad parking lot, now unhooked from the tow. *At least we don't have to manage that.* He nodded at me. One by one we crawled down the hallway, hugging the wall next to the stairs, and then we bolted for the front door, some twenty feet away.

We had nearly reached the front door before Traver's gang noticed, but then they leapt into action. All I had was one thought: *Crap. Damn shitknuckles.*

Darling was first to the car. She moved faster than lightning. A single man sat in the driver's seat, possibly trying to get the engine to start or figure out what the line of dashboard gadgets did.

"Hallelujah, look at me!"

She was yelling and running straight at him, waving her arms like she was capable of blocking a shot on a basketball court, despite her five-foot frame.

"I'm talking to you! Yes you!"

Sitting there slack-jawed, he was completely unprepared for what happened next. She punched him on the side of his head, right in the eye socket.

I might have screamed a little.

For his part, he collapsed onto the seat. Mr. Van Doren looked shocked, too. *At least it's not just me.*

I shut the door as fast as I could, fumbling to get the lock pick in the keyhole. I had wedged my foot against the bottom of the door when the first thump fell from the other side. With one hand I held the pick and with my other, I guided it to the hole. I wouldn't be able to hold this door for more than two seconds unless I could break the pins inside. From a window to the side of the front door, I saw Dr. Traver leering at me, his anger at me plain and intense. He pounded on the glass. They were like zombies, ready for some good ole human brains.

The pick slipped in, and I twisted it hard, feeling the works inside go crunch.

I turned and ran as hard as my legs could manage. Mr. Van Doren and Darling had thrown the would-be driver onto the parking lot surface, where he still looked completely confused about what had just happened to him.

"Open the hood," I shouted. Mr. Van Doren looked confused for one second and then folded it back.

I ran up to the engine and saw that as predicted, the manifold had come off and was hanging by one line. I shoved wires in place as fast as I could, hearing the pounding on the door behind me. I was in mid-air, jumping in over the door into the driver's seat, when the first shot rang out. They'd shot their way out of the building. *Terrific.*

"All this hard work and they just shoot it up," I said, fumbling with the starter. Darling and Mr. Van Doren tumbled into the car, which rumbled but resisted firing. My heart pounded as the engine cranked. The men ran toward us. Fifty yards away.

"Come on, come on," I said to the car.

"It's a good time to get going," said Darling.

"What a hilarious lady you are," I said.

Mr. Van Doren put his body in front of Darling and mentioned that we should move.

Crank, crank, crank. Crap, something else must be wrong. Ten yards, one of them got down on one knee and aimed his shotgun at us.

"Please," I said, as if that would make any difference to the engine inside. An image of a faraway Catholic school in Ohio, one that wouldn't be built for another twenty years, sprang into my mind, reminding me of the easy life I'd once lived.

Ha. Nothing was simple now.

"Saint Catherine of Alexandria," I shouted.

Finally, the engine caught, and I popped the transmission into gear, squealing off across the parking lot around the corner of the building. The gunman tried to follow us with his barrel but missed us by quite a bit. *Amateurs!*

"Who is that?" asked Darling.

"Patron saint of car mechanics," I said, aiming for the loading dock. Their shots whizzed past us, but Mr. Van Doren groaned.

"I've been hit." He held onto his right shoulder, dark red blood streaming down his arm, squeezing out from between his clenched fingers. Darling, from the back seat, put pressure on his wound and apologized for causing him any more pain.

"Go," said Lucas's father, but I was already speeding off, skittering around the corner of the building, where a hundred yards away we could see Jackson, Lucas, and Mr. Dawkins, hunkered down behind a stack of moldering wooden crates, as four of Dr. Traver's guards sprayed bullets at them.

"Hold on," I told my passengers. Mr. Van Doren was putting up a good fight, but the color was draining out of his face.

"We'll be shot to pieces," said Darling, leaning over Mr. Van Doren, like his bodyguard.

I could barely get my sentence out before we were directly in the field of fire.

"I have a plan." *Always with the stupid plans.*

I drove straight toward the men and their guns, calling for my passengers to slide down in their seats, which they did mostly on their own anyway. This totally stupid strategy surprised the shooters, who needed a little bit of time to adjust, and decide if they should hold their ground and fire at their new target, or run.

Two of them hurried back to the building. Peeking her head up a little Darling watched them, and said to me, "Like rats fleeing a fire." One of them tried to take shots at us, but his magazine jammed and with his gun useless, he launched himself to the side so he wouldn't get run over by me. But the last man dropped his weapon and jumped into the car, right up over the hood, landing in the back seat, next to Darling.

He lunged at me from behind, clawing at my throat. Pain pierced my voice box and I felt faint. *No, no, no,* I thought, *I can't jump now, there's too much at stake.* Then the pressure disappeared, all in a moment. It took me a long second to realize I was still driving the car, and I hadn't left. I turned at the last instant before we hit the old tannery building, and I took a glance at the back seat, where Darling had him in a vice grip, some kind of turnabout in which his neck was trapped in the tiny crook of her elbow. *Do not mess with the Guardians, apparently.*

I spun around, seeing that the two men in the doorway were readying their guns again. I flipped a switch and toggled a lever on the dash, the guard doing his best to distract me by thrashing, and Mr. Van Doren holding a blood-stained handkerchief to his wound. I didn't know what such a small square of cloth was supposed to do for him, but it did seem that the flow had subsided a little.

Before he could ask me what I was preparing, two canisters shot out from the front fender of the car and rolled over to them, which they looked at with heads tilted, like curious dogs. Small pops from each of them and thick smoke billowed out, and I headed right for the crates where our friends were stationed.

The guards at the building coughed and shouted to each other as the white cloud filled the air in front of them. I positioned the car behind the crates, where Mr. Dawkins and Jackson hauled the interloper out, dumping him on the ground and climbing in.

"I could have used you in the trenches," said Jackson from the seat behind me.

"You served in the Navy," said Darling.

"So I did."

Just then Dr. Traver and his other henchmen came bounding around the side of the building in two cars.

"Get in," I said to Lucas, who was having trouble scrambling to his feet from where he had crouched. He saw the waxy complexion on his father's face and the broad stain on his shoulder.

"Father!"

Mr. Van Doren told him in a scratchy voice that he was fine, and then the next series of events happened almost at once—Lucas grabbed on to the rumble seat at the back, his legs dragging on the ground behind us because I just couldn't wait any longer, as Dr. Traver was almost upon us. I peeled out, leaving the hot stench of rubber in our nostrils. Lucas held on to the car, managing to climb into the rumble seat. Many more pops from the thugs' guns echoed off the building walls, making it difficult to count how many bullets were heading our way. Lucas made a gurgling sound and slumped over in the seat far enough that I worried he'd fall to the ground. Jackson reached back to grab his shoulder and held him in the car.

I don't remember shouting, but I must have because later I was hoarse, although maybe it was from my neck being so sore after my attack.

Jackson picked up the thug's shotgun from the floor of the backseat and fired twice, taking out the tires from Dr. Traver's car. It ground to a halt and the other car crashed into it and fell over on its side.

Dr. Traver screamed at the driver who tried in vain to explain that without wheels they weren't going anywhere.

Then Dr. Traver shot the driver in the head, and aimed next at us. *Holy shit. He's a lunatic.*

I dropped the car into third gear, then fourth, as we sped back up the driveway to the old factory, and it was only once we were out of sight that anyone said anything at all.

"Well done," said Jackson.

"I wouldn't go that far," I said. I wished I had a rear-view mirror to use, because I wanted to see how everyone was doing. *Lucas. How was Lucas?*

We were ten miles out and the gas gauge blinked at me. *Good glory hell, why is the gas tank so tiny?* I pulled onto a wider road, hoping that it led to a populated area. Maybe even one with a doctor who wasn't a psychopath or the town drunk, or both. Mr. Van Doren seemed to be holding his own. But turning around I saw that Lucas was in terrible shape. Darling and Arthur Dawkins were trying to hold him together.

"Where is he hit?" I asked. The engine grumbled; I was running out of gas, and there was no town in sight. Just mountains that in any other circumstance I would think were beautiful. Cattle. Green fields and thick woods. Lucas was going to die here. *I can't let Lucas die.*

"One shot through his leg," said Darling, "that seems to have kept on going into the seat. One bullet in his side, and one in his chest."

His chest. Three bullets and no hospital, no trauma team. No oxygen, or blood transfusions. No penicillin to stem infection, for that matter.

"Just hold on," said Mr. Dawkins to Lucas. Lucas tried to speak, a trickle of blood making its way from the corner of his mouth.

"Don't worry about me," he said, his voice low. The engine sputtered, the new turbocharger unable to help with no gas.

"Keep going," I said to the car. All of my little gadgets and skills and I couldn't have seen some way out of this disaster? "Keep going!"

Mr. Van Doren turned around in his seat, wincing as he moved. "Lucas?"

No answer from the back of the car. Darling and Mr. Dawkins shook their heads at each other. At last the engine gave out, having run itself dry, and we lost speed until we were stopped, leaning half-in a ditch on the side of the road. My throat closed up.

"Lucas," I called out. "You have to hang on!" *For what, hang on? For some country veterinarian to tell me he's dead?*

"Lucas," I said, reaching behind me to touch him. I flailed in the air; the rumble seat was too far away for me to reach him.

I faced forward again, as if there was anything ahead of me that could help us. I jumped out of my seat and ran around to take his hand. His eyes were glassy, nothing in them except a dull reflection of myself. He was gone. I needed to roll back time once more. Or I needed to just stop. Maybe this wasn't a house fire, but Lucas was gone all the same. Watching him die like this, it was worse somehow. I screamed to nobody in particular.

"Jacqueline, we still need help for his father," said Mr. Dawkins in a quiet tone, as if I were liable to explode again. In the front passenger seat sat Lucas's father, crying silently into one hand. I didn't begin to know how to comfort him.

"We're out of fuel. I don't know what to do," I said.

Darling gently took my hand off of Lucas's, and she closed his eyes for him. We hadn't seen a car or wagon the whole time we sat at the edge of the ditch next to the road.

Jackson climbed out of the vehicle and headed off, in the direction we'd been traveling.

"Where are you going?" I asked him.

"I think I know where we are," he said, not breaking his pace. He walked with his hands in his pockets, which stiffened his gait and made him seem more like an old man. I watched him walk away and searched my mind for what to do next. Eventually he reached the top of the rise in the ground, and then each step drew him more out of my view. First his legs were gone, then his torso, and then his crop of strawberry blond hair.

I looked at Mr. Van Doren, not sure what to say to him. He put his good arm around me and drew me in, and we stayed there for many minutes, while Darling and Arthur gingerly lifted Lucas out of the car. I wanted to say something to him. Anything.

"We can't leave him to the wolves," I said, thinking of my own encounters with the animals in the Kentucky woods.

Darling looked at me sternly. "We would never do that," she said. "We just need to move him while he's limber." *Oh, wow. No. No. NO.*

Mr. Van Doren cried out at that, trying unsuccessfully to swallow the noise. A small tree stood nearby so we found a spot under it and sat in silence. As if our thoughts would contaminate the group of us, we didn't talk to each other. Hours passed and the dark crept in, and it got colder and colder until my bones hurt and my legs went numb. I cried until I was dry.

The fight had gone out of us, at least until we heard the low-pitched rumble of an engine, coming at us from beyond the hill ahead, two headlights cutting out ahead of it. My pulse pounded. I couldn't think of what to do before the truck was upon us.

Jackson sat in the passenger seat, waving us off from attacking them, which we were already not prepared to do, and in the driver's seat was Mother, hair tied in her usual tight bun, wearing a flowered housedress and the widest smile I'd ever seen on her face. The pickup truck sputtered and coughed as it speeded toward us, but the down slope of the hill gave it some extra momentum.

Mother did not appear particularly capable of driving, but I presumed she'd insisted on it. Off in the distance I heard a roll of thunder.

She continued to bounce down the slope, headed straight for us. I waved at her, which in hindsight I suppose amounted to nothing more than stupid hope that she could correctly steer away from us. Hopefully we weren't about to get steamrolled.

At the last instant, just as Jackson was reaching over to grab the wheel from her, my mother yanked hard to the side, driving into the field and scattering road dirt all over us. I coughed and took swipes at my head to get the dust out of my hair.

"You're too late," I told them. "He's . . . Lucas is gone."

She got out of the car without putting it in park, leaving Jackson to slam on the brakes from his side of the seat. Then I was enveloped in her arms.

"I'm so sorry about Lucas," she said with her head next to mine. Without meaning to I cried into her shoulder. *Guess I could find more liquid in me after all.*

"It's all my fault," I said.

"None of this is your fault, child. God will bring justice to Lucas's killers." Justice would need to seek me out as well, then. But I didn't want to argue with her.

I pulled away. Above us the sky had darkened, waves of thunder continuing to echo from miles away, headed in our general direction. It was hard to tell in the bad light where the edge between the clouds and the nighttime was.

"I can't wait for God," I said. "Every moment that goes by, more people die or disappear. When does it end?"

Jackson popped out of the vehicle and grabbed something from the truck bed. A can of gas. Arthur pulled off the cap and began filling up my car, and Jackson and Lucas's father placed his body in the back of the truck, loading him in with kid gloves again, and then covering him with a blanket. I heaved in a couple quarts of air or whatever it takes to fill two lungs.

"We have to stop them," I said, sure that nobody was listening to me anymore.

Darling walked up to me.

"We will stop them, Jacqueline, but first things first. We need to bury Lucas. How many times have you failed to stop Dr. Traver from his evil work?"

"Twice. Although so far this time fewer people have . . . died." I swallowed hard.

She looked at me and I tried to figure out what expression she had. Sadness? Wisdom? Frustration? If she was a Guardian, why didn't she have answers?

"Honey, you need to go back earlier then. Find Dr. Traver before he became Dr. Traver. And stop looking to me to be some magical black woman, because I am too tired to be that for you."

"I just don't know what I'm doing."

She smiled at that. "I keep telling you, you are more capable than you credit yourself. Now let's put that sweet boy that you love so much to rest."

In the back of Mother's truck, they'd piled a few spades and shovels. We moved them to the side and gently lowered Lucas into the bed.

I looked at him again, like he was just sleeping, and the rain fell down on us.

CHAPTER TWENTY-FIVE

MR. VAN DOREN TOLD US he knew where Lucas would have wanted to be buried. I didn't have any image in my head of where that could be until the familiar line of trees cropped up on the horizon, and then I understood: these were the woods where we'd met. I couldn't imagine holding sacred a place where I'd sustained a life-threatening injury, but Lucas's dad was allowed his preference.

The rain tapered off, then strengthened again, but we were determined not to let it slow us down. We'd drawn a thick canvas over the top of the car, and as the storm dragged on it sagged under the weight of the water. Why these cars didn't include roofs, I didn't know. All this effort over insignificant horse power increases, and nobody thought, "Put in a freaking roof"?

Arthur and Jackson finished digging a hole that seemed too small for Lucas. I realized that the whole moment lacked any sense of ritual. In Catholic school I learned there was always a ritual, and a garment, and frankincense. *I wish Pie was here.* I wanted to ride as far as her muscles could take me. If only I could just disappear again and forget. Maybe this was part of being a Traveler.

Arthur and Jackson lowered Lucas into the ground, which was saturated from the pouring rain. Lucas's father stood over his son, unable to help with his wounded arm. There was no way to cover Lucas gently. My eyes lost focus as they shoveled black dirt over him, making his skin messy and then hiding him. It was close to dawn by the time we finished. I walked away from the group, but I only made it to the next shade tree over. I'd thought I had so much time, time to spend with Lucas once we exposed Dr. Traver and instead he was gone from me. If all of my efforts ended in disaster, what was the point?

Darling walked up after me after they were done filling in the earth.

"There will be a day, a long time from now, when you will notice you feel a little better," she said, her arm around my shoulders.

"No, Darling, I won't ever feel any better."

"As a Traveler, you will have more grief to handle than most. And sometimes you will grieve a loss that later will never have occurred. You need to become as strong as the forest here."

"Strong for what? Lucas is dead, his father is shot, and still Traver has all these people in his grip. What are we supposed to do now?"

"All of this force from the man, it means he's losing."

"Losing? Lucas is gone! I want him back! I . . . I need him." I was so weak.

"You have not made contact with your Guardian in your own time. You've been on your own. But you're not alone. You remember what I said earlier, on the road?" She looked worried for me.

I nodded, biting my lip.

"You find out why this man turned to such evil. I think that is the key."

"I am so tired of fighting, Darling. If I'm not all alone, why is it all up to me to stop him? And I think he knows about Guardians and Travelers somehow."

"That's possible."

"Possible? How can you not know?"

She frowned at me, her wire-rimmed glasses slipping down her nose a little.

"Child, you mind your elders and don't speak to me that way. I already told you I don't know everything, I provide guidance and some protection."

"Protection for me or from me?"

"Both," she said. I didn't like her answer. Lucas was gone and now I was being lectured?

I wrenched out of her hold and fought my way through thick brambles to reach the next tree, a long oak. The flash of white light that took over my vision didn't even register as lightning at first. I had a fraction of a second to realize I'd been struck dead on, the current running the length of my body, down through my left heel, sucked into the ground.

In an instant, I was gone.

* * *

I blinked, adjusting to the dark, and was met with a glop of black oil on my face, which I half-inhaled. Coughing and sputtering, I pushed out from under the car, two other grime-covered people laughing at me. I knew this mechanic's shop. I went to rub my eyes because the car on the lift was wild-looking to me, but I stopped before I smeared any more slime on myself. This was going to be the worst post-nasal drip ever.

"Who opens the oil pan while he's in the way?" said one man, a squat fellow with hair as black as the waste I'd just snorted. All of us wore blue jump suits with our names sewn on the front. I looked down and saw "Jack" on mine. His read "Armand," and the other fellow, who moved lizard-slow, even as he was laughing, had a tag with "Frank" on it. These were the guys who'd worked in my Dad's auto body shop.

"It's dark down there," I said, trying not to show that I was startled by my deep voice. "Can someone grab me a light?"

"Sure, here you go," said Frank, pulling a lamp down from the ceiling. It was attached to a pulley and could be set at any height. "You feeling okay?"

"I'm fine." I thought I should duck back under the car so I could collect my thoughts in semi-privacy, but apparently these two were used to chit-chat.

"He used to get the shakes as a kid," Armand said to Frank, as if I weren't even in the room. "Remember that, Jack?"

"Yup." Already I didn't much care for Armand.

"You didn't have one of them there fits down there, did you?"

I leveled my stare at him. "Seizures, Armand. They're not fits or shakes, they're seizures. And no, I didn't have one just now."

"Geez, someone's a little pissy today."

Really?

"I had a rough night. Go easy on me today, okay?"

"No problem, Jack. Whatever you say." He shook his head a little, presumably writing me off. "Rough night, I bet," he said under his breath. I needed to find Jeannine and Sanjay. They'd know what was going on.

Some kind of electronic synthesizer started beeping, and Frank moved like a glacier to the desk in the corner. Turns out it was a phone. Like, without a bell. *Ugh, whatever. I need to find out about Lucas and find my Guardian.*

Armand was on the plastic phone.

"Yes, ma'am, you can bring your car in later this week. Let's see, it's March—"

I glanced at the calendar on the wall next to the desk, where he pointed as he spoke. My eyes read the numbers in the year.

1992.

It was 1992. It had been nine years since I jumped back the last time. I did the math in my head. I was twenty-six years old.

"Look guys, I'm not feeling well. Do you mind if I head out for the rest of the day?"

Armand and Frank exchanged glances. Armand answered me, being quicker to speak.

"Sure, sure. You want us to just lock up at five?"

"That would be fantastic."

I'd presumed one or the other of these guys was my boss. I walked out of the car bay and looked at the shop from the outside. A bold neon sign ran the width of the garage: *Inman & Son Auto Service*

I started walking, not sure where I was in town, or even if I was in the same town as a decade ago.

"Uh," Frank began, "don't you want to take your car?" He pointed, raising his finger at a black Mustang with silver racing stripes. We must be doing well for ourselves.

"I sure do," I said, feeling for keys in my pockets. Armand snatched up a key ring from the desk and tossed them over to me.

"Thanks," I said. "Catch you guys tomorrow."

"Feel better, man," said Armand. Frank nodded slowly.

I drove off, hoping I'd picked a direction that made sense.

Ten blocks or so away, I came to an intersection I remembered. I flicked the turn signal, and made a right, and then I was back to my development, which had not aged well in the last decade. Yellowed lawns and faded siding gave the street a washed-out, tired look. All of the cars had turned over from what used to be parked here when I was in high school, so I couldn't determine if the same families or new ones lived in these homes now. I drove to the middle of the block, noting that concrete sidewalks were crumbling away. I knocked on the door to my old house, presuming I couldn't just walk inside. There was a deadbolt installed in the front door that hadn't been there before. No answer. I tried the doorbell, but it didn't work. Maybe I should leave a note. I considered looking in through the window to the side of the front door, but didn't want any of the neighbors to think I was an intruder.

From inside the house, I heard movement, and then someone fumbling with the locks. An older woman greeted me.

"Can I help you, young man?"

"I was wondering, did you know the Inmans who lived here?" I asked.

"The Inmans? Oh, the family from this house. No, I didn't know them. They were the sellers, though." She waited for me to ask another question or bid her good day.

"Thank you. Do you by any chance know where they moved?"

She narrowed her eyes at me. "Now why would you want to know that, son? What was is your name?"

"Lucas Van Doren," I said without pausing. "I'm an old friend of Jack's." *Close to true.*

"Oh, the boy. Well, I suppose you could find out at the county office that they bought another home in Lakewood. Is that all? *General Hospital* is on."

I thanked her and went across the street to find out if Jeannine or Sanjay's families were still here. Jeannine's family had moved away, but Sanjay's mother greeted me and seemed happier to see me than ever before. Perhaps the intervening years had made her like me more.

"Sanjay is studying civil engineering at Columbia," she said with a clap and a smile. New York City. It was the first easy to follow lead I'd gotten, and with a car as fun to drive as my Mustang, I hopped onto the I-90 and drove across Ohio and New York, and found the university in a matter of hours.

Except Sanjay wasn't studying engineering, wasn't even a student there.

* * *

I found him in a small, dingy coffee shop in the East Village, seated around a communal table with half a dozen other people, none of whom I knew. I waved at him, trying to find a way to break into their intense conversation. One of them, a petite woman with very short hair and black plastic glasses, sneered at me, then tapped Jay on the arm. "This strange man seems to want your attention." I was still wearing my mechanic's uniform. I didn't exactly fit in.

Jay started talking before he saw me. "Look, if you're here to harass us, we don't—Jack?"

"Hey, Jay, can we talk?"

"His name is Sanjay," said the woman in the glasses. "Don't Anglicize him."

"Corrine, it's okay," he said. "I'll be right back."

"This is important," she said.

He nodded, reassuring her, then pushed back from the table, squeaking on the old linoleum floor. We walked outside and stood on the sidewalk, where I marveled at how much had changed since the early 1980s. The cars were all ugly as hell, for one.

"What are you doing here, man? How did you find me?" Jay asked, looking around as if spies were scoping us out from the corner.

"Why haven't you told your mother you dropped out of school? I went to the engineering school and two of your classmates said I'd find you here."

"You're stalking me? Don't tell my mother." He crossed his arms. After all these years, this wasn't the conversation I thought we'd be having.

"No, I just wanted to see you. What are you up to these days?"

"Seriously, Jack, nobody does hot and cold like you do."

"I've only just now jumped back."

He inhaled and dropped his arms. "Wow. It's been how long now?"

"Nine years?"

"Nine years. Shit, that's a long time."

"I didn't think I'd lose that much time. I apologize for anything I've done in the interim that hurt you."

Jay laughed, then looked at the door to the coffee house. "You want blanket immunity? You haven't done me wrong, Jack." *That's good to know,* I thought. "But you haven't been around, you're so focused on your job and your parents."

I jumped in my skin.

"Are they okay?"

"Yeah, yeah, sure, they're fine. I think you bought them a nicer house in some posh suburb. I really wish my parents would move, our home town isn't a good place to be anymore."

I nodded, telling him I'd seen it.

"Who are those people in there?" I asked.

"Oh, that's the ACT UP group," he said. He noticed my blank look. "Right, you jumped in '83. I don't have time to explain AIDS to you, man, but people are dying from a virus, a really bad one. My friends are dying, I lost my partner two years ago, and the politicians are like just ignoring this epidemic. So engineering can wait. It's why I dropped out of school."

"You're doing okay, though? You don't have this AIDS thing?"

"Watch how you talk, Jack," he said, checking out the people around us again. "A lot of people in the Village would be offended if they thought you were making light of it. Thousands of people have died in the last twelve years. It's a . . . really terrible way to die."

"I'm sorry. That's awful."

He gave me a brief hug. "You don't even know. Straight people treat gay people like lepers now, tell us it's our fault we're sick. Look, I have to get back to it. You want to catch up? Meet me back here in an hour, and we can get a beer."

I nodded, and walked back to my car a few blocks away. Gay people versus straight people? Lepers? Synthesizer phones? I pulled down the vanity mirror over the steering wheel and checked myself out. I had really packed on some muscle. If I bent my elbows my biceps pushed against the sleeves of my overalls. My jaw seemed wider, and unzipping my uniform a few inches I saw I was covered with almost as much chest hair as a chimpanzee. From ear to ear I had black stubble on my face, but my eyes looked the same, thank god. I looked at the car clock. Forty-eight minutes to meet Jay. I shut my eyes and even though I was stressed and sick about Lucas, I fell asleep. It was the line of drool down my chin that woke me up, and I checked the clock on my dashboard. I sprang out of the car and raced to the corner. Sanjay stood there, frowning when he saw me.

"I was about to give up on your punk ass," he said.

"I'm glad you waited."

"Let's get a drink," said Jay, and I followed him. He pushed open a heavy, tall door and then we were inside a dark bar. A counter ran the length of the narrow space, and I flashed back to the marble counter at Mr. Van Doren's tavern pre-Prohibition. I turned to Sanjay.

"So you're still gay, huh?"

He smiled. "Still gay. Super gay, even." We sat down at the bar. He ordered a beer, and I asked for a soda. When he raised an eyebrow in my direction, I explained that I'd never actually had any alcohol. I didn't even know what to order or what I would like.

"Well, I know what I like," he said, raising his glass.

We talked about life after high school, how he loved the city.

"It's overwhelming to me."

"Really?" he asked. "All the people?"

"All the people, how packed in everything is, all the smells."

"Please honey, you're not even here in summer. Then it really takes on some precious new odors."

"I guess I'm not used to it."

"I guess not. It grows on you. Like a fungus!" Jay laughed, and the bartender rolled his eyes.

"You know everyone here, eh?"

"It gets easier to know people when the community gets smaller every day," he said, turning grim.

"You seem so grown up, Jay. Sanjay." He waved me off.

"You can call me Jay, it's all right. Liberal white people get way more offended about it than I do."

I nodded, trying to follow along with him. His next question threw me well off track.

"So what's it like being back in your body instead of that girl's?"

"Jeannine told you?" I asked, attempting to sound casual.

He swallowed hard, but hadn't sipped at anything. "Yes, she did. It must have been an adjustment."

"It was, at first," I said. I played with the base of my pint glass. "And then I was okay with it." *And I never minded it when I was curled into Lucas. In fact I like it a lot.*

Jay leaned in toward me. "Did you like it better?"

"I've never thought of it that way. I don't really know. I fell in love back there, though."

"You did? But wait, if you were a girl, did that make you a lesbian?"

I grinned. "His name was Lucas."

"Ooh, there's hope for you yet." He sipped at his beer, wiping the foam off of his lip.

Lucas in past tense. I watched them bury him. I have to undo his death. I can't take it.

"He died."

Jay looked at me, and I worried he was going to tease me or call me crazy.

"Jack, I'm so sorry. That's really hard."

"I'm sorry you lost your partner."

"The country is such a fucking mess, man."

"I should see what Jeannine thinks about all of this," I said, running my finger along the top of my glass.

He sighed, pulling his glasses off and wiping them with the tail of his shirt. "Well, you can't do that, Jack. Jeannine's dead."

Chapter Twenty-Six

HE OPENED THE DOOR a little at a time, stopping after only a few inches. The wharf smell hanging in the air from Lake Erie was more intense inside the warehouse where he lived. Maybe he didn't notice it anymore. He was smaller than I remembered, and disheveled, and smelled funky.

The bottom of the door scraped along the entryway floor, carving itself along a well-worn groove in the tile.

"Well, I wondered when you would turn up again," said Dr. Dorfman. His thick mutton chop sideburns were gone, as was most of the hair on his head. Only his eyes defied his age, hedged in as they were with deep wrinkles that pointed to them like arrows.

"It's good to see you," I said, glancing around the room. It smelled terrible in here. His home was some kind of half-converted warehouse in the industrial district of Cincinnati, a mixture of reheated takeout and whatever wafted in from the waterway outside, none of which smelled good.

"Mm, is it?" he asked. He directed me to sit down. I found a spot on his couch that seemed the least dirty. "You're a dainty thing for such a strapping young man."

"If I knew how to respond to that, I would," I said. "I know it's been a long time."

Dr. Dorfman dropped himself into an old easy chair across from me. The armrests had been shredded, the back cushion held together with half a roll of duct tape.

"Yes, Jack, it has. A very long time. I'm glad you're well. You look well." He said all of this like he didn't particularly mean it.

"I suppose I am. I wouldn't know. I only just jumped back two days ago."

Now he sat forward, and his cheek twitched.

"You don't say. Two days. That's a long jump for this side." For some reason he untied and retied his shoes. "Damn laces always coming undone." I'd never heard him swear before. I played with my hands in my lap.

"You see," he said to me, his head still bowed toward his shoes, "I know you're just a figment of my imagination. You're not real, Jack."

"I promise, I'm real."

"No, you're a fantasy. It's okay. Sometimes I talk to you, and my doctor says that's okay. Time travel is a great idea, and it's even theoretically possible, but nobody's done it, not least a little boy in a neurological study I conducted twelve years ago. So have a nice day, Jack. You can leave now."

"But I'm actually here, doctor. You helped me jump back before, about nine years ago."

"Yes, yes I did. I even escaped from the hospital and corralled you poor kids into that house, to keep my delusion going. I'm sorry I behaved that way."

He refused to make eye contact with me. Sanjay had told me the doctor had come up with this plot of taking responsibility for leaving the ward so that none of us would get in trouble. But Jay hadn't realized that Dr. Dorfman believed the lie at this point.

"You have nothing to be sorry for," I said, and he cut me off.

"Now, now, here you go, getting me all confused about what's right and what's wrong. It's time for you to leave, Jack." He stood up, waving me toward the door.

"Dr. Dorfman, I have questions for you." I couldn't go like this.

"Later, Jack, they'll have to come later. I want you to leave."

"Dr. Dorfman," I began, but he cut me off.

"Leave!" He clenched his eyes shut, gripping his ears with his thin hands, his skin translucent enough to show the blood thumping through his veins. "Leave, leave, leave!"

I stood up. "Okay, I'm going. Stop shouting at me."

I walked through the creaky warehouse, the floorboards giving way to poured concrete and then the few scraped tiles by his door. It was then that I saw the bookcase, filled with dust and medical textbooks, and one journal that caught my eye. The journal from his study that I used to see him scribble in at the ends of our sessions. He stopped groaning, checking to see if his delusion still stood in his home.

"Oh, you came for it, didn't you? Just like the others."

I turned to face him. "Others?"

"Yes, years ago now. They took all of my notebooks, but they didn't take *the* notebook."

"I don't understand."

"How can my own imagination not understand?" He looked about to begin moaning again.

"No, no, I get you. The notebook. The important one, right?"

"I knew, I knew," he said. "I would get confused soon. I should call my doctor."

"Why didn't they take the notebook?" I asked, figuring I already knew the answer.

"Oh, Jackie Jack," he said, walking over to me, "you are a stubborn delusion today. They didn't find it because it was hidden."

"You're a smart fellow, doctor."

"That's right."

"Doctor, I'll make you a promise," I said.

"What's that?"

"Let me take this notebook and I'll never come back again."

He considered my proposal. "Since you're only in my imagination, I'm not really giving you the notebook, I suppose." Another pause as he stroked his chin. "Deal."

I shut the door as hard as I could so that he would know his dream state was over.

It was my fault that I'd ruined him. And all of my going back and forth wasn't making any of this any better. Not only did I need to stop Lucas from dying, but I wanted to see if there was anything I could do to save Jeannine, and now Dr. Dorfman.

I really hate time travel.

Where is my damn Guardian?

* * *

The cemetery crept up the side of a bright green hill, small slabs of granite poking out of the short grass. From a distance it could have been Easter Island for all I knew, but it was peppered with gifts left by the living: bright flowers, a teddy bear, rocks set at the tops of some grave markers. I'd never thought about who came to these places, or what it would feel like to be a visitor in a graveyard.

Birds chirped in the trees around me. I searched through the rows of markers, trying to orient myself with the map the groundskeeper had handed me, but I wound up navigating by date of death. And there it was—Jeannine's tombstone. I sat down on the lawn.

Jay had told me the story, mostly said through rough swallows of his throat. Helping out a stranger with a flat tire, her back to the road, she'd been struck by a truck driver who didn't see her in her dark clothes. She'd pulled over because the driver of the wayward car was elderly and looked distraught. But the woman hadn't driven her car far enough to the shoulder. Perhaps Jeannine should have known better, should have moved the car herself. We would all make different choices if we could roll back time. Except I had direct experience with that crap. Shit never works out anyway.

"I'm so sorry, Jeannine," I said to the carved stone. Jeannine Maria Hernandez. August 14, 1964–March 18, 1989. Beloved daughter and wife. Standing up, I touched the stone, and tiny flecks of it came off on my fingerprints. Someday, I knew, weathering would erase this rock. At the foot of the marker I left a small bouquet of daffodils, her favorite flower. I touched the top of her marker and tried to push away the image of her dead, buried a few feet under me.

"I'm going to fix this, Jeannine." I tried to believe myself.

* * *

The garage doors were shut on my car shop and the neon open sign unlit, so I unlocked the side entry and let myself in. I thumbed through the card index at the edge of my desk. Everything, including this, had a thin film of oil, grease, or lubricant on it. I wasn't the cleanest mechanic around. I found the phone number for my parents and noticed that the phone had push buttons on it instead of a rotary dial. Also my index finger could hit two buttons at a time, it was so big. There was too much junk to adjust to in this time.

My father picked up. "Hey, Jack, how are you? When are you coming over for supper?"

"When works for you, Dad?" I tried to sound as casual as possible.

"Oh," he said, sounding like he was looking over toward my mother to assess her condition, "any evening is fine. How about tonight?"

"Sounds good. Everything okay over there?"

"Sure! The shop okay?"

I wasn't sure if Armand or Frank had said anything to him. I'd called them saying I was going to be out all week.

"It's fine. I took a couple days off because I haven't had a vacation in a while." *I hope that's true.*

"Well, you're entitled to it, Jack. Everyone needs a little R&R sometimes. Just don't forget nobody will take care of the place like you will."

This must be why Dad never took vacations, I thought. That and he didn't know how to be close to his wife.

"Okay, I'll see you tonight around six."

"Love you, son," he said. How long had it been since I'd heard that from him?

"I love you too, Dad."

I set the receiver down and looked at my desk. No pictures of any loved ones. No trinkets or personal touches. Maybe those weren't things to be found at a tough man's work area. Also no ring on my finger. All the time in Jacqueline's life expressing emotions, experiencing things from her perspective, now this body felt foreign to me. *Who is Jack? What am I about?* If I could help prevent suffering, why had I only made things worse?

Lucas and Jeannine were dead. I shouldn't blame myself about Jeannine, but I was sure her death was connected to me in some way. Dr. Dorfman's life was a shambles, and Sanjay seemed happy but also very angry and grieving for the loss of his friends and boyfriend. Could I bear to go see my parents?

I fumbled through the mail that had piled up, and I found a utility bill for my parents' house. I tucked the address into my pocket, and drove to a hotel I'd seen on the highway. There was no point in finding my own home. The doctor's notebook turned out to be full of nonsense—rambling, scrawly handwriting about physics and string theory and then a bunch of shit about aliens. I felt responsible that he'd lost everything, but man, what a waste of time trying to get my hands on absolutely nothing.

* * *

The house looked pleasant: brick with brown shutters and a wide door at the front, nestled between two evergreens. I knocked on the door and let myself inside. Calling out to let them know I was there was met with silence. Sweat popped up on my forehead as I made my way through the kitchen and family room. *I hope this is the right place.*

I saw them sitting out on the porch, laughing. Laughing. I slid the door aside and joined them.

An older man reclined on a long chair.

"Hi Mom, hi Dad," I said.

"Well, don't leave out your namesake," said the man. I blinked.

"Grandfather. Hello."

My mother stood up, stretching her arms out for a hug. She was warm and smelled like coffee grounds and perfume.

"How are you, Mom?"

"Oh, fine," she said. Seeing my shock, she tousled my hair. "I'm going to get dinner started." My father headed to a charcoal grill on the other side of the porch, fiddling with the coals.

"Come sit with me," said Jackson. *He shouldn't be alive.* I took the chair next to him.

"Well, hello," I said.

"You look like you've seen a ghost," he said, smiling.

"It's good to see you. And the last time I left . . . well, Mom is happy. I can't remember ever seeing her happy and ..."

"Lucid?"

"Yes," I said, stopping because I was choking up. He put his hand on mine and patted me.

"Imagine my surprise when my daughter had a baby boy."

"Oh, right. About that—"

"It doesn't matter, Jack. I am so grateful I've had all this time."

I considered him. His ears looked floppier than when he was in his youth; he was less tan, the skin under his chin not very attached to his head. Maybe he'd spent less time in the sun. He'd kept all of his hair, which had gone white. The staring got to him.

"What?" he demanded.

"Has anyone told you that you look like Nick Lowe?"

"You're the first. This isn't what we should be talking about."

"You're right, grandpa," I said, marveling at the word. I'd never used it before. "It's good to see you. Again."

"I'm really glad to see you, though you know, I've watched you grow up."

I nodded. "Have we discussed our past before?"

"This is the first time you've brought it up," he said. "I've been waiting. I'm a Guardian now, so I felt you come through."

I thought it through. Had my time jumps from 1980 and 1983 changed time enough that Jackson Hartle realized he needed to live his life differently? Had they changed my own childhood? My mother certainly seemed to be living in a different existence. I still had so much left to do, but I wanted a few minutes with him.

"Well, let's talk then. How's Pie?"

He laughed a little. "She lived a good, long life. As have I, with the benefit of knowing which habits weren't good for me."

"I take it you didn't go work for a white bread company?"

"Ha, no, and I don't eat that shit, either." I noticed he sounded just like my mother did when she found something funny, all bobbly and musical. "Back in the 20s they marketed it as "White bread for the White Race. Stuff and nonsense. I refused to smoke cigarettes, too. And here I am, as old as a stump. So thank you for that."

"I just got back," I said. "Like you noticed. I'm still adjusting."

"Well, Jack, I hate to say it, but I think you need to go back again."

"I know I do. I can't leave things like this. And I love Lucas."

He nodded a little bit, tapped me on my knee.

"I know you do."

"I have an idea about how to make it all right, but I'm not sure. And I don't know who my Guardian is in this time. Is it you?"

"No, it's not me," he said, and he grinned.

"I'm your Guardian," said my mother, sitting down on a blue lawn chair. She rested her hands on her lap. "I suppose you have questions for me."

I just stared at her. My own mother, my Guardian? My neck felt hot all of a sudden.

"Why didn't you tell me?"

She looked into her lap, twisting a dish towel.

"I was afraid."

"I was in danger! How could you say nothing? You must have known every time I jumped."

She nodded, dabbing her eyes with the towel.

"I'd heard so much about how Travelers were persecuted when they were discovered, and then I felt the time shifts, just tiny ones, once you were a toddler. Usually Guardians and Travelers are at most distantly related, like cousins or across one or more generations. I almost didn't believe it when I felt you moving through time. Travelers don't have real abilities until they're teenagers. I was scared for you. And then I needed to change my medication, and I was in such a fog and I couldn't help you, and you didn't tell me anything was wrong."

I stood up, feeling dizzy for the first time in ages.

"Because I thought I was crazy, Mom! Hopping around time, it's not normal."

"I'm sorry, honey. I should have prepared you better. I made the wrong decision."

"I thought I was losing my mind."

"I know, I'm sorry. I was trying to protect you. It was a mistake."

Now it was my turn to look down. I needed to think. My Guardian was with me all along and I never knew it. I reached out and took my mother's hand. I couldn't tell if I was angry or sad or what.

"It's okay, Mom." *Mostly. Even with all this time travel I never feel like I have any rest.*

"I'm so proud of you, my dear. You're such a wonderful young man."

"Or woman," said Jackson, grinning on half of his face.

"That too," she said. I sighed.

"I have been stacking up the questions for my Guardian."

"Like?" she asked.

"What happens when I'm in someone else's body? Am I losing time or do I just have really bad aim? Can I die or can I jump forever?"

Mom smiled, a real smile, without a medication haze or a cover for something bad. A real, genuine smile.

"There are answers to all of these questions, Jack."

"Good, because I have a lot more."

"Okay. We're here to help."

"And another thing—I have no real idea how to stop Dr. Traver."

Grandpa sat up and he held my gaze, and played with the chain on his old pocket watch.

"I do," he said.

Chapter Twenty-Seven

THE TRACKS STRETCHED SO FAR toward the horizon that the individual rails seemed to merge into one point, and then they disappeared, becoming lost to the wilderness. I followed the railroad ties, using a scrap of paper I'd received a couple of hours earlier. Edgar camped out where the tracks took on a look of modern sculpture, the result of a terrible derailing several years ago. Not that modern art was anything anyone had heard of yet. The old conductor told me I couldn't miss it.

I'd been tracing his steps for a week, and I was running out of time. I crunched through a stream of broken glass and pottery. Moonshine bottles, brown beer glass, and growler jugs, or so I guessed. I was getting close. If the story was right then he hadn't started to spiral down yet, but this was the last week for his fragile sobriety.

The tracks rose up from the ground, twisting and climbing like an iron vine. Scraps from trains lay half-buried in the weeds and wildflowers, glinting from my lantern light. I'd come all the way out to Montana to find him, and now the sun was setting. I called out his name. His new name.

A crackling sound off to my right and I saw the lean-to, a few bums feeding a small fire in front of their shelter. I walked over to them and asked if anyone knew where Melvyn was.

"Who wants to know?" asked a scrawny young man. Those green eyes. The self-proclaimed Dr. Traver.

"I need to speak with you, please," I said. He seemed to doubt my sincerity. "It's of the utmost importance."

"It must be if you ventured to this hellacious place," he said, and he stepped forward, closer to the light of the fire and my lantern. His sunken cheeks and brittle appearance surprised me. He'd never looked particularly healthy in any of our previous encounters, but I hadn't seen him malnourished before, either. Melvyn stepped toward me with care, as if checking that the ground underneath would hold his light frame. "Pray tell," he said once he was in front of me, "who are you and why have you come here?"

He wore wool knickers that by my research, were a good decade out of style, a prickly cotton shirt that seemed about two sizes too large for him, a beat-up brown leather jacket, not made for the cold temperatures, and a wool cap that stunk more than it covered his head. These were runaway clothes, assembled on the road, or stolen from his abusive half-brother or father. He put his hands in his pockets, waiting for my response.

"My name is Brock Tillman," I said, hoping I'd remembered that correctly. "I'm here on behalf of your family."

"I don't have a family," he said, stiffening up. This wasn't going well.

"Sir, you do, and I need to explain a few things."

He sighed. "Explain then."

"You're working at a lumber yard, yes? The M. J. Dwight Company?"

"You work for them? You have me exasperated, Mr. Tillman."

"My sincere apologies," I said. "You're going to sleep very little tonight, and rush to your job tomorrow, and make a mistake on the saw that will cost a man his life."

"You're a crackpot," he said, and began walking away.

"Wait!"

He continued to pace away from me, aiming to take cover with the older men at the fire.

"Edgar, please!" This stopped him in his tracks, and he hurried back over to where I stood.

"Who are you?"

"I am a time-traveler, as impossible as that seems."

"You are not well, whoever you are." His anger was so familiar. He had the same sneer on his face that I saw when he and his men surrounded us, years later.

"I promise, Melvyn, I understand more than you know. How awful your brother was to you, why you ran away—"

"Stop. It is of no consequence anymore. I am now my own man." He puffed out his chest. Which was not saying much.

"I know you are. That is why I've come to speak with you."

"It is a strange audience you request, Mr. Tillman." He paused, thinking. "Accidents happen at mills all the time, and this cold ground is no place for a decent night's sleep, so you've said nothing that isn't obvious. I've heard of you psychics and soothsayers. You are all charlatans." He waved his hand in the air like I was a bad smell. He was really pissing me off. But I couldn't hate him for crimes he hadn't yet committed.

"Tomorrow, before noon, you will kill the yard owner's son by accident, unless you seek to avoid it. Come find me on the corner outside the general store at three o'clock tomorrow. You'll believe me by then." I fished in my knapsack. He continued to frown at me, but he'd quit yelling.

"I feel sorry for you, sir," he said, holding his ground. "You ought to thank your lucky stars you're not in a sanitarium."

"Maybe I should," I said, handing him a small wrapped sandwich.

"What is this?" he asked. He sniffed the brown paper.

"Supper. Made just like Mrs. Ellison prepared them for you in Detroit. You haven't eaten in two days, after all."

"You're the devil," he told me, as I walked away, back along the tracks and into the tiny town in the mountains.

Call me what you want, I thought, *but I gave you the opportunity to prevent a death tomorrow. And all of the deaths after that.*

* * *

I sat on the porch of the general store, nursing a not-sweet-enough iced tea that the young daughter of the owner had made for anyone willing to pay two cents. Light brown dust covered everything out here, and was slowly crawling up the length of my boots. I pulled my wide-brimmed hat down a little lower on my face, and wished that someone had invented sunglasses before now. *I will never complain again about how much it sucks in the suburbs.*

At the end of the row of stores, two men pushed at a Ford Model T that was stuck in thick mud. It lurched forward, finding traction for only a second before getting stuck again. This unexpected motion caused the man leaning against the left rear fender to fall face-down onto the ground. He let out a stream of curses and I stifled a laugh, not wanting to bring any attention to myself. His friend got the bright idea to hitch two horses to the vehicle.

As they worked, Melvyn walked up to me. I checked the clock in the tower of the bank across the street, and saw that it was only 2:00 pm.

"Fancy meeting you here," I said, still covered by my hat.

Melvyn leaned against the railing at the boundary of the porch. "It is an evil man who would sabotage equipment he knows working men require to use."

"I didn't sabotage anything," I said with confidence. I pushed back the brim of my hat and sat forward, looking at him. "I've been here all day. Ask the shop owner."

"Have you no concern of the poor soul who could have been killed today?"

"I take it he's still alive, then."

"No thanks to you." He scowled at me, made all the more intense by the fact that the sun had turned his eyes into small darts.

"Actually, it is entirely thanks to me. Were it not for my warning to you yesterday you would not have left your sad state of a bed early to examine the mill's workings as is part of your job, but which you almost never do. So hooray, you then realized that two bolts had fallen off of the steam engine. Were it not for me, in fact, you would not have sought to call this to the attention of the mill foreman in time before the start of the morning shift. And now the foreman knows your name and is considering promoting you."

By the end of this stream of explanation, the fight had left him. His fists unclenched, his jaw relaxed, and he stood in the dust of the street, expressionless.

"What do you want of me?" he asked, almost as an exhale.

"A woman once told me, a long time from now, that every person has everything inside of them—curiosity and apathy, triumph and defeat, goodness and wickedness."

"I have attended Bible study, I assure you," said Melvyn.

"Well, at some point, you forgot what it said. You stopped asking where your own actions were leading you."

"You are the most confounding person I can remember encountering."

"Thank you. I try."

Melvyn's cheek twitched. He was one nervous cat.

"Let me ask you this. Why are you here in this godforsaken place? Why have you run all the way from Michigan to the wilds of the West? Because you are attempting to distance yourself from the truth." At this his head nodded, almost without his consent, but he stood silent. "And yet with all the miles you've put between here and there, still you are haunted."

"What you say is true," said Melvyn, digging his toe in the brown dust. "But you have no solution for me."

I stood up, brushing off my trousers and setting down my drink.

"I do, in fact, have ideas for you, Edgar. But you have given up on self-determination, and I suggest you give it a second chance. Come with me."

Walking away, I didn't look back, because I knew even though he needed to consider my request, he would follow me. After a few moments, he trotted to catch up to me. We made crunching sounds on the rough surface.

I headed toward the bank, in the middle of the line of shops. The teller nodded at me as we entered and the bank vice president stood up to greet us. Melvyn leaned in to my ear.

"I have no business with these people."

"Oh, yes you do." I handed the banker a key, and he walked into the vault, bringing back a box to us. He set it on a heavy mahogany table next to where we stood, and walked away. "Open it," I told Melvyn.

He gave me a look but then pulled back the cover of the metal container on its hinge, and gasped as he inspected the contents.

"I thought you were a devil or a carpet bagger."

I shook my head. "Maybe I have my moments," I said.

Melvyn read and re-read the birth certificate with both of his parents' names typed in as amended. He rubbed at his eyes, which made me reach out to pat him on his shoulder. I handed him a short stack of money. It wasn't much, but it was enough to give him a start as something other than a runaway servant's child. It had taken me two weeks of popping in and out of time to arrange, but I knew my trouble would pay off.

"What do I take from this?" he asked. I guessed he was talking about the bills that came in denominations he'd likely never seen before.

"That forgiveness beats anger," I said. "Never pretend to be someone else." I jumped away before he could respond, before he even had a chance to look up and see I had disappeared.

* * *

I saw her from a block away, her hair cut short, spiky on top. Jeannine spotted me and waved, shutting her car door and trotting across the intersection.

"You should be careful, look both ways."

"Okay, Grandma, I'll try to remember," she said, laughing at me. I sat on a chilly metal chair out on the sidewalk. If it was supposed to be a fancy café, it wasn't. I didn't give a flip, I was just here to see Jeannine.

I stood up and hugged her and then she told me enough already. I waited for her while she went inside and came back with a fancy espresso thing.

"Since when did you start drinking lattes?"

"Since why don't you ever stop drinking soda pop? It's terrible for you."

"You should try them when they still had cane sugar in them. Whole different experience."

She rolled her eyes at me.

"So tell me the whole story of what happened after Dr. Dorfman sent you back from Aimée's house."

I could deal with this new normal, I figured.

Epilogue

NATE RUNS INTO THE FIELD of flowers cackling with laughter and I rush off to catch him before he wanders into the patch of poison ivy near the little stream that gurgles by the end of the clearing. He's strong as he squirms to get out of my hold.

"Did he make a break for it?" asks Lucas, who is absentminded at best.

I walk up to him with the fidgeting toddler and place the child in front of him. We parent in zones.

"You know he did," I say.

The phone rings in the kitchen and I make eye contact with my spouse to make sure he'll watch the little one while I dash off. I could feel like I spend my days hurrying to the phone or the child, but I'm too busy to think about it.

"I've got him," he says to the space I very recently occupied.

I answer the call and the operator connects us. Date, time, location, quite brief description of what's gone wrong, and we disconnect. I make my way to the root cellar, walking through the living room of our farm house as I study my notes. My mother looks up from her knitting. She makes and gives away a sweater a week and is happy to be done with tending to chickens and cows.

"Another call?" she asks without taking her eyes off her stitches.

"Yes, but I'll be back soon."

"Don't work yourself too hard," she says. People spend a lot of time talking to me as I'm moving.

"Promise," I say as I descend the stairs.

"Nineteen thirty-seven," I whisper. I'm sitting in a plush burgundy chair, my favorite spot to focus before I leave. "October 7th. Harvey Koss, Hell's Kitchen. Harvey." He's been pretending to go to a job every day that he hasn't had in more than a year. I wonder what his face looks like, if I'll be Harvey or someone he knows well. And before I can blink, I'm gone.

I am Jacqueline Leigh Bishop Van Doren, and I can travel through time.

MORE GREAT READS FROM BOOKTROPE

Revision 7: DNA **by Terry Persun** (Science Fiction) Time traveling robots, a walking medical experiment turned detective genius, and a kidnapped psychic combine in a story that will tear at your heart and get your adrenaline pumping.

Charis: Journey to Pandora's Jar **by Nicole Walters** (Young Adult - Fantasy) Thirteen-year-old Charis Parks has five days to face her fears against the darker forces of Hades and reverse the curse of Pandora's Jar to save mankind.

Essence **by A.L. Waddington** (Young Adult) Jocelyn Timmons does not believe she is anything special. She's about to find out how wrong she is. Our minds often wander, but can our souls?

Forecast **by Elise Stephens** (Young Adult, Fantasy) When teenager Calvin finds a portal that will grant him the power of prophecy, he must battle the legacies of the past and the shadows of the future to protect what is most important: his family.

Godspeed **by Febraury Grace** (Steampunk) In a steam-powered society, medical advancement is the last forbidden frontier. Can a young doctor working in secret rebuild his shattered heart by saving that of another? Or will ghosts of the past rise again, endangering all he holds dear?

Discover more books and learn about our new approach to publishing at:*www.booktrope.com*

THE LIBRARY
NEW COLLEGE
SWINDON
WITHDRAWN

Lightning Source UK Ltd.
Milton Keynes UK
UKOW04f1533120216

268247UK00004B/66/P

9 781620 152072